DICK TRACY®

DEAD OR ALIVE

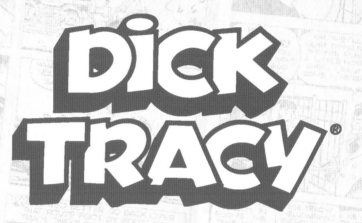

Become our fan on Facebook **facebook.com/idwpublishing**
Follow us on Twitter **@idwpublishing**
Subscribe to us on YouTube **youtube.com/idwpublishing**
See what's new on Tumblr **tumblr.idwpublishing.com**
Check us out on Instagram **instagram.com/idwpublishing**

www.IDWPUBLISHING.com

COVER ARTIST
MICHAEL ALLRED

COVER COLORIST
LAURA ALLRED

COLLECTION EDITORS
JUSTIN EISINGER
AND **ALONZO SIMON**

COLLECTION DESIGNER
CLAUDIA CHONG

PUBLISHER
CHRIS RYALL

Chris Ryall, President, Publisher, & CCO
John Barber, Editor-In-Chief
Robbie Robbins, EVP & Sr. Art Director
Cara Morrison, Chief Financial Officer
Matthew Ruzicka, Chief Accounting Officer
Anita Frazier, SVP of Sales and Marketing
David Hedgecock, Associate Publisher
Jerry Bennington, VP of New Product Development
Lorelei Bunjes, VP of Digital Services
Justin Eisinger, Editorial Director, Graphic Novels & Collections
Eric Moss, Sr. Director, Licensing & Business Development

Ted Adams, IDW Founder

ISBN: 978-1-68405-414-5   22 21 20 19   1 2 3 4

Originally published as DICK TRACY: DEAD OR ALIVE issues #1–4.

Special thanks to Scott Cameron and Tracy Clark at Tribune Content
Agency for their invaluable assistance.

For international rights, contact licensing@idwpublishing.com

DICK TRACY

DEAD OR ALIVE

WRITERS
LEE & MICHAEL ALLRED

PENCILER
RICH TOMMASO

INKER
MICHAEL ALLRED

COLORIST
LAURA ALLRED

LETTERER
SHAWN LEE

SERIES ASSISTANT EDITORS:
ELIZABETH BREI AND **ANNI PERHEENTUPA**

SERIES EDITOR:
DENTON J. TIPTON

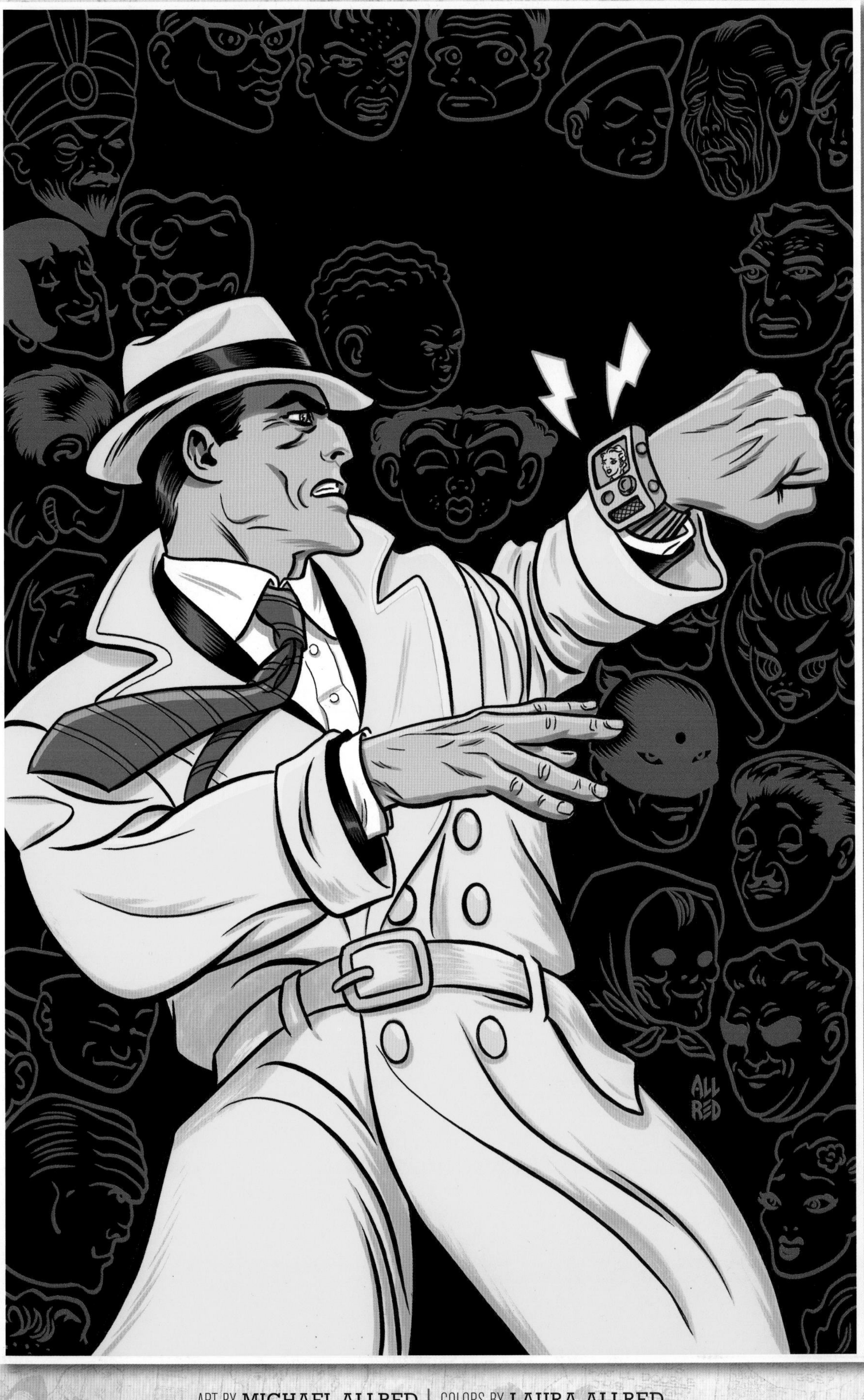
ALL
RED

ART BY **MICHAEL ALLRED** | COLORS BY **LAURA ALLRED**

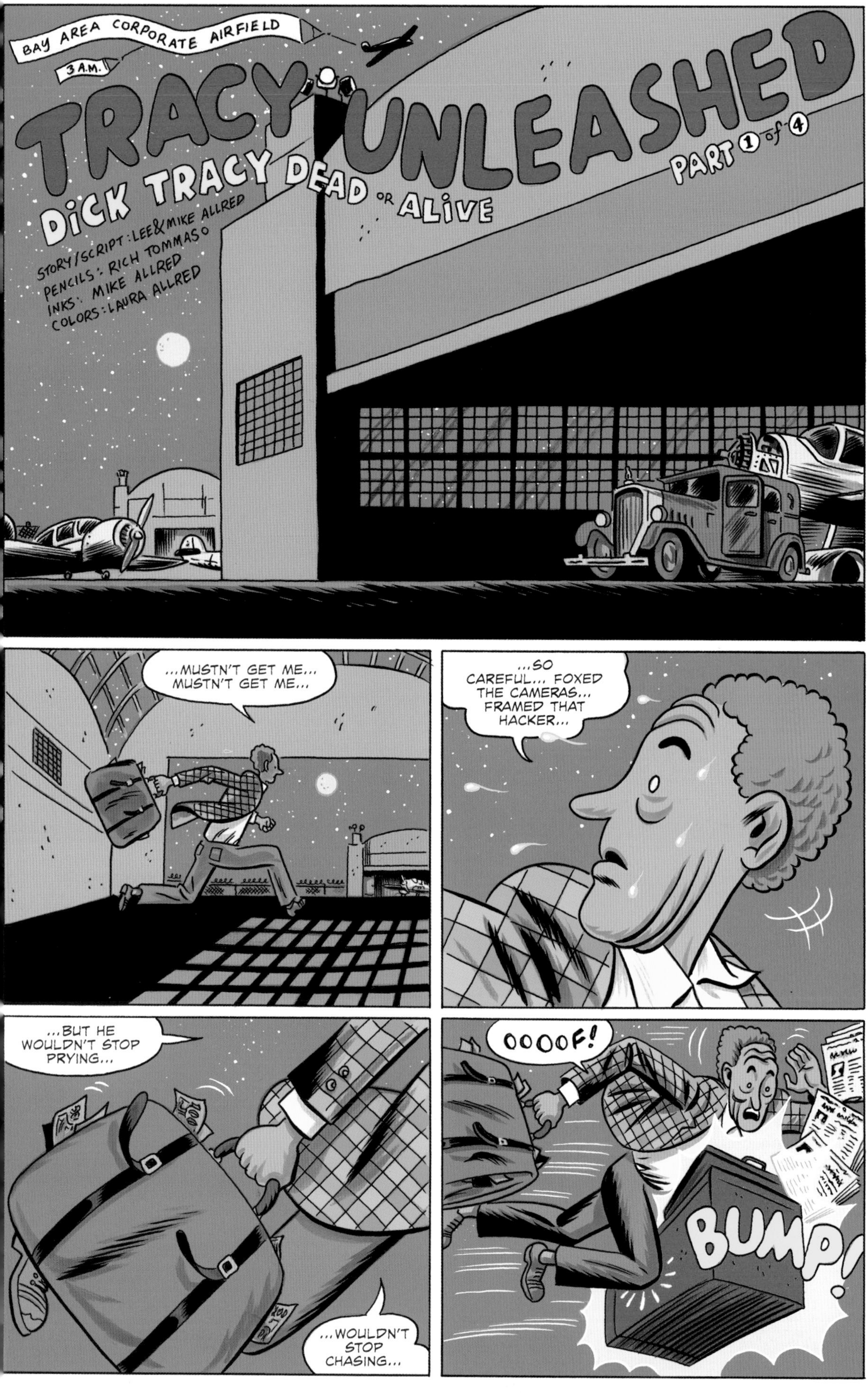

BAY AREA CORPORATE AIRFIELD
3 A.M.
TRACY UNLEASHED
PART 1 of 4
DICK TRACY DEAD OR ALIVE
STORY/SCRIPT: LEE & MIKE ALLRED
PENCILS: RICH TOMMASO
INKS: MIKE ALLRED
COLORS: LAURA ALLRED
...MUSTN'T GET ME... MUSTN'T GET ME...
...SO CAREFUL... FOXED THE CAMERAS... FRAMED THAT HACKER...
...BUT HE WOULDN'T STOP PRYING...
...WOULDN'T STOP CHASING...
OOOOF!
BUMP!

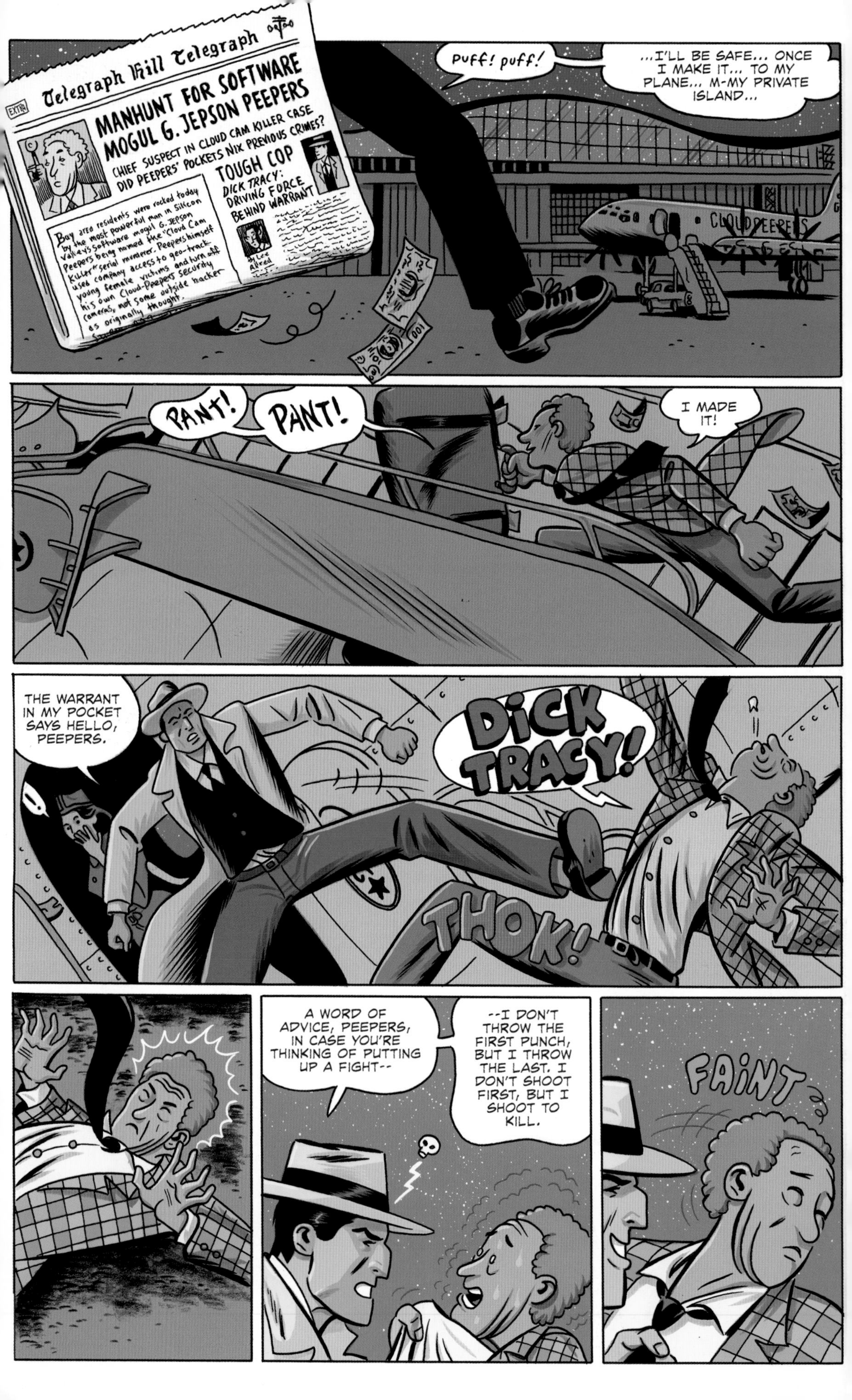
Telegraph Hill Telegraph
EXTRA
MANHUNT FOR SOFTWARE MOGUL G. JEPSON PEEPERS
CHIEF SUSPECT IN CLOUD CAM KILLER CASE
DID PEEPERS' POCKETS NIX PREVIOUS CRIMES?
Bay area residents were rocked today by the most powerful man in Silicon Valley's software mogul G. Jepson Peepers being named the "Cloud Cam Killer" serial murderer. Peepers himself used company access to geo-track young female victims and turn off his own Cloud-Peepers security cameras, not some outside hacker as originally thought.
TOUGH COP
DICK TRACY: DRIVING FORCE BEHIND WARRANT
By Lee Allred
Puff! puff!
...I'LL BE SAFE... ONCE I MAKE IT... TO MY PLANE... M-MY PRIVATE ISLAND...
CLOUDPEEPERS
PANT!
PANT!
I MADE IT!
THE WARRANT IN MY POCKET SAYS HELLO, PEEPERS.
DICK TRACY!
THOK!
A WORD OF ADVICE, PEEPERS, IN CASE YOU'RE THINKING OF PUTTING UP A FIGHT--
--I DON'T THROW THE FIRST PUNCH, BUT I THROW THE LAST. I DON'T SHOOT FIRST, BUT I SHOOT TO KILL.
FAINT

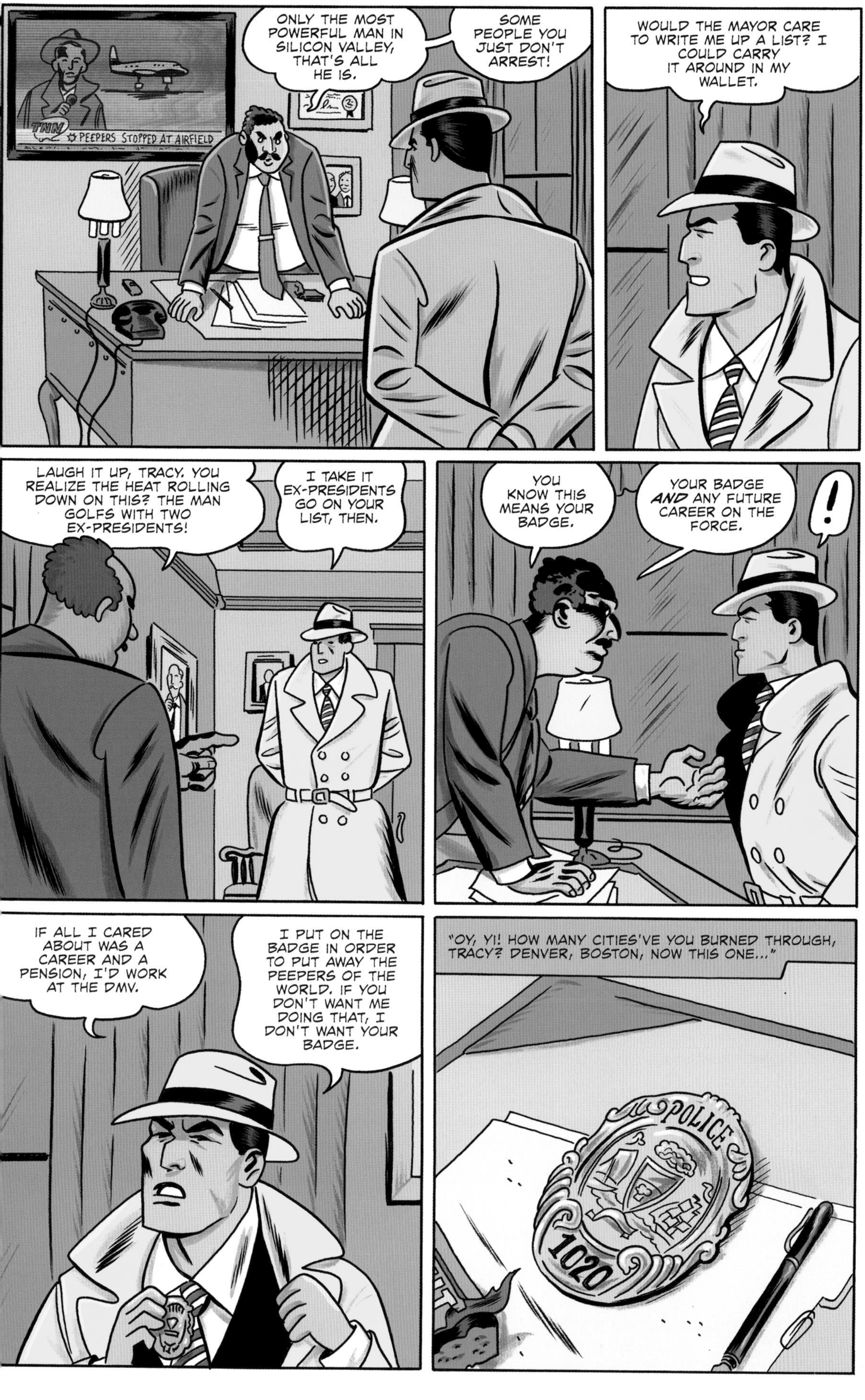
PEEPERS STOPPED AT AIRFIELD
ONLY THE MOST POWERFUL MAN IN SILICON VALLEY, THAT'S ALL HE IS.
SOME PEOPLE YOU JUST DON'T ARREST!
WOULD THE MAYOR CARE TO WRITE ME UP A LIST? I COULD CARRY IT AROUND IN MY WALLET.
LAUGH IT UP, TRACY. YOU REALIZE THE HEAT ROLLING DOWN ON THIS? THE MAN GOLFS WITH TWO EX-PRESIDENTS!
I TAKE IT EX-PRESIDENTS GO ON YOUR LIST, THEN.
YOU KNOW THIS MEANS YOUR BADGE.
YOUR BADGE AND ANY FUTURE CAREER ON THE FORCE.
!
IF ALL I CARED ABOUT WAS A CAREER AND A PENSION, I'D WORK AT THE DMV.
I PUT ON THE BADGE IN ORDER TO PUT AWAY THE PEEPERS OF THE WORLD. IF YOU DON'T WANT ME DOING THAT, I DON'T WANT YOUR BADGE.
"OY, YI! HOW MANY CITIES'VE YOU BURNED THROUGH, TRACY? DENVER, BOSTON, NOW THIS ONE..."
POLICE
1020

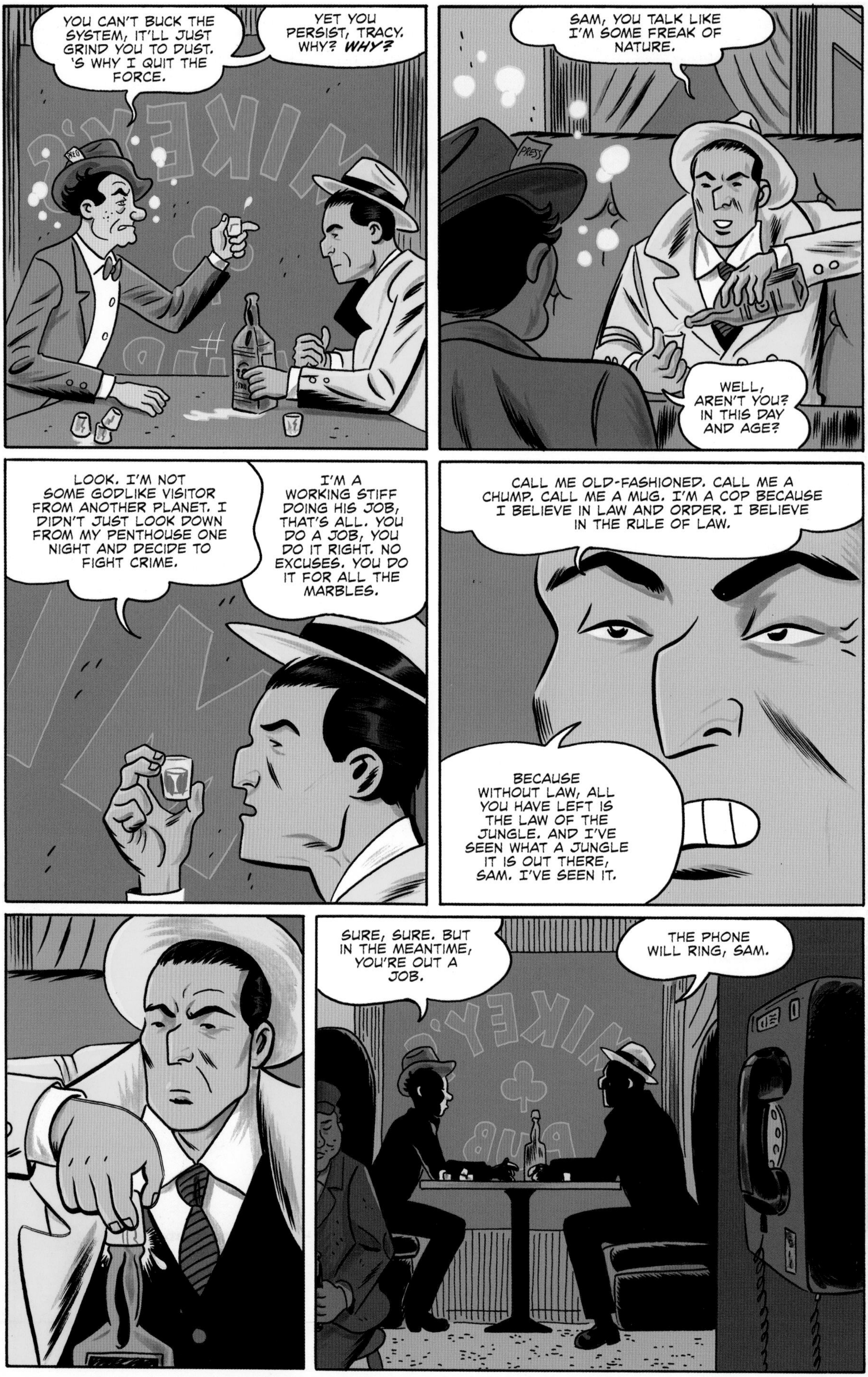
YOU CAN'T BUCK THE SYSTEM, IT'LL JUST GRIND YOU TO DUST. 'S WHY I QUIT THE FORCE.
YET YOU PERSIST, TRACY. WHY? WHY?
SAM, YOU TALK LIKE I'M SOME FREAK OF NATURE.
WELL, AREN'T YOU? IN THIS DAY AND AGE?
LOOK. I'M NOT SOME GODLIKE VISITOR FROM ANOTHER PLANET. I DIDN'T JUST LOOK DOWN FROM MY PENTHOUSE ONE NIGHT AND DECIDE TO FIGHT CRIME.
I'M A WORKING STIFF DOING HIS JOB, THAT'S ALL. YOU DO A JOB, YOU DO IT RIGHT. NO EXCUSES. YOU DO IT FOR ALL THE MARBLES.
CALL ME OLD-FASHIONED. CALL ME A CHUMP. CALL ME A MUG. I'M A COP BECAUSE I BELIEVE IN LAW AND ORDER. I BELIEVE IN THE RULE OF LAW.
BECAUSE WITHOUT LAW, ALL YOU HAVE LEFT IS THE LAW OF THE JUNGLE. AND I'VE SEEN WHAT A JUNGLE IT IS OUT THERE, SAM. I'VE SEEN IT.
SURE, SURE. BUT IN THE MEANTIME, YOU'RE OUT A JOB.
THE PHONE WILL RING, SAM.
MIKEY'S
PUB

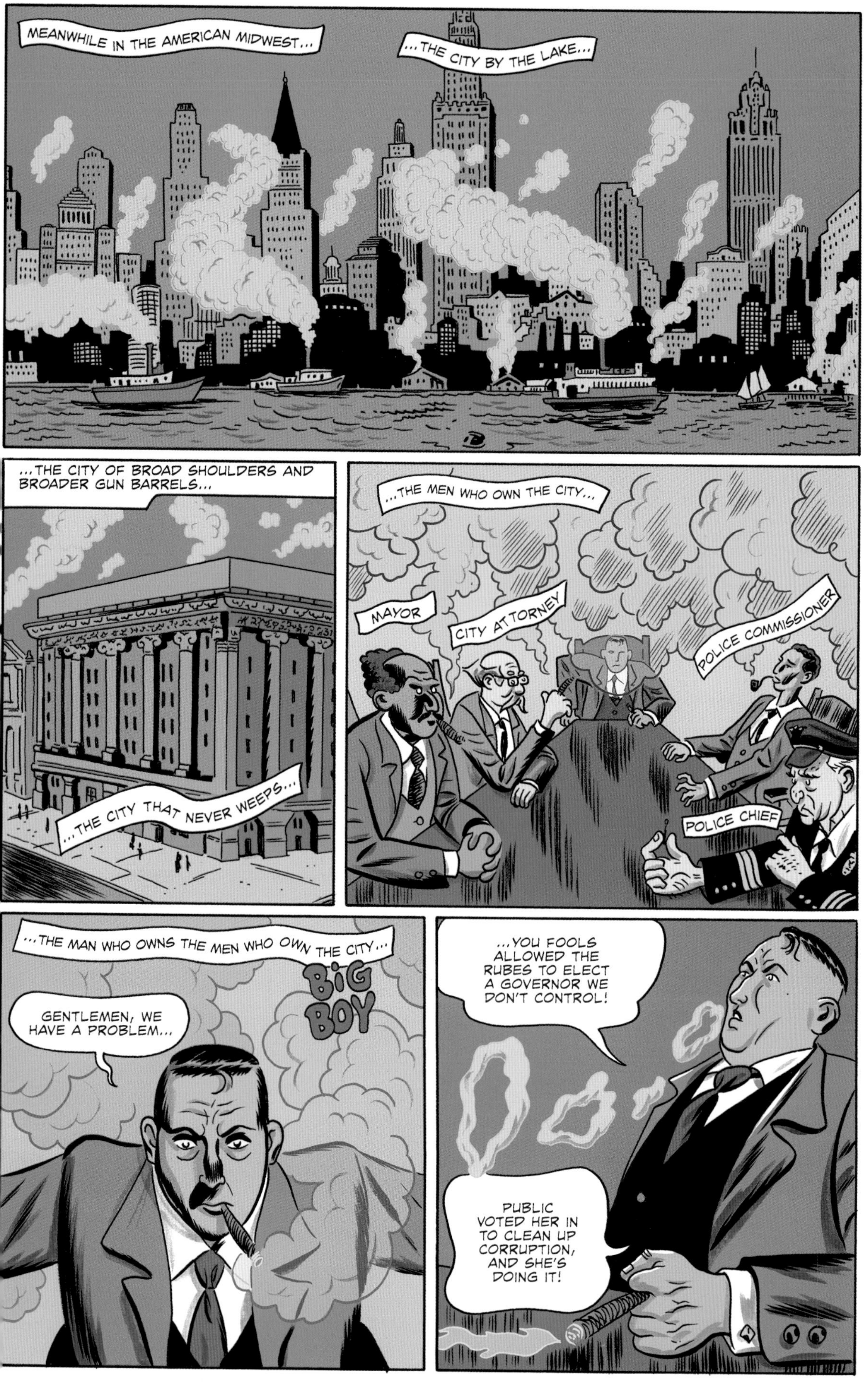
MEANWHILE IN THE AMERICAN MIDWEST...
...THE CITY BY THE LAKE...
...THE CITY OF BROAD SHOULDERS AND BROADER GUN BARRELS...
...THE CITY THAT NEVER WEEPS...
...THE MEN WHO OWN THE CITY...
MAYOR
CITY ATTORNEY
POLICE COMMISSIONER
POLICE CHIEF
...THE MAN WHO OWNS THE MEN WHO OWN THE CITY...
BIG BOY
GENTLEMEN, WE HAVE A PROBLEM...
...YOU FOOLS ALLOWED THE RUBES TO ELECT A GOVERNOR WE DON'T CONTROL!
PUBLIC VOTED HER IN TO CLEAN UP CORRUPTION, AND SHE'S DOING IT!

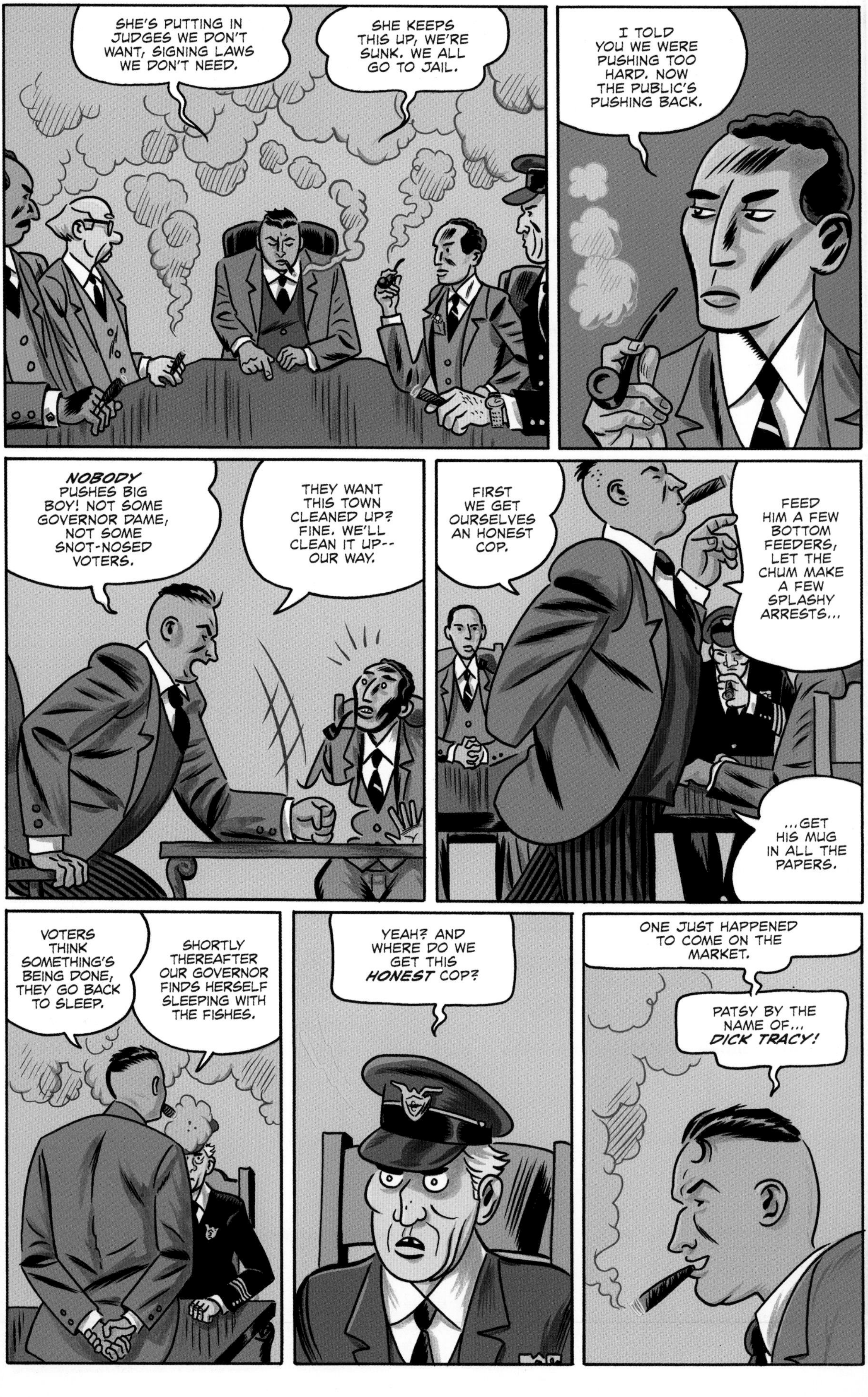
SHE'S PUTTING IN JUDGES WE DON'T WANT, SIGNING LAWS WE DON'T NEED.
SHE KEEPS THIS UP, WE'RE SUNK. WE ALL GO TO JAIL.
I TOLD YOU WE WERE PUSHING TOO HARD. NOW THE PUBLIC'S PUSHING BACK.
NOBODY PUSHES BIG BOY! NOT SOME GOVERNOR DAME, NOT SOME SNOT-NOSED VOTERS.
THEY WANT THIS TOWN CLEANED UP? FINE. WE'LL CLEAN IT UP-- OUR WAY.
FIRST WE GET OURSELVES AN HONEST COP.
FEED HIM A FEW BOTTOM FEEDERS, LET THE CHUM MAKE A FEW SPLASHY ARRESTS...
...GET HIS MUG IN ALL THE PAPERS.
VOTERS THINK SOMETHING'S BEING DONE, THEY GO BACK TO SLEEP.
SHORTLY THEREAFTER OUR GOVERNOR FINDS HERSELF SLEEPING WITH THE FISHES.
YEAH? AND WHERE DO WE GET THIS HONEST COP?
ONE JUST HAPPENED TO COME ON THE MARKET.
PATSY BY THE NAME OF... DICK TRACY!

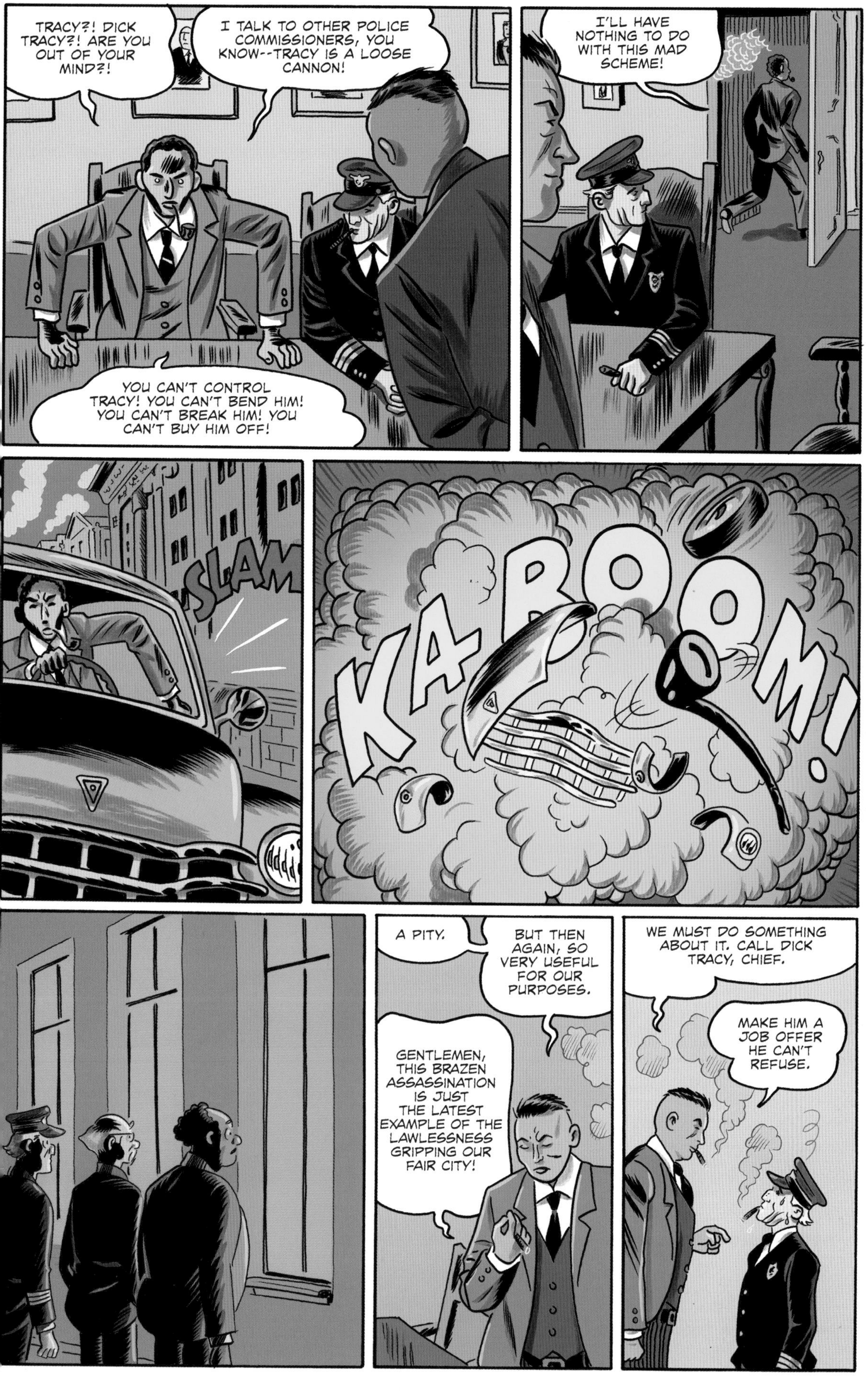
TRACY?! DICK TRACY?! ARE YOU OUT OF YOUR MIND?!
I TALK TO OTHER POLICE COMMISSIONERS, YOU KNOW--TRACY IS A LOOSE CANNON!
YOU CAN'T CONTROL TRACY! YOU CAN'T BEND HIM! YOU CAN'T BREAK HIM! YOU CAN'T BUY HIM OFF!
I'LL HAVE NOTHING TO DO WITH THIS MAD SCHEME!
SLAM
KABOOM!
A PITY.
BUT THEN AGAIN, SO VERY USEFUL FOR OUR PURPOSES.
GENTLEMEN, THIS BRAZEN ASSASSINATION IS JUST THE LATEST EXAMPLE OF THE LAWLESSNESS GRIPPING OUR FAIR CITY!
WE MUST DO SOMETHING ABOUT IT. CALL DICK TRACY, CHIEF.
MAKE HIM A JOB OFFER HE CAN'T REFUSE.

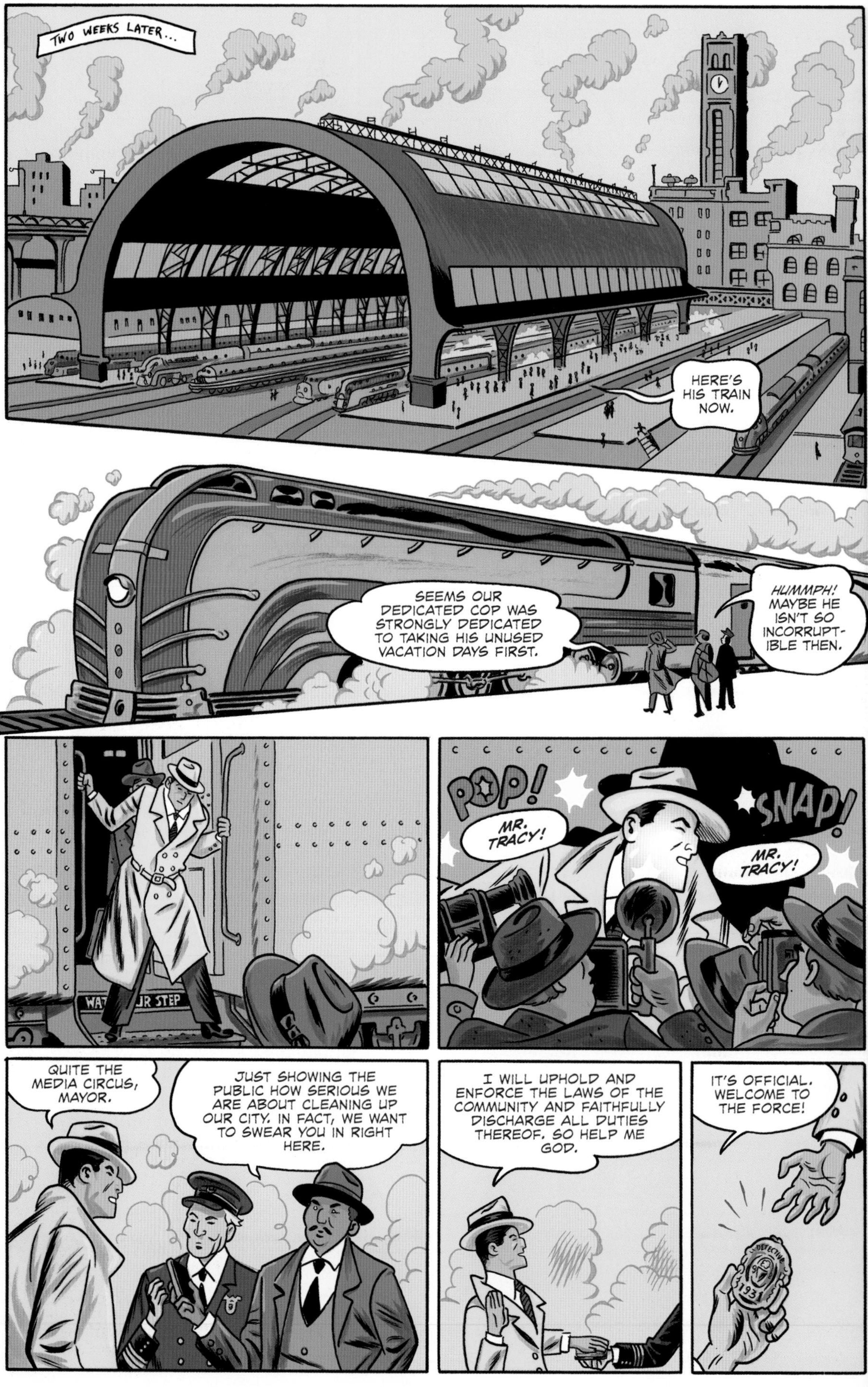
TWO WEEKS LATER...
HERE'S HIS TRAIN NOW.
SEEMS OUR DEDICATED COP WAS STRONGLY DEDICATED TO TAKING HIS UNUSED VACATION DAYS FIRST.
HUMMPH! MAYBE HE ISN'T SO INCORRUPT-IBLE THEN.
WAT UR STEP
POP!
MR. TRACY!
SNAP!
MR. TRACY!
QUITE THE MEDIA CIRCUS, MAYOR.
JUST SHOWING THE PUBLIC HOW SERIOUS WE ARE ABOUT CLEANING UP OUR CITY. IN FACT, WE WANT TO SWEAR YOU IN RIGHT HERE.
I WILL UPHOLD AND ENFORCE THE LAWS OF THE COMMUNITY AND FAITHFULLY DISCHARGE ALL DUTIES THEREOF. SO HELP ME GOD.
IT'S OFFICIAL. WELCOME TO THE FORCE!
DETECTIVE
1931

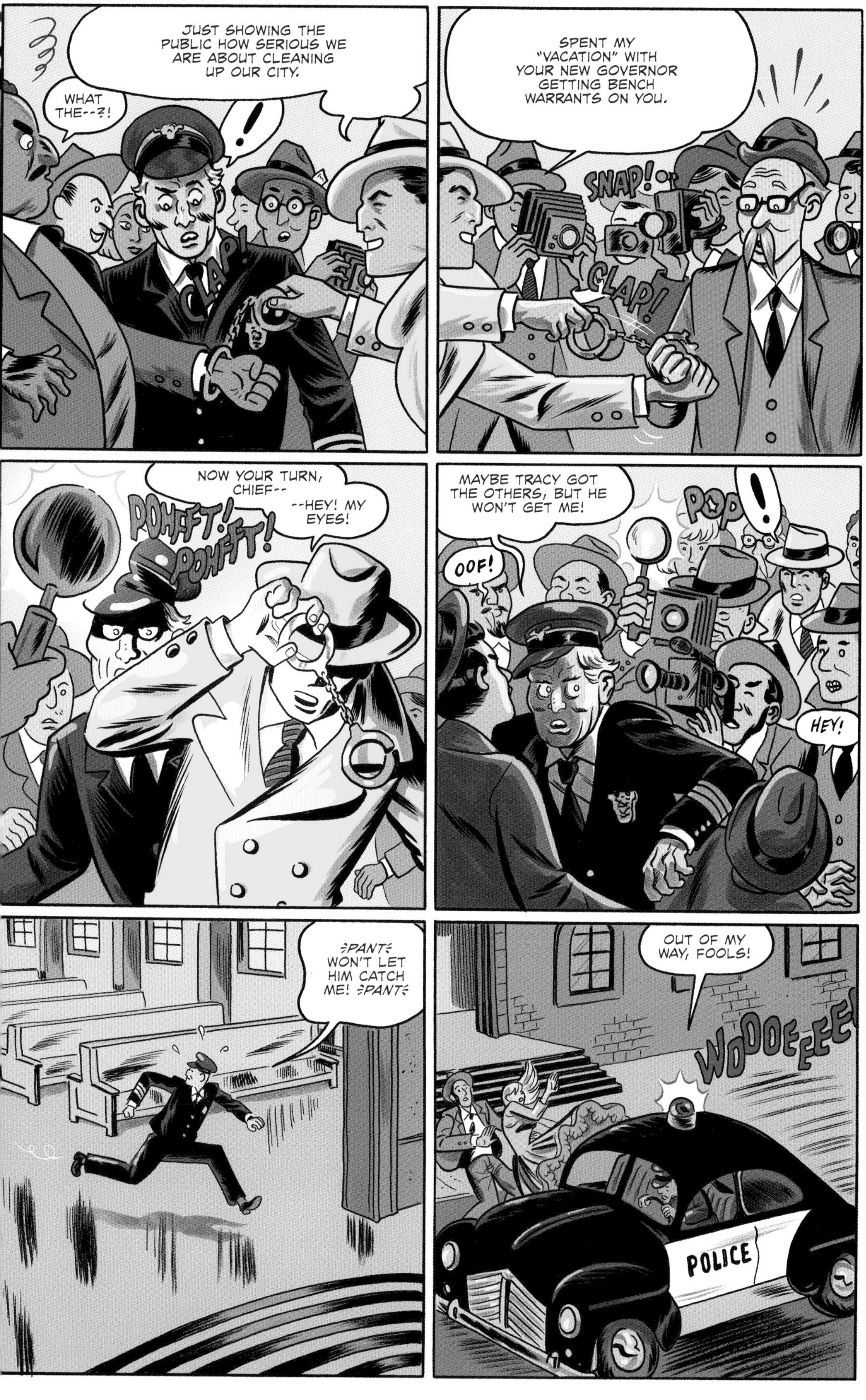
JUST SHOWING THE PUBLIC HOW SERIOUS WE ARE ABOUT CLEANING UP OUR CITY.
WHAT THE--?!
!
CLAP!
SPENT MY "VACATION" WITH YOUR NEW GOVERNOR GETTING BENCH WARRANTS ON YOU.
SNAP!
CLAP!
NOW YOUR TURN, CHIEF--
POHFFT! POHFFT!
--HEY! MY EYES!
MAYBE TRACY GOT THE OTHERS, BUT HE WON'T GET ME!
POP!
!
OOF!
HEY!
=PANT= WON'T LET HIM CATCH ME! =PANT=
OUT OF MY WAY, FOOLS!
WOOOEEEE
POLICE

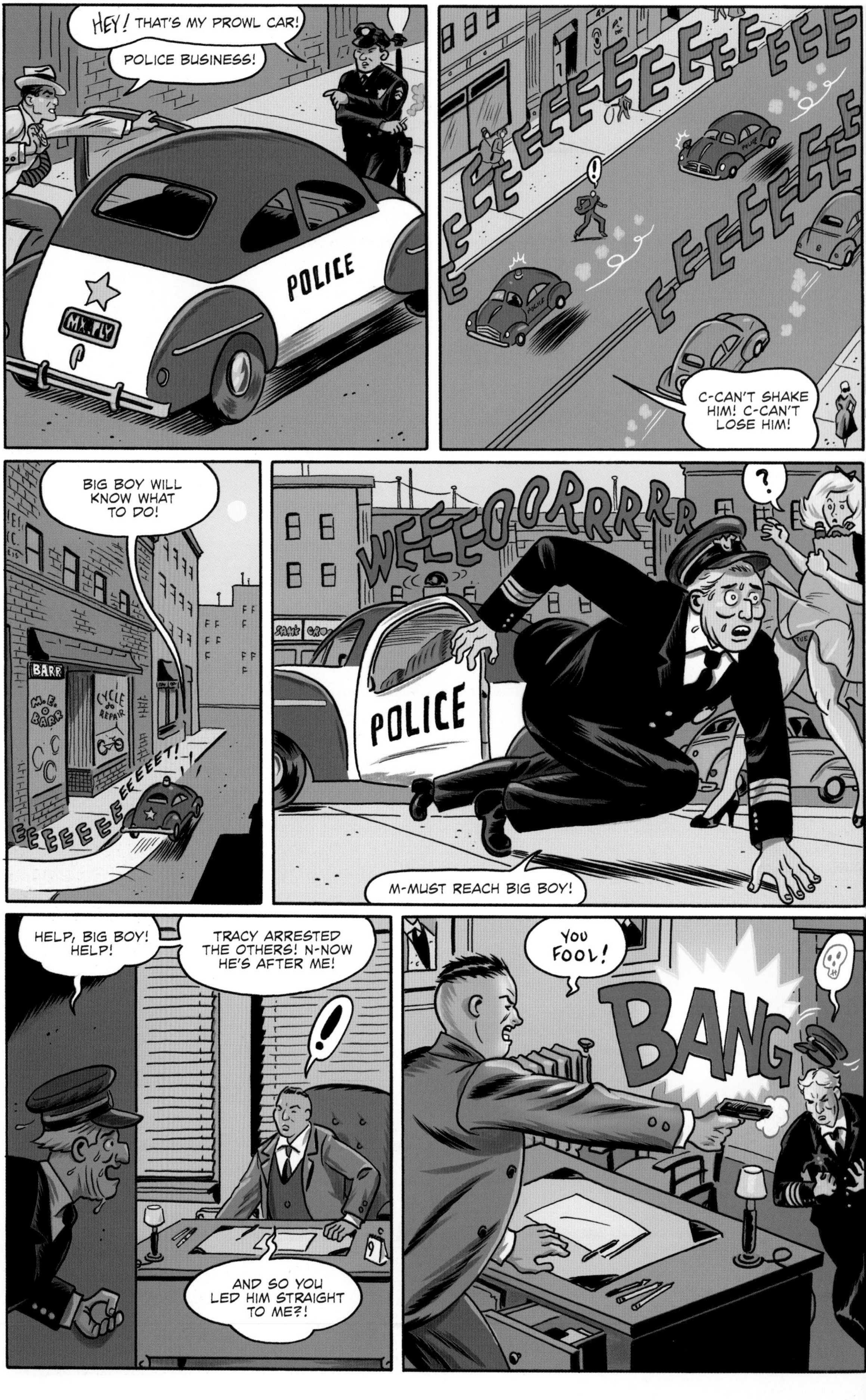
HEY! THAT'S MY PROWL CAR!
POLICE BUSINESS!
POLICE
MX.FLY
EEEEEEEEEEEEEEEEEEE
C-CAN'T SHAKE HIM! C-CAN'T LOSE HIM!
BIG BOY WILL KNOW WHAT TO DO!
BARR
M.E. BARR
CYCLE REPAIR
EEEEEEEEEEEET!
WEEEOORRRRRR
?
POLICE
M-MUST REACH BIG BOY!
HELP, BIG BOY! HELP!
TRACY ARRESTED THE OTHERS! N-NOW HE'S AFTER ME!
!
AND SO YOU LED HIM STRAIGHT TO ME?!
YOU FOOL!
BANG

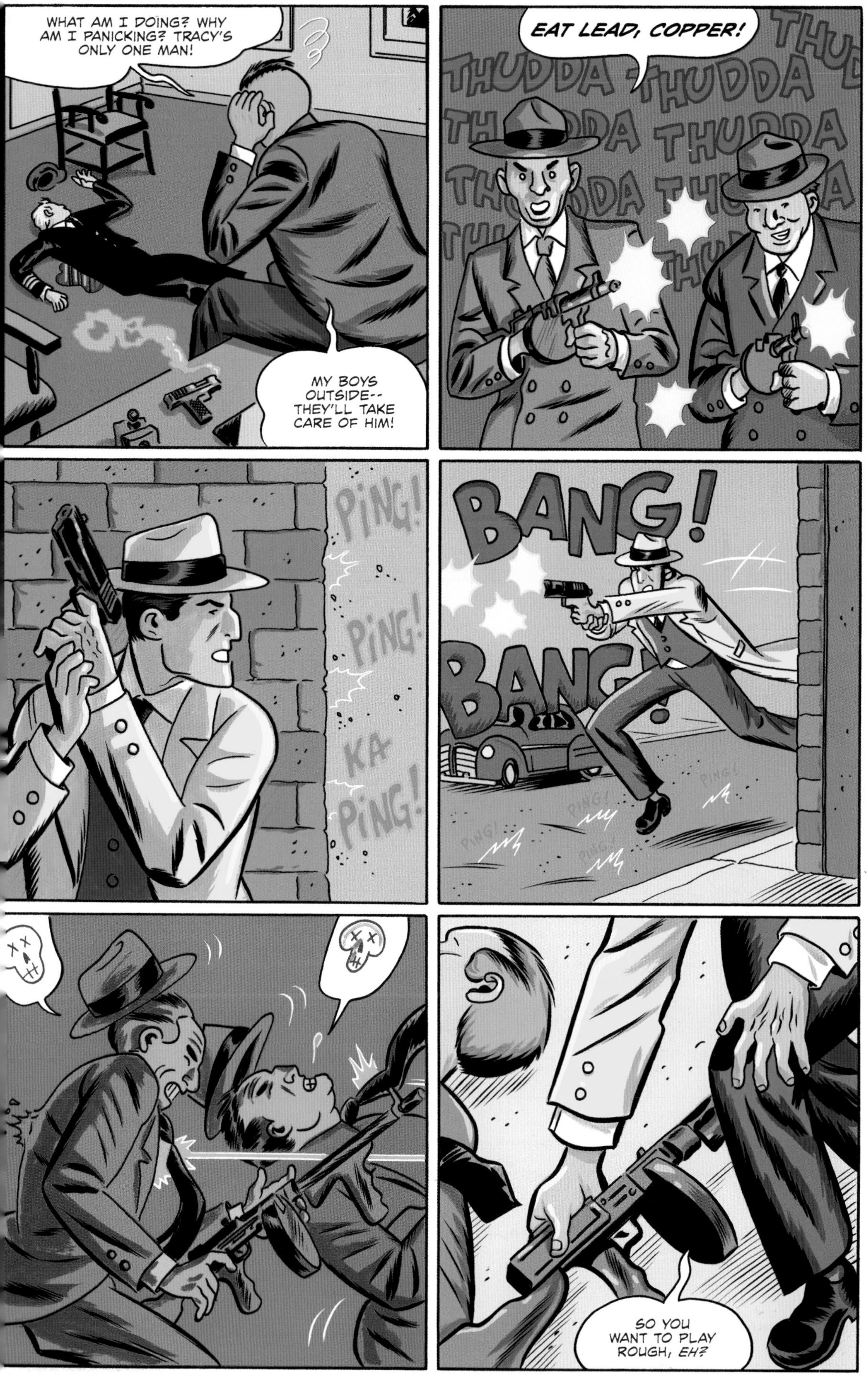
WHAT AM I DOING? WHY AM I PANICKING? TRACY'S ONLY ONE MAN!
MY BOYS OUTSIDE-- THEY'LL TAKE CARE OF HIM!
EAT LEAD, COPPER!
THUDDA THUDDA THUDDA THUDDA THUDDA THUDDA
PING! PING! KA PING!
BANG! BANG!
PING! PING! PING! PING!
SO YOU WANT TO PLAY ROUGH, EH?

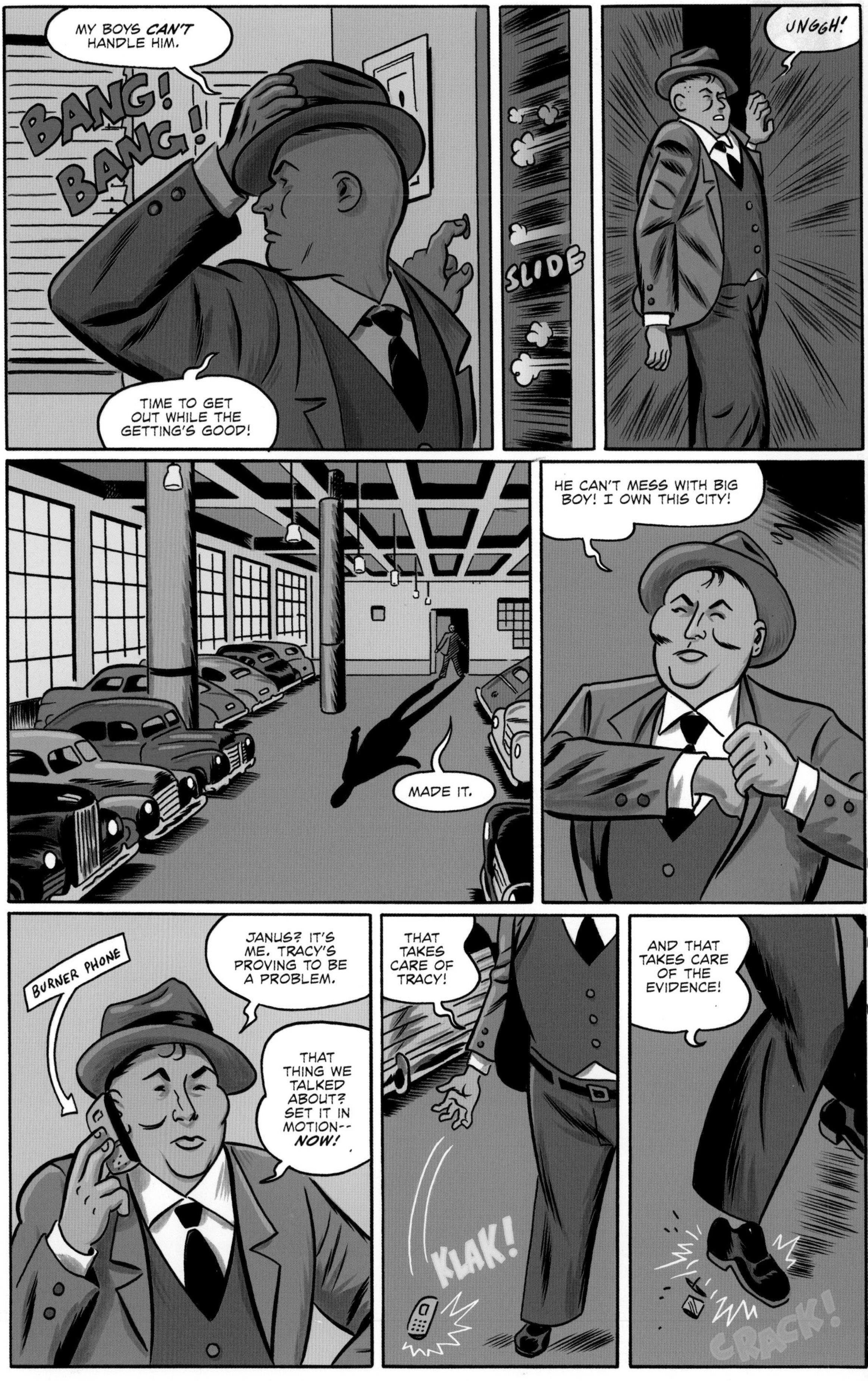
MY BOYS CAN'T HANDLE HIM.
BANG! BANG!
TIME TO GET OUT WHILE THE GETTING'S GOOD!
SLIDE
UNGGH!
MADE IT.
HE CAN'T MESS WITH BIG BOY! I OWN THIS CITY!
BURNER PHONE
JANUS? IT'S ME. TRACY'S PROVING TO BE A PROBLEM.
THAT THING WE TALKED ABOUT? SET IT IN MOTION-- NOW!
THAT TAKES CARE OF TRACY!
KLAK!
AND THAT TAKES CARE OF THE EVIDENCE!
CRACK!

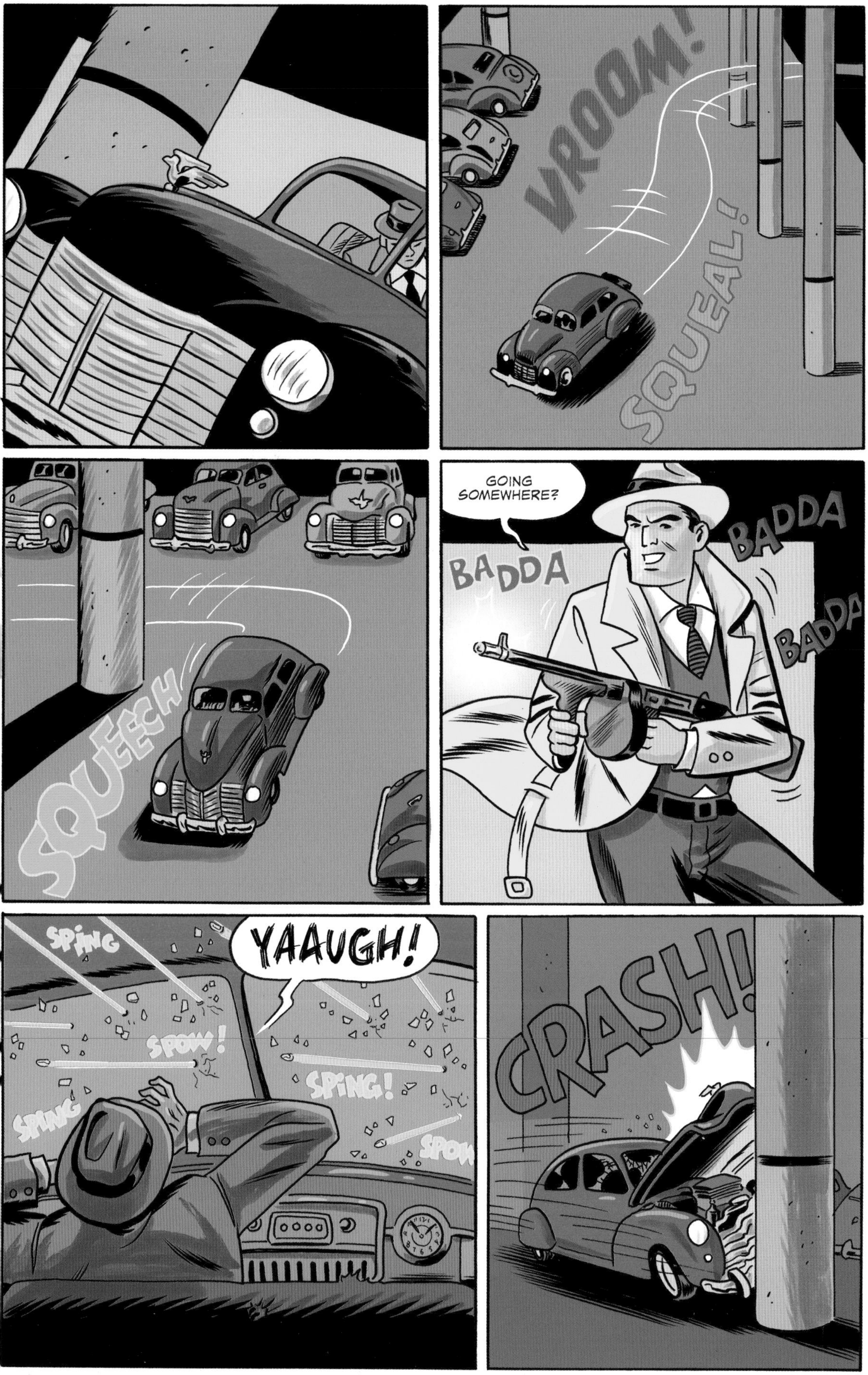
VROOM!
SQUEAL!
SQUEEECH
GOING SOMEWHERE?
BADDA
BADDA
BADDA
YAAUGH!
SPING
SPOW!
SPING!
SPING
SPOW
CRASH!

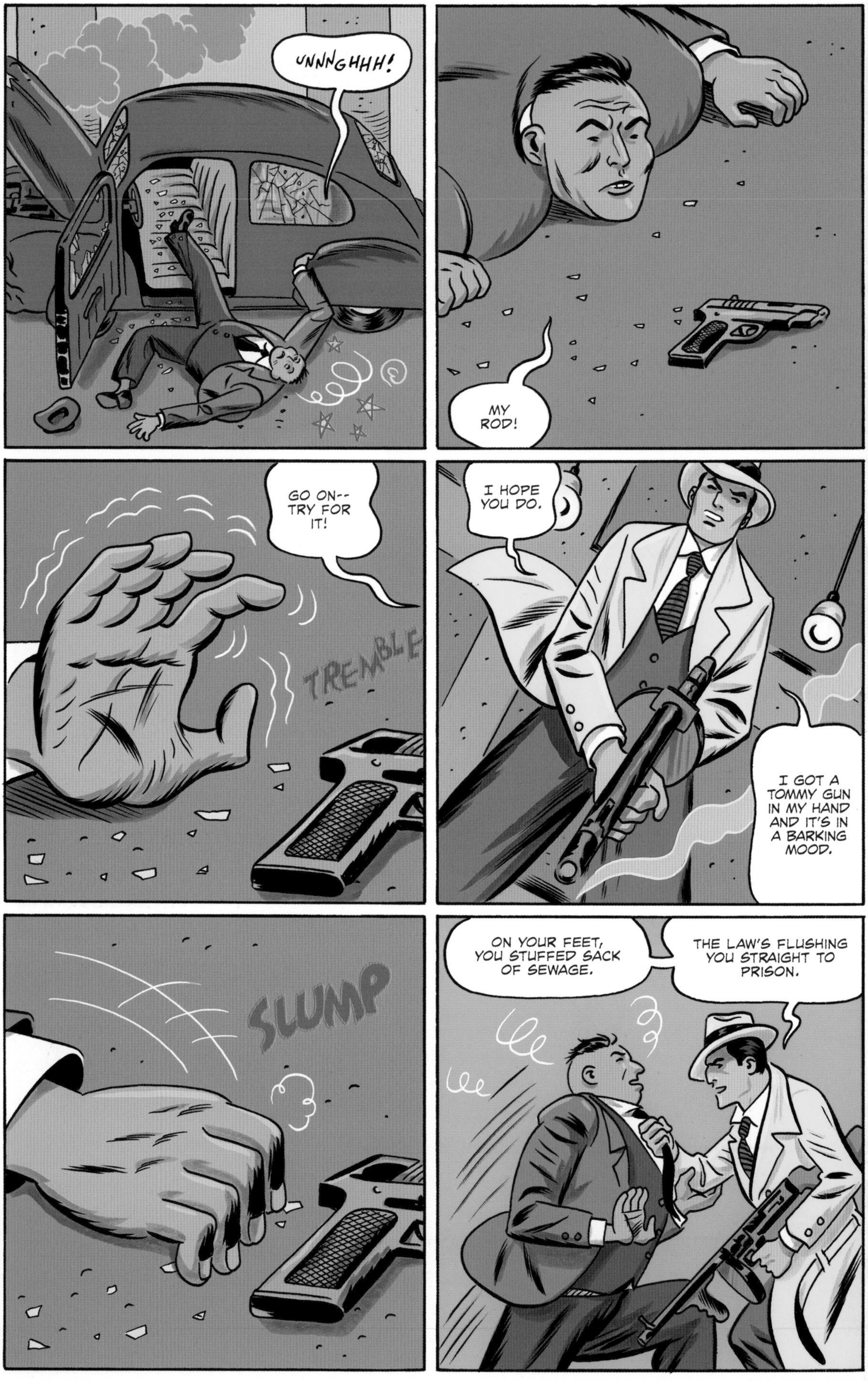
UNNNGHHH!
MY ROD!
GO ON--
TRY FOR
IT!
TREMBLE
I HOPE
YOU DO.
I GOT A
TOMMY GUN
IN MY HAND
AND IT'S IN
A BARKING
MOOD.
SLUMP
ON YOUR FEET,
YOU STUFFED SACK
OF SEWAGE.
THE LAW'S FLUSHING
YOU STRAIGHT TO
PRISON.

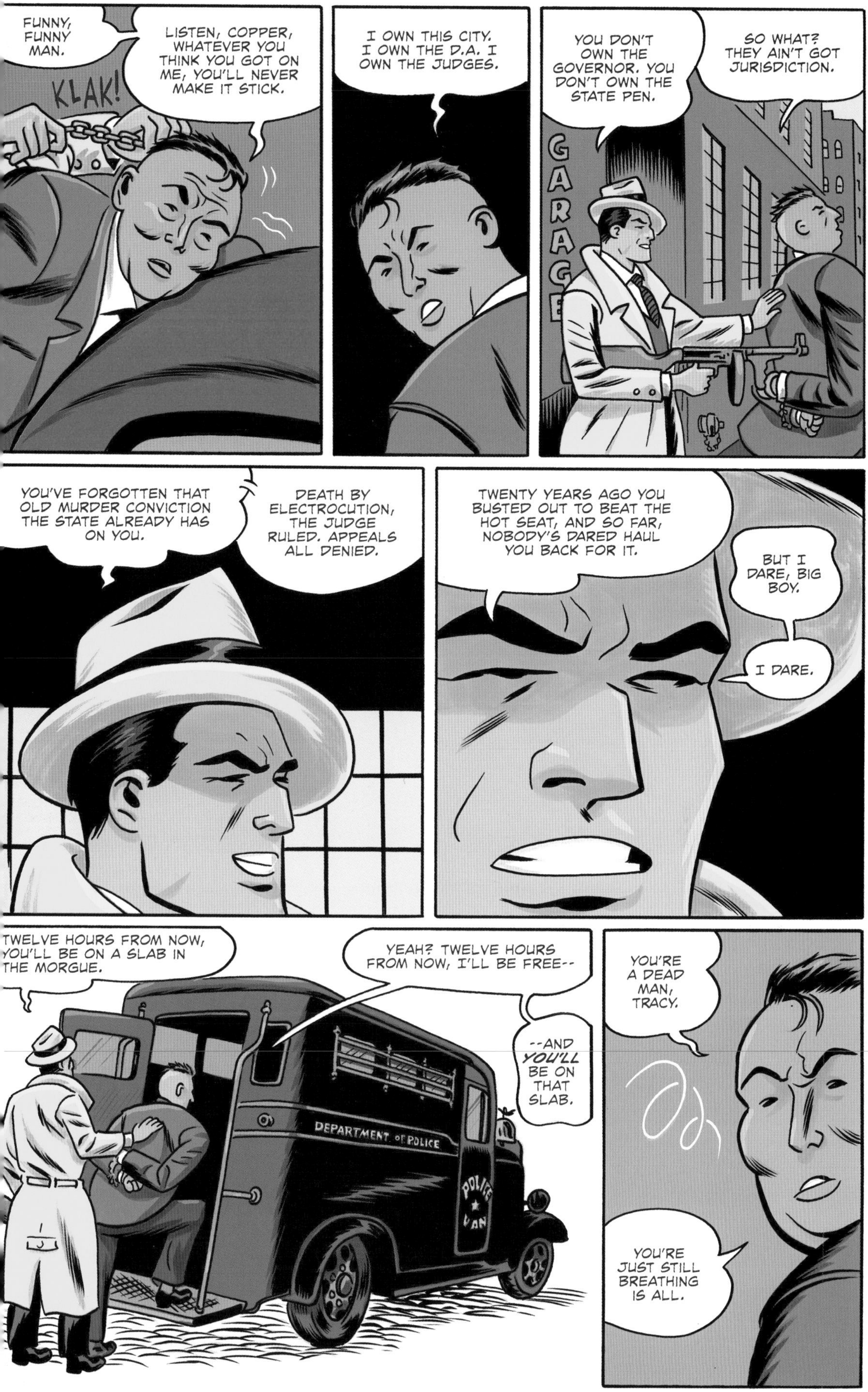
FUNNY, FUNNY MAN.
KLAK!
LISTEN, COPPER, WHATEVER YOU THINK YOU GOT ON ME, YOU'LL NEVER MAKE IT STICK.
I OWN THIS CITY. I OWN THE D.A. I OWN THE JUDGES.
YOU DON'T OWN THE GOVERNOR. YOU DON'T OWN THE STATE PEN.
SO WHAT? THEY AIN'T GOT JURISDICTION.
GARAGE
YOU'VE FORGOTTEN THAT OLD MURDER CONVICTION THE STATE ALREADY HAS ON YOU.
DEATH BY ELECTROCUTION, THE JUDGE RULED. APPEALS ALL DENIED.
TWENTY YEARS AGO YOU BUSTED OUT TO BEAT THE HOT SEAT, AND SO FAR, NOBODY'S DARED HAUL YOU BACK FOR IT.
BUT I DARE, BIG BOY.
I DARE.
TWELVE HOURS FROM NOW, YOU'LL BE ON A SLAB IN THE MORGUE.
YEAH? TWELVE HOURS FROM NOW, I'LL BE FREE--
--AND *YOU'LL* BE ON THAT SLAB.
DEPARTMENT OF POLICE
POLICE VAN
YOU'RE A DEAD MAN, TRACY.
YOU'RE JUST STILL BREATHING IS ALL.

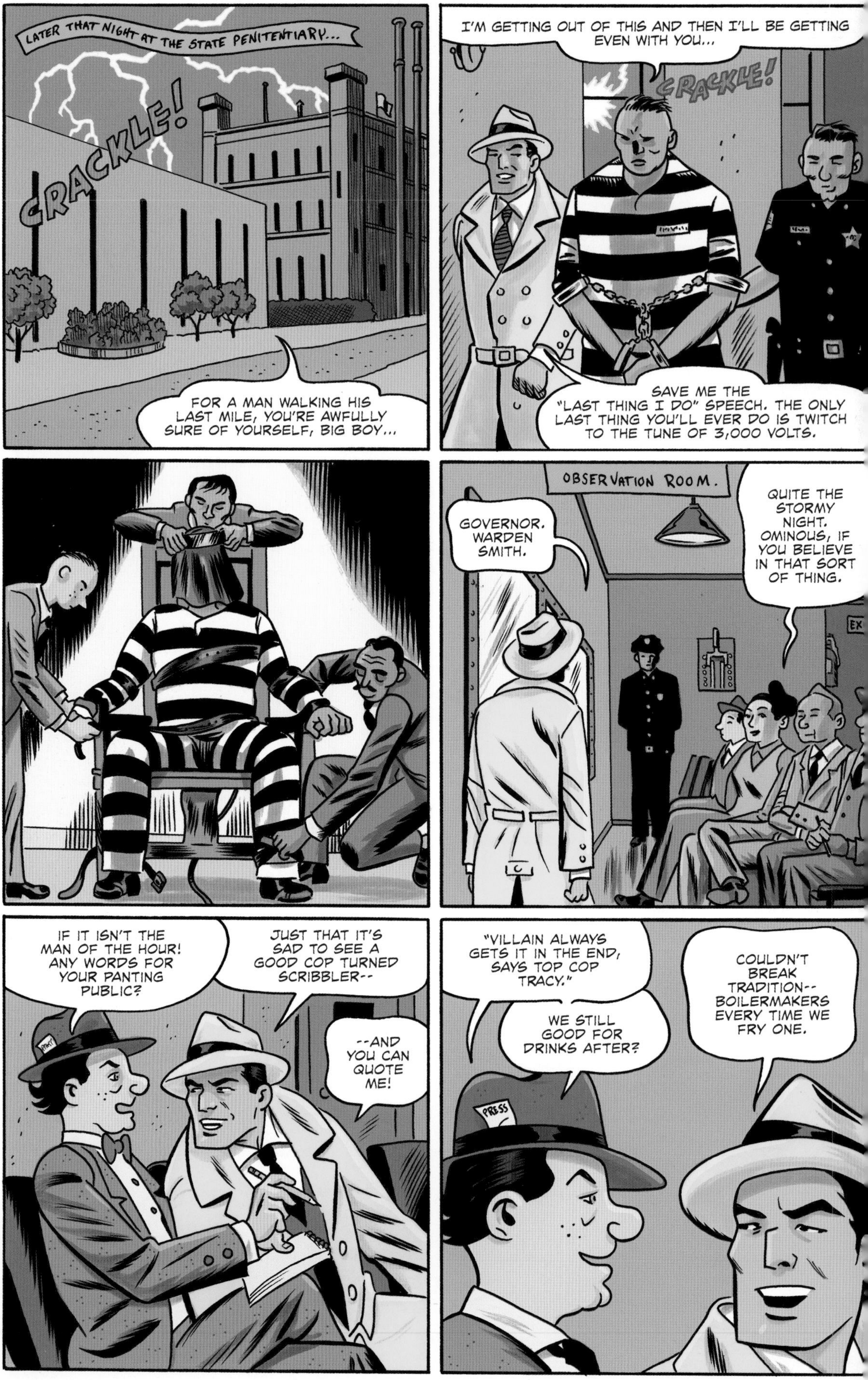
LATER THAT NIGHT AT THE STATE PENITENTIARY...
CRACKLE!
FOR A MAN WALKING HIS LAST MILE, YOU'RE AWFULLY SURE OF YOURSELF, BIG BOY...
I'M GETTING OUT OF THIS AND THEN I'LL BE GETTING EVEN WITH YOU...
CRACKLE!
SAVE ME THE "LAST THING I DO" SPEECH. THE ONLY LAST THING YOU'LL EVER DO IS TWITCH TO THE TUNE OF 3,000 VOLTS.
OBSERVATION ROOM.
GOVERNOR. WARDEN SMITH.
QUITE THE STORMY NIGHT. OMINOUS, IF YOU BELIEVE IN THAT SORT OF THING.
IF IT ISN'T THE MAN OF THE HOUR! ANY WORDS FOR YOUR PANTING PUBLIC?
JUST THAT IT'S SAD TO SEE A GOOD COP TURNED SCRIBBLER--
--AND YOU CAN QUOTE ME!
"VILLAIN ALWAYS GETS IT IN THE END, SAYS TOP COP TRACY."
WE STILL GOOD FOR DRINKS AFTER?
COULDN'T BREAK TRADITION--BOILERMAKERS EVERY TIME WE FRY ONE.
PRESS

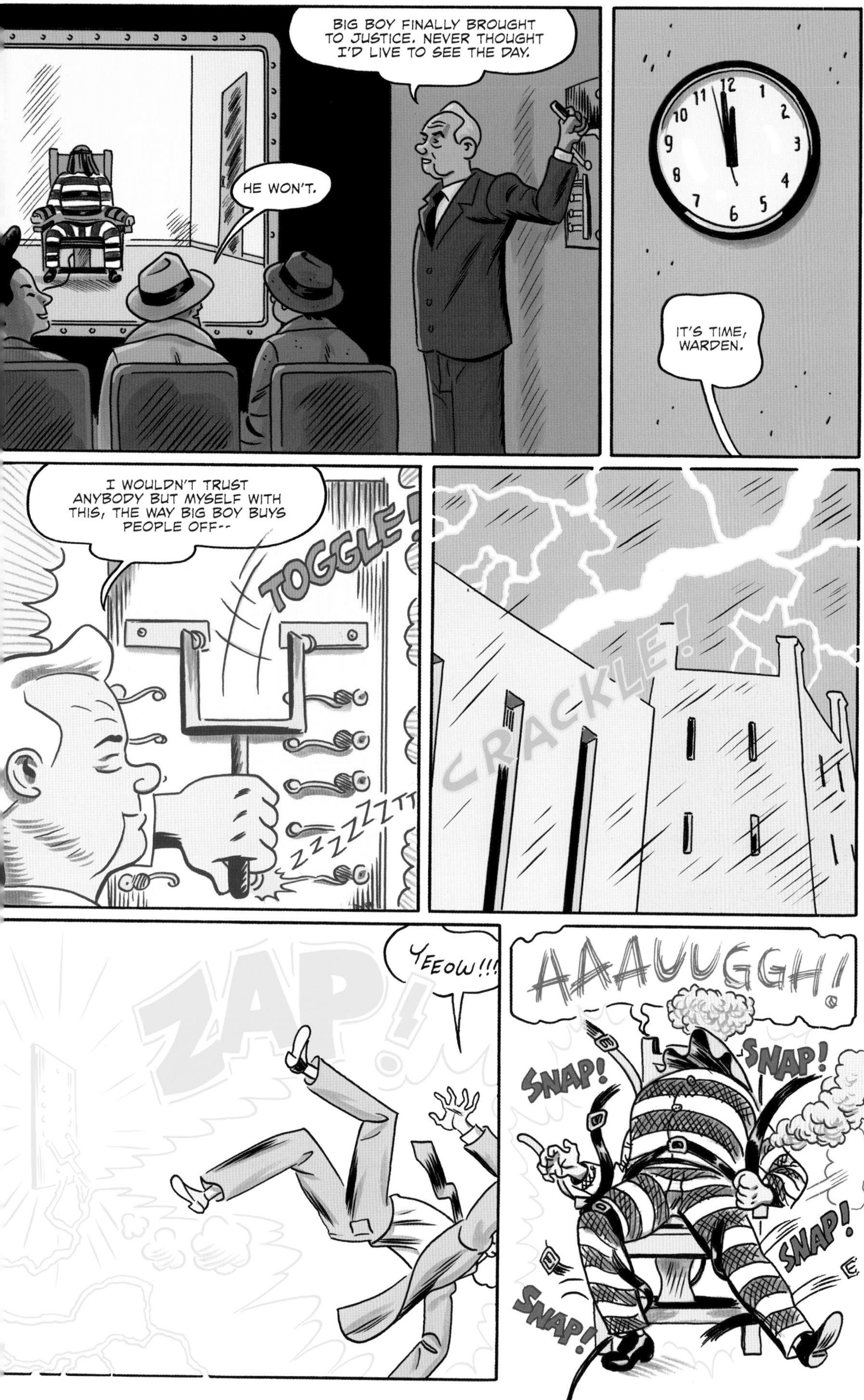
BIG BOY FINALLY BROUGHT TO JUSTICE. NEVER THOUGHT I'D LIVE TO SEE THE DAY.
HE WON'T.
IT'S TIME, WARDEN.
I WOULDN'T TRUST ANYBODY BUT MYSELF WITH THIS, THE WAY BIG BOY BUYS PEOPLE OFF--
TOGGLE!
ZZZZZZTT
CRACKLE!
ZAP!
YEEOW!!!
AAAUUGGH!
SNAP!
SNAP!
SNAP!
SNAP!

WARDEN!

NEVER MIND ME--I'M OKAY. WHAT ABOUT BIG BOY?

THE PRISON CORONER IS EXAMINING HIM NOW...

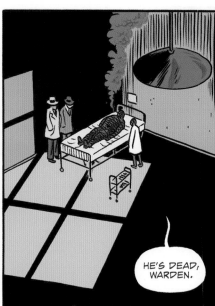

HE'S DEAD, WARDEN.

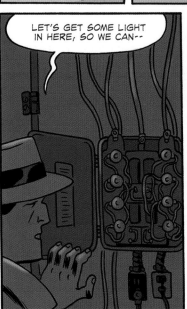

LET'S GET SOME LIGHT IN HERE, SO WE CAN--

KLIK!

WHAT THE--?!

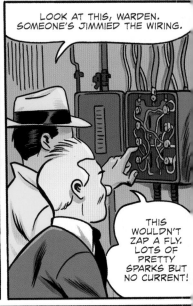

LOOK AT THIS, WARDEN. SOMEONE'S JIMMIED THE WIRING.

THIS WOULDN'T ZAP A FLY. LOTS OF PRETTY SPARKS BUT NO CURRENT!

BUT WHO--?

SOMEONE WORKING FOR BIG BOY, OF COURSE. ALL IT'D TAKE IS TWO MINUTES' ACCESS TO THIS ROOM.

WARDEN, YOU HAVE A MOLE IN YOUR PRISON.

AND HE WOULD HAVE GOTTEN AWAY WITH IT, TOO, IF IT HADN'T BEEN FOR THAT FREAK LIGHTNING STRIKE!

YOU MENTIONED OMENS FROM ABOVE, GOVERNOR? I THINK THIS QUALIFIES.

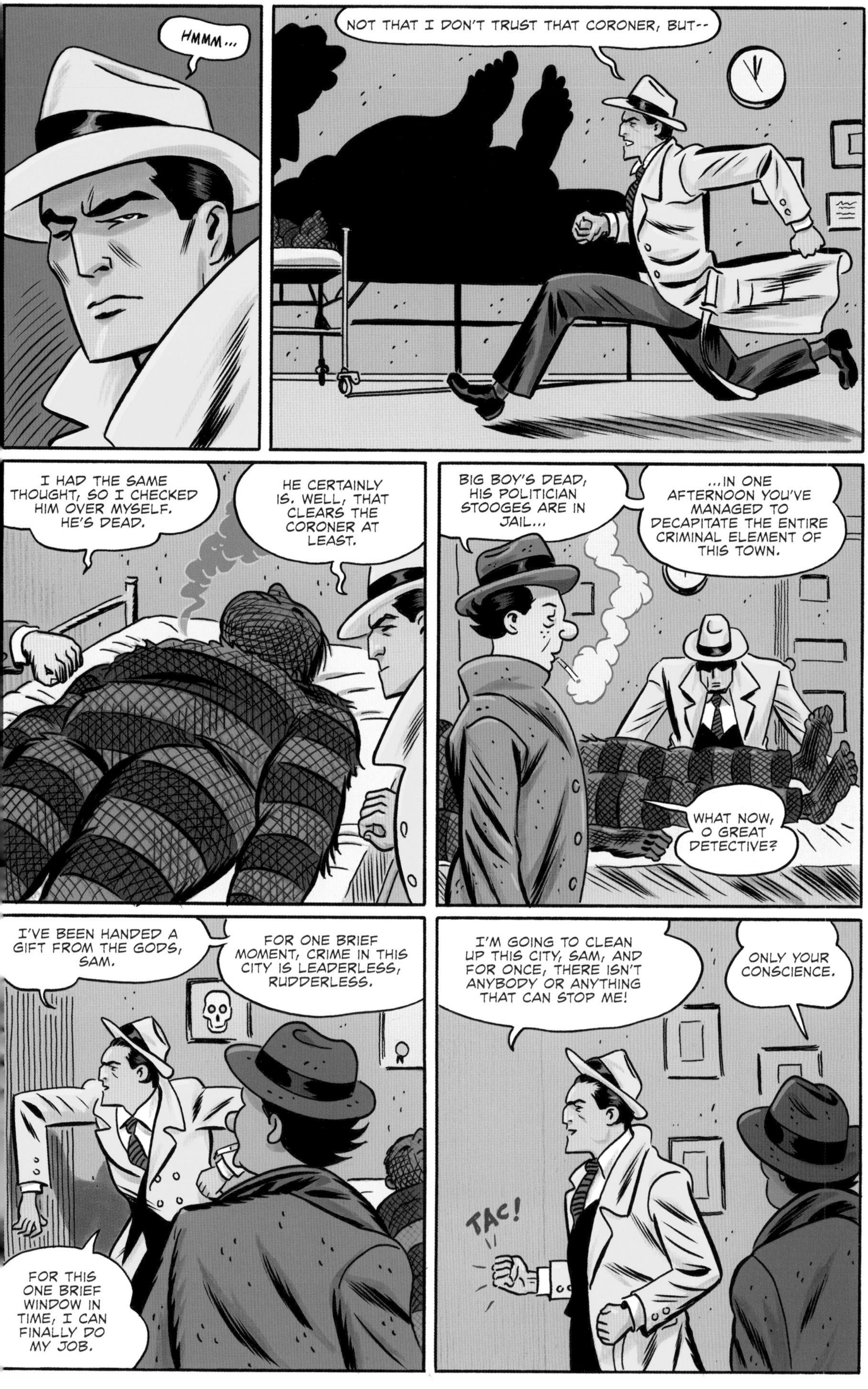
HMMM...
NOT THAT I DON'T TRUST THAT CORONER, BUT--
I HAD THE SAME THOUGHT, SO I CHECKED HIM OVER MYSELF. HE'S DEAD.
HE CERTAINLY IS. WELL, THAT CLEARS THE CORONER AT LEAST.
BIG BOY'S DEAD, HIS POLITICIAN STOOGES ARE IN JAIL...
...IN ONE AFTERNOON YOU'VE MANAGED TO DECAPITATE THE ENTIRE CRIMINAL ELEMENT OF THIS TOWN.
WHAT NOW, O GREAT DETECTIVE?
I'VE BEEN HANDED A GIFT FROM THE GODS, SAM.
FOR ONE BRIEF MOMENT, CRIME IN THIS CITY IS LEADERLESS, RUDDERLESS.
FOR THIS ONE BRIEF WINDOW IN TIME, I CAN FINALLY DO MY JOB.
I'M GOING TO CLEAN UP THIS CITY, SAM, AND FOR ONCE, THERE ISN'T ANYBODY OR ANYTHING THAT CAN STOP ME!
ONLY YOUR CONSCIENCE.
TAC!

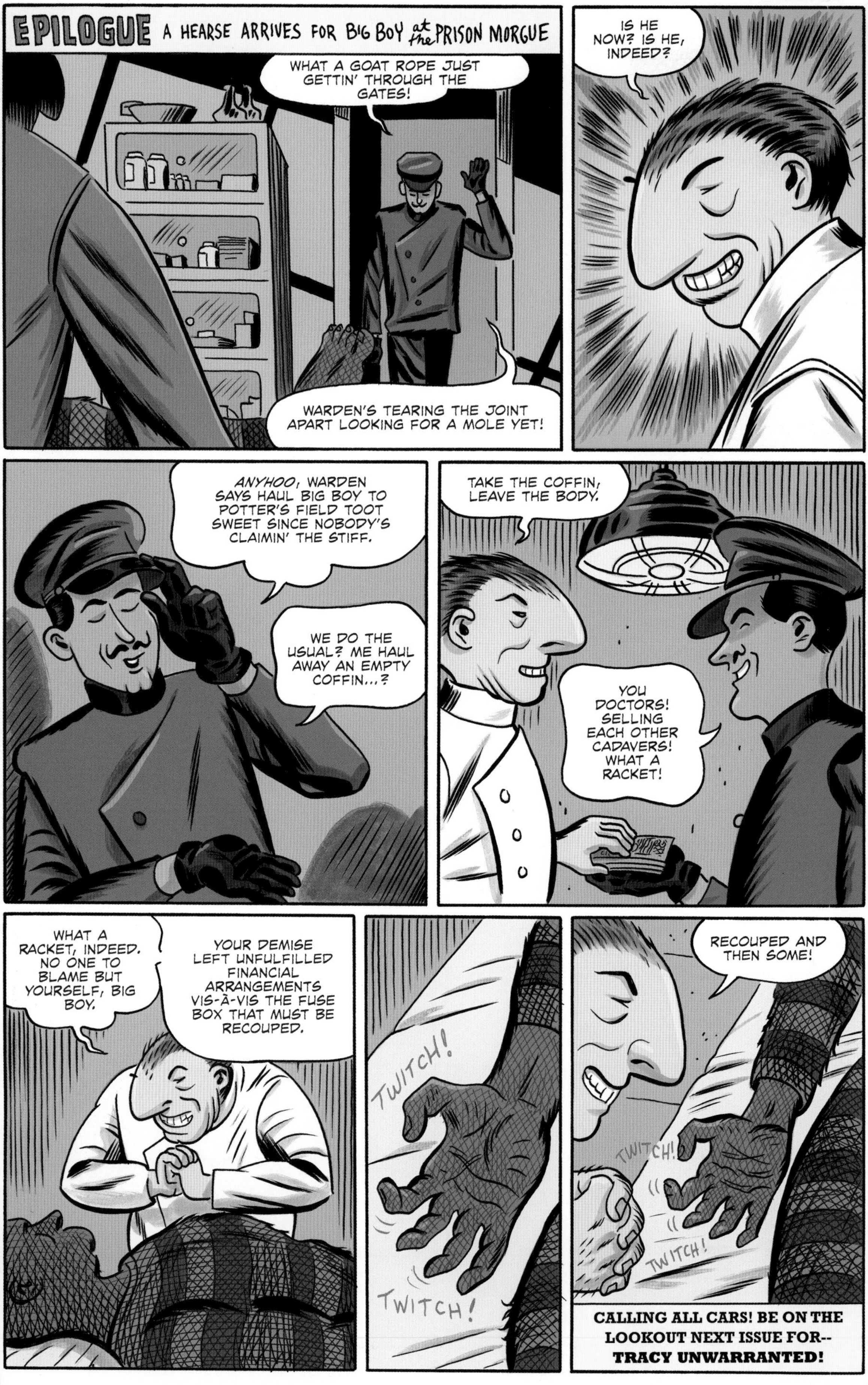
EPILOGUE A HEARSE ARRIVES FOR BIG BOY at the PRISON MORGUE
WHAT A GOAT ROPE JUST GETTIN' THROUGH THE GATES!
WARDEN'S TEARING THE JOINT APART LOOKING FOR A MOLE YET!
IS HE NOW? IS HE, INDEED?
ANYHOO, WARDEN SAYS HAUL BIG BOY TO POTTER'S FIELD TOOT SWEET SINCE NOBODY'S CLAIMIN' THE STIFF.
WE DO THE USUAL? ME HAUL AWAY AN EMPTY COFFIN...?
TAKE THE COFFIN, LEAVE THE BODY.
YOU DOCTORS! SELLING EACH OTHER CADAVERS! WHAT A RACKET!
WHAT A RACKET, INDEED. NO ONE TO BLAME BUT YOURSELF, BIG BOY.
YOUR DEMISE LEFT UNFULFILLED FINANCIAL ARRANGEMENTS VIS-À-VIS THE FUSE BOX THAT MUST BE RECOUPED.
TWITCH!
TWITCH!
TWITCH!
RECOUPED AND THEN SOME!
TWITCH!
TWITCH!
CALLING ALL CARS! BE ON THE LOOKOUT NEXT ISSUE FOR--
TRACY UNWARRANTED!

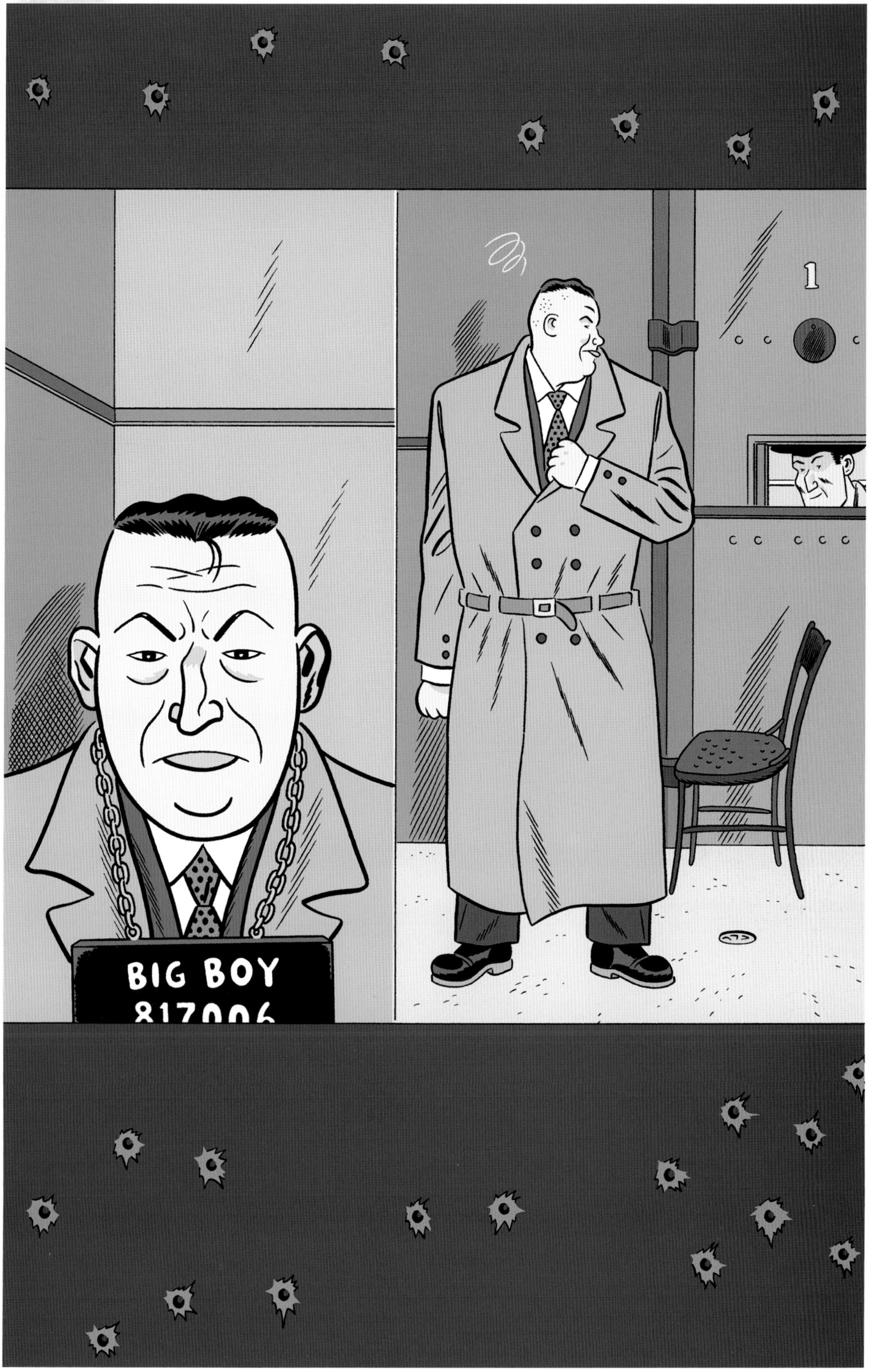

1
BIG BOY
817006

ART BY **RICH TOMMASO** | COLORS BY **AMY PLASMAN**

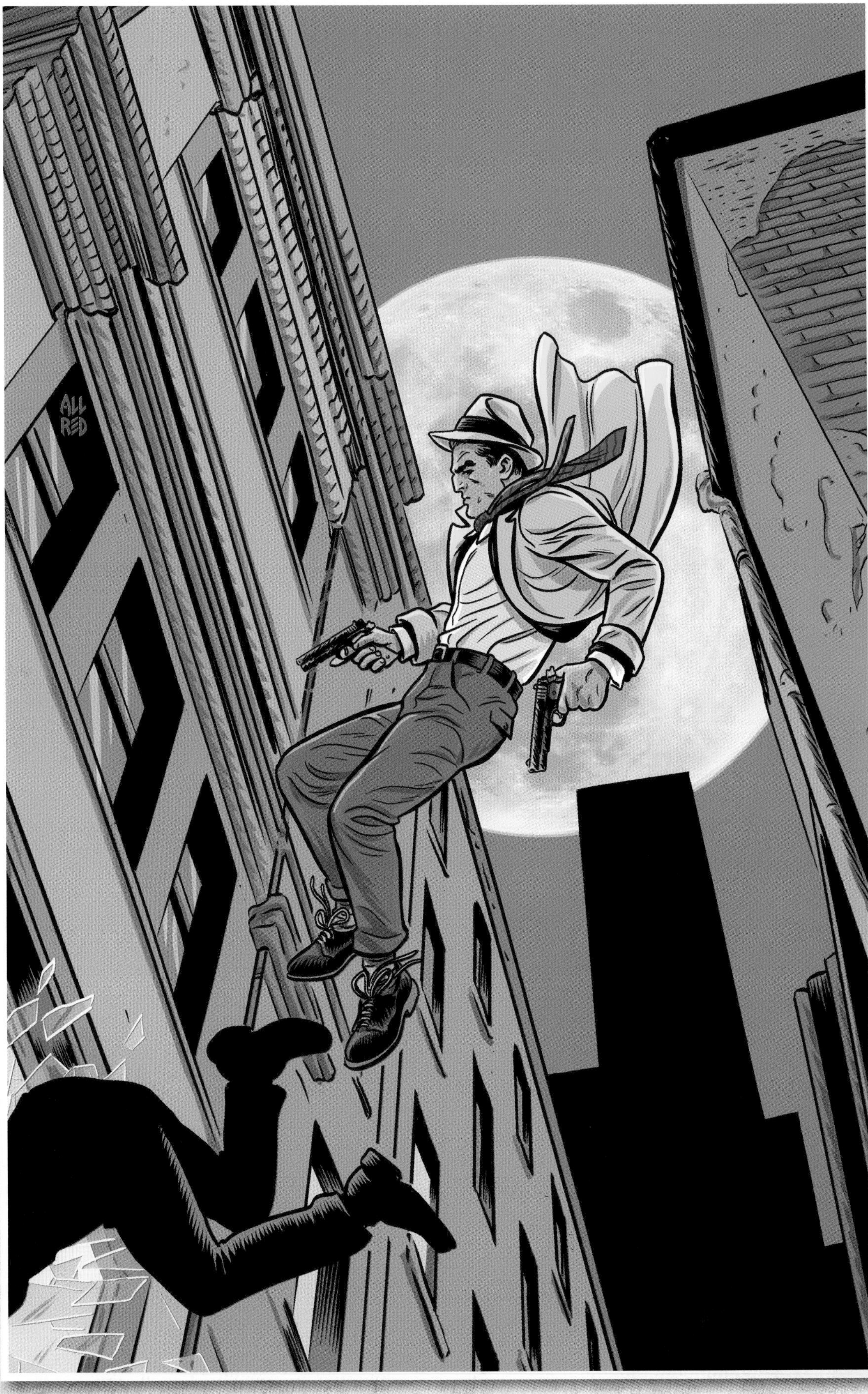
ALL
RED

ART BY **MICHAEL ALLRED** | COLORS BY **LAURA ALLRED**

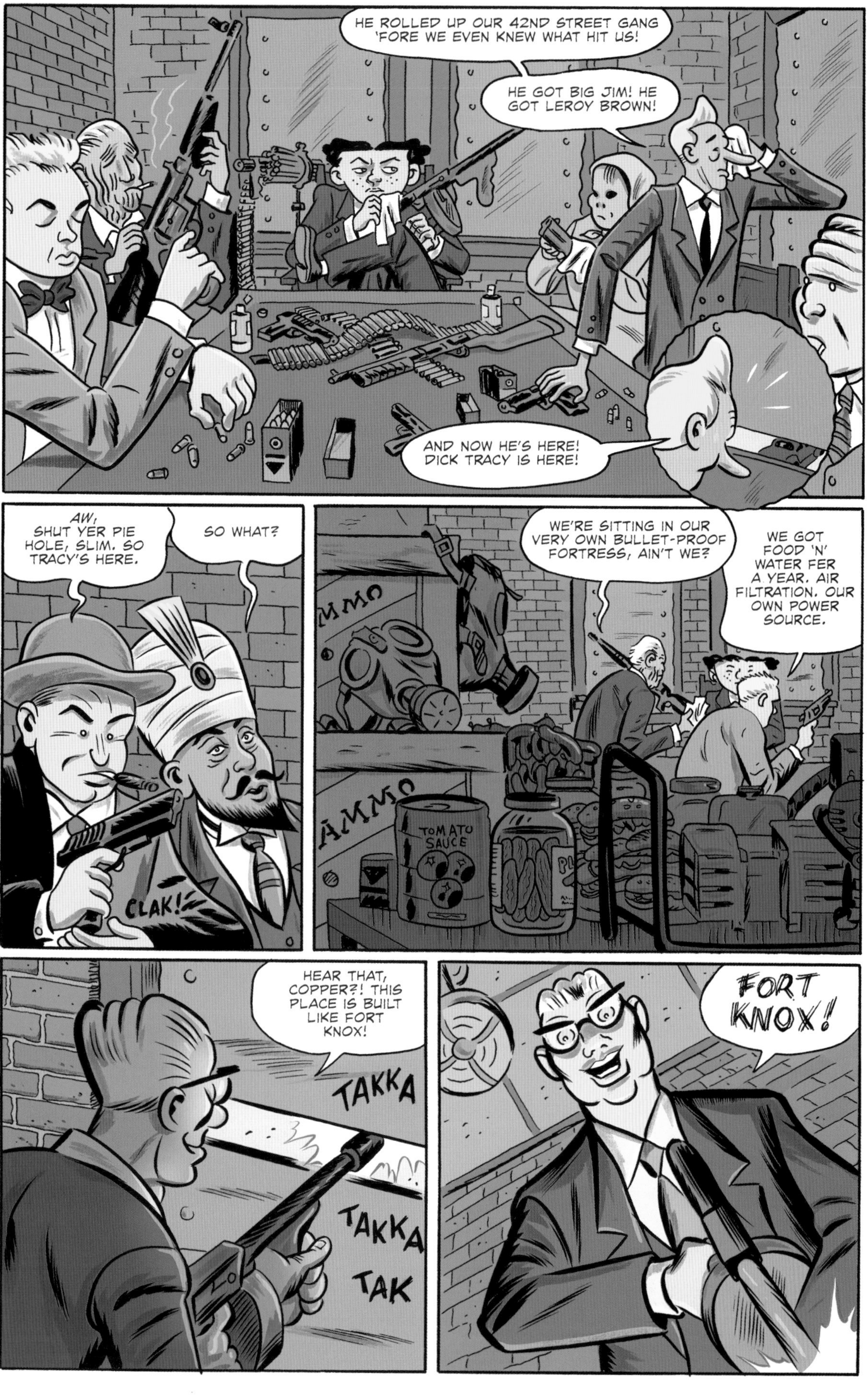
HE ROLLED UP OUR 42ND STREET GANG 'FORE WE EVEN KNEW WHAT HIT US!
HE GOT BIG JIM! HE GOT LEROY BROWN!
AND NOW HE'S HERE! DICK TRACY IS HERE!
AW, SHUT YER PIE HOLE, SLIM. SO TRACY'S HERE.
SO WHAT?
CLAK!
WE'RE SITTING IN OUR VERY OWN BULLET-PROOF FORTRESS, AIN'T WE?
WE GOT FOOD 'N' WATER FER A YEAR. AIR FILTRATION. OUR OWN POWER SOURCE.
AMMO
AMMO
TOMATO SAUCE
HEAR THAT, COPPER?! THIS PLACE IS BUILT LIKE FORT KNOX!
TAKKA
TAKKA
TAK
FORT KNOX!

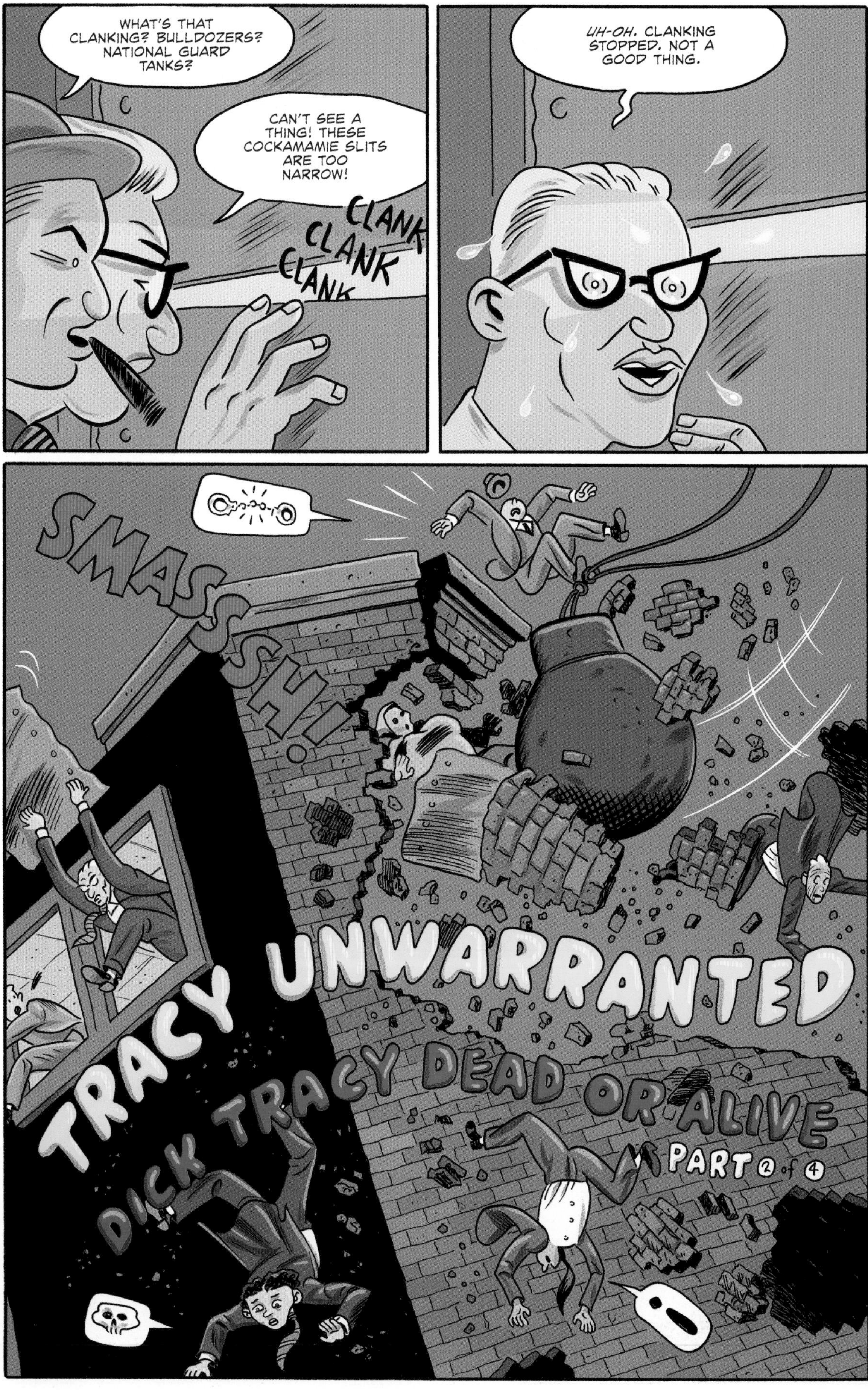

WHAT'S THAT CLANKING? BULLDOZERS? NATIONAL GUARD TANKS?
CAN'T SEE A THING! THESE COCKAMAMIE SLITS ARE TOO NARROW!
CLANK CLANK CLANK
UH-OH. CLANKING STOPPED. NOT A GOOD THING.
SMASSSSH!
TRACY UNWARRANTED
DICK TRACY DEAD OR ALIVE
PART 2 of 4

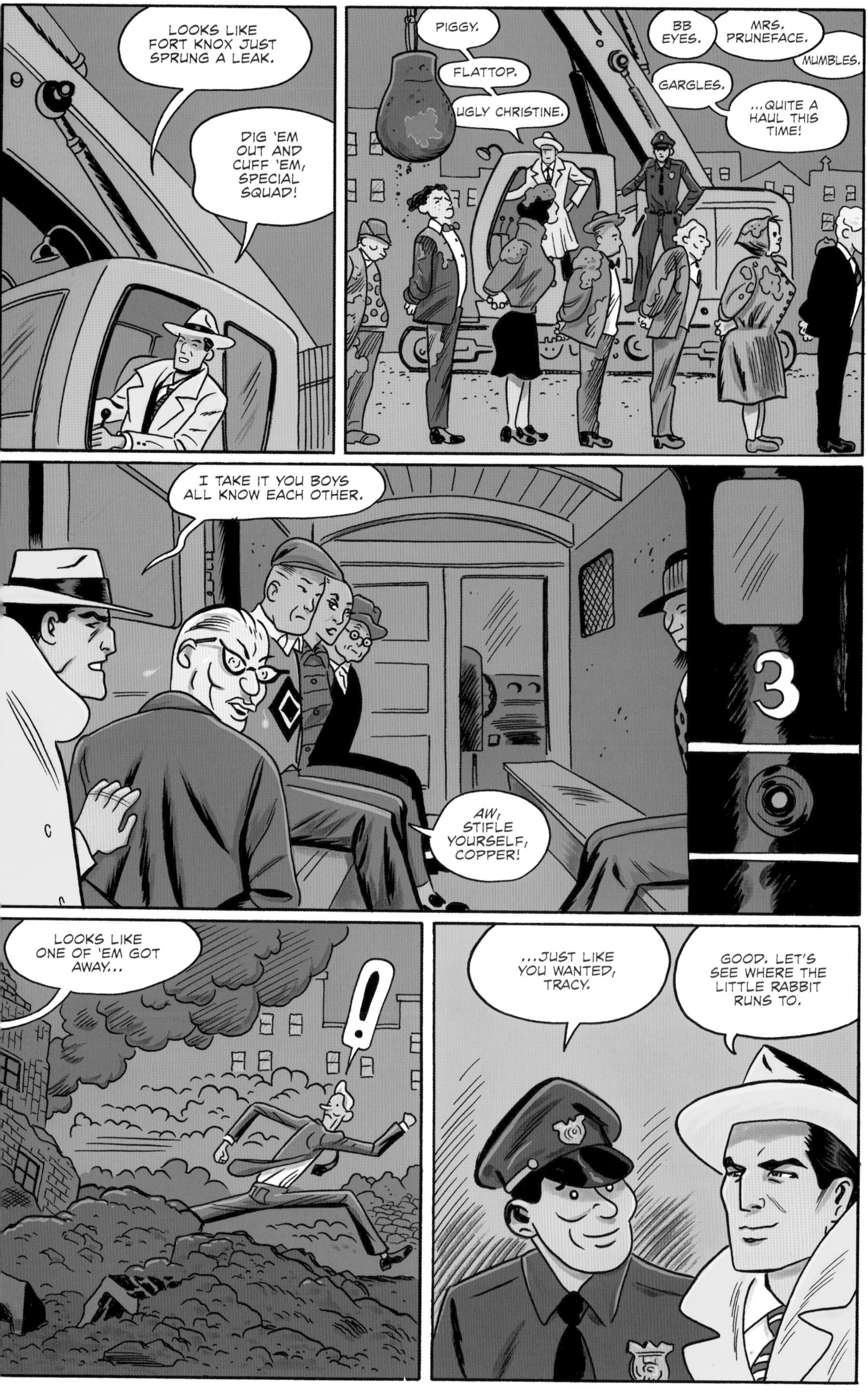

LOOKS LIKE FORT KNOX JUST SPRUNG A LEAK.
DIG 'EM OUT AND CUFF 'EM, SPECIAL SQUAD!
PIGGY.
FLATTOP.
UGLY CHRISTINE.
BB EYES.
MRS. PRUNEFACE.
MUMBLES.
GARGLES.
...QUITE A HAUL THIS TIME!
I TAKE IT YOU BOYS ALL KNOW EACH OTHER.
AW, STIFLE YOURSELF, COPPER!
3
LOOKS LIKE ONE OF 'EM GOT AWAY...
!
...JUST LIKE YOU WANTED, TRACY.
GOOD. LET'S SEE WHERE THE LITTLE RABBIT RUNS TO.

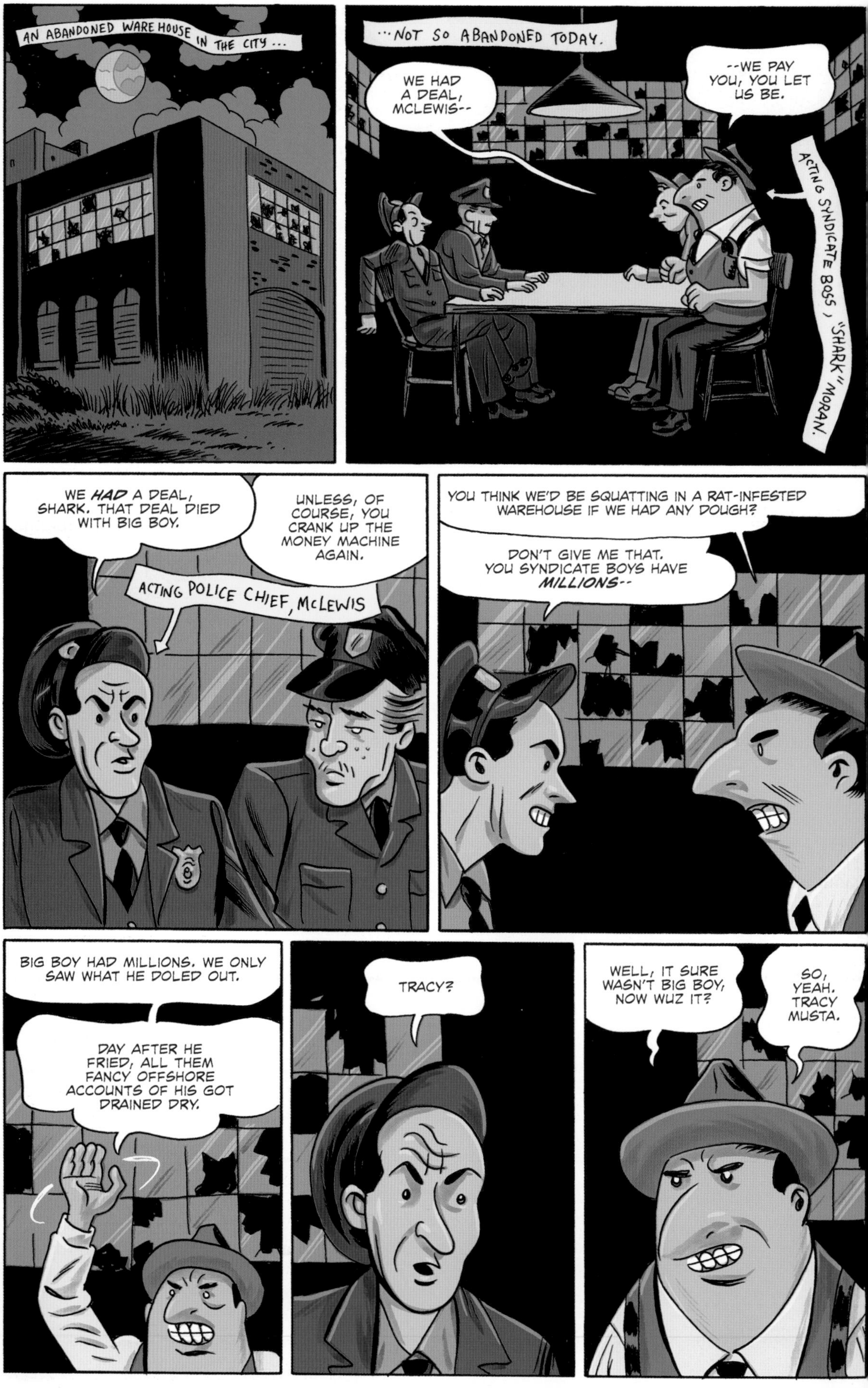
AN ABANDONED WAREHOUSE IN THE CITY...
...NOT SO ABANDONED TODAY.
WE HAD A DEAL, MCLEWIS--
--WE PAY YOU, YOU LET US BE.
ACTING SYNDICATE BOSS, "SHARK" MORAN.
WE HAD A DEAL, SHARK. THAT DEAL DIED WITH BIG BOY.
UNLESS, OF COURSE, YOU CRANK UP THE MONEY MACHINE AGAIN.
ACTING POLICE CHIEF, McLEWIS
YOU THINK WE'D BE SQUATTING IN A RAT-INFESTED WAREHOUSE IF WE HAD ANY DOUGH?
DON'T GIVE ME THAT. YOU SYNDICATE BOYS HAVE MILLIONS--
BIG BOY HAD MILLIONS. WE ONLY SAW WHAT HE DOLED OUT.
DAY AFTER HE FRIED, ALL THEM FANCY OFFSHORE ACCOUNTS OF HIS GOT DRAINED DRY.
TRACY?
WELL, IT SURE WASN'T BIG BOY, NOW WUZ IT?
SO, YEAH. TRACY MUSTA.

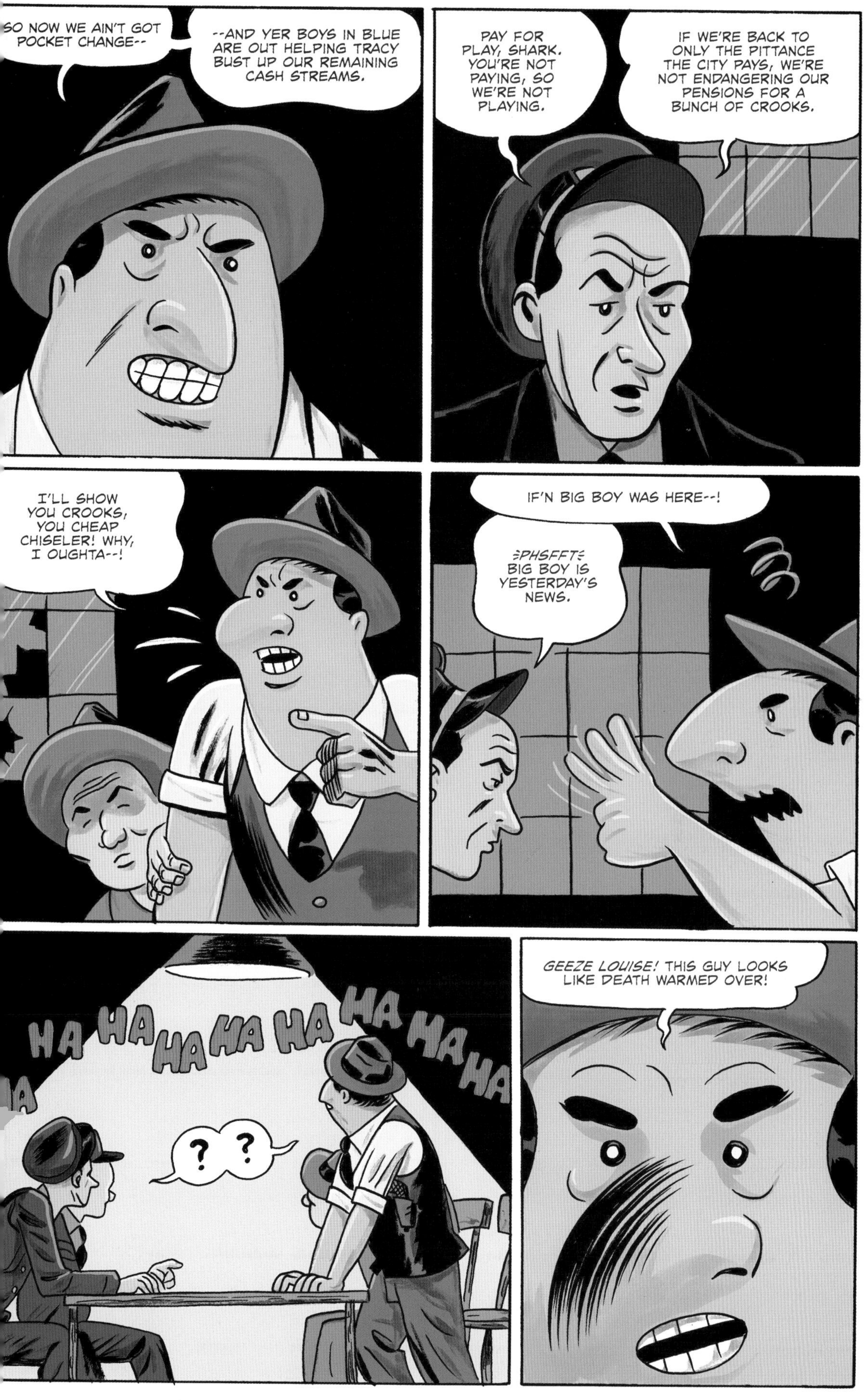
SO NOW WE AIN'T GOT POCKET CHANGE--
--AND YER BOYS IN BLUE ARE OUT HELPING TRACY BUST UP OUR REMAINING CASH STREAMS.
PAY FOR PLAY, SHARK. YOU'RE NOT PAYING, SO WE'RE NOT PLAYING.
IF WE'RE BACK TO ONLY THE PITTANCE THE CITY PAYS, WE'RE NOT ENDANGERING OUR PENSIONS FOR A BUNCH OF CROOKS.
I'LL SHOW YOU CROOKS, YOU CHEAP CHISELER! WHY, I OUGHTA--!
IF'N BIG BOY WAS HERE--!
PHSFFT BIG BOY IS YESTERDAY'S NEWS.
HA HA HA HA HA HA HA HA HA HA HA
? ?
GEEZE LOUISE! THIS GUY LOOKS LIKE DEATH WARMED OVER!

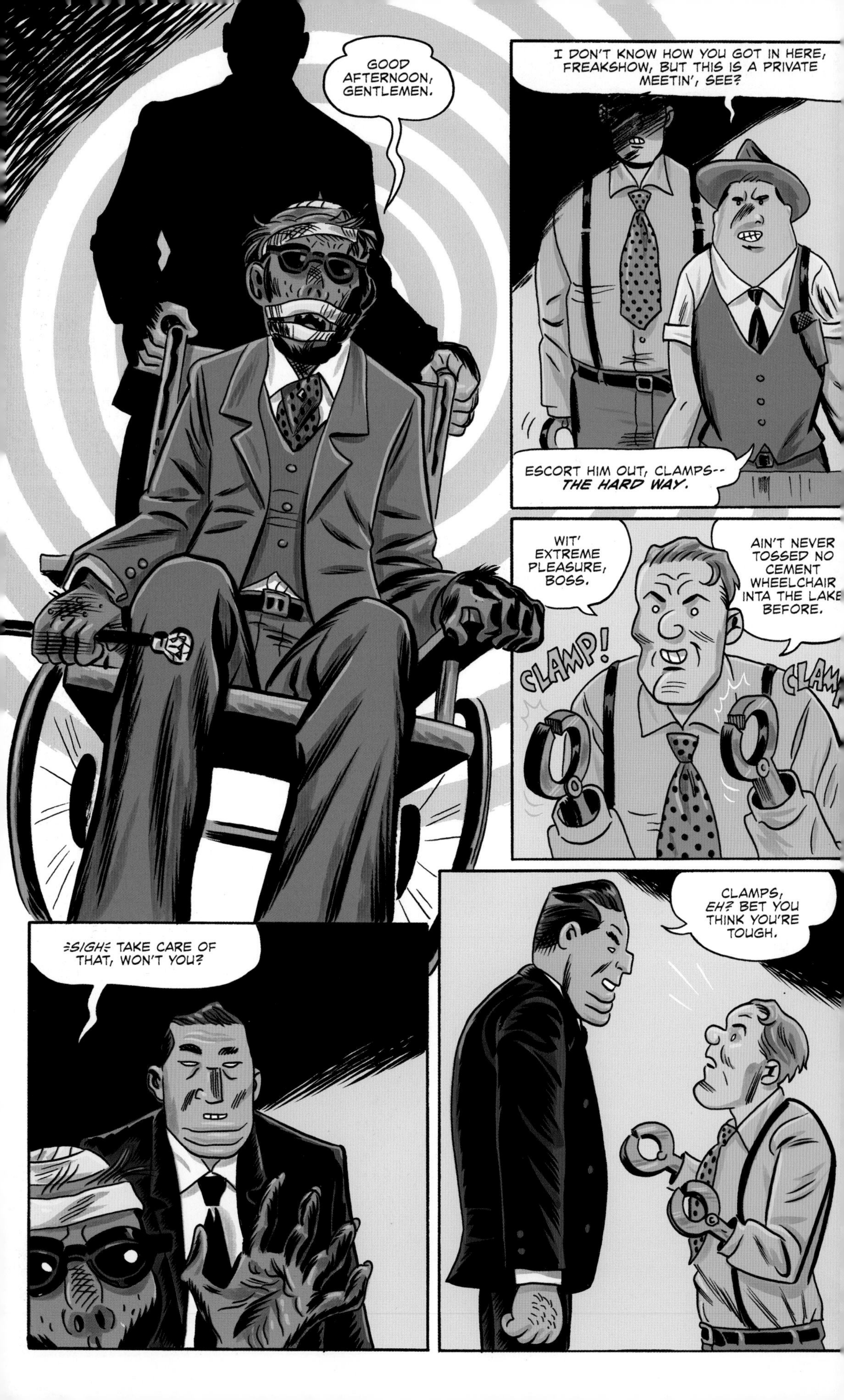
GOOD AFTERNOON, GENTLEMEN.
I DON'T KNOW HOW YOU GOT IN HERE, FREAKSHOW, BUT THIS IS A PRIVATE MEETIN', SEE?
ESCORT HIM OUT, CLAMPS-- THE HARD WAY.
WIT' EXTREME PLEASURE, BOSS.
AIN'T NEVER TOSSED NO CEMENT WHEELCHAIR INTA THE LAKE BEFORE.
CLAMP!
SIGH TAKE CARE OF THAT, WON'T YOU?
CLAMPS, EH? BET YOU THINK YOU'RE TOUGH.

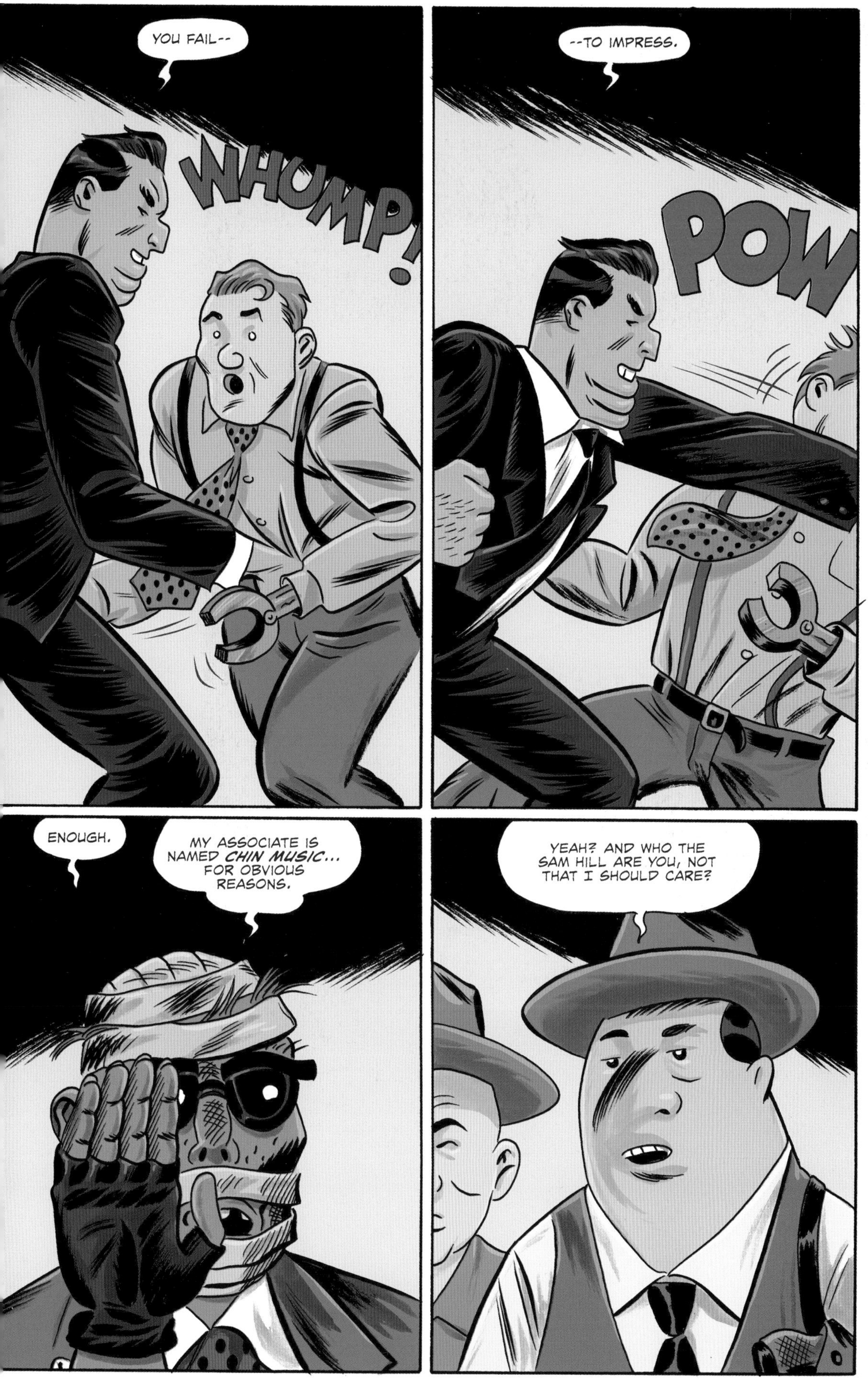
YOU FAIL--
WHOMP!
--TO IMPRESS.
POW
ENOUGH.
MY ASSOCIATE IS NAMED CHIN MUSIC... FOR OBVIOUS REASONS.
YEAH? AND WHO THE SAM HILL ARE YOU, NOT THAT I SHOULD CARE?

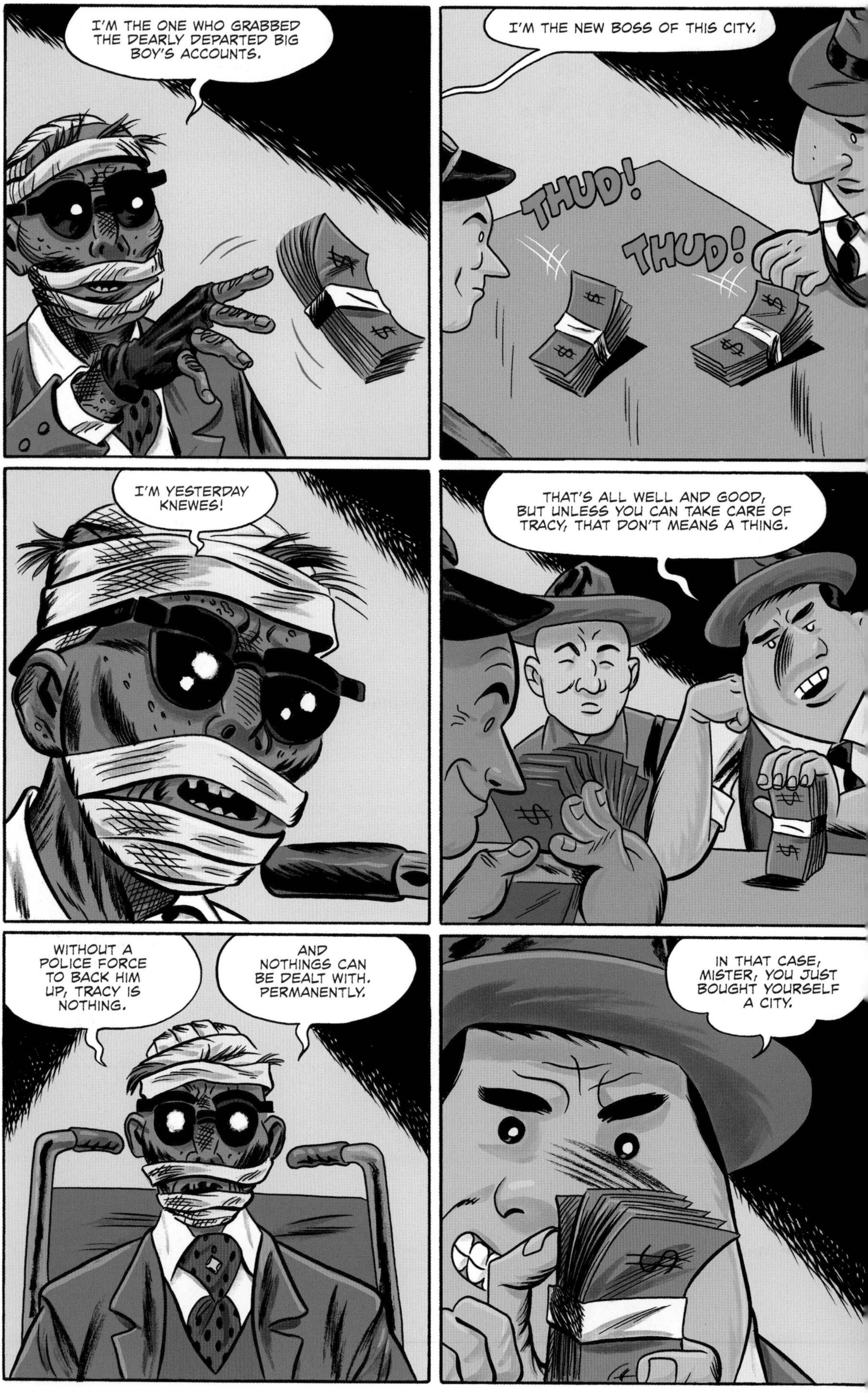
I'M THE ONE WHO GRABBED THE DEARLY DEPARTED BIG BOY'S ACCOUNTS.
I'M THE NEW BOSS OF THIS CITY.
THUD!
THUD!
I'M YESTERDAY KNEWES!
THAT'S ALL WELL AND GOOD, BUT UNLESS YOU CAN TAKE CARE OF TRACY, THAT DON'T MEANS A THING.
WITHOUT A POLICE FORCE TO BACK HIM UP, TRACY IS NOTHING.
AND NOTHINGS CAN BE DEALT WITH. PERMANENTLY.
IN THAT CASE, MISTER, YOU JUST BOUGHT YOURSELF A CITY.

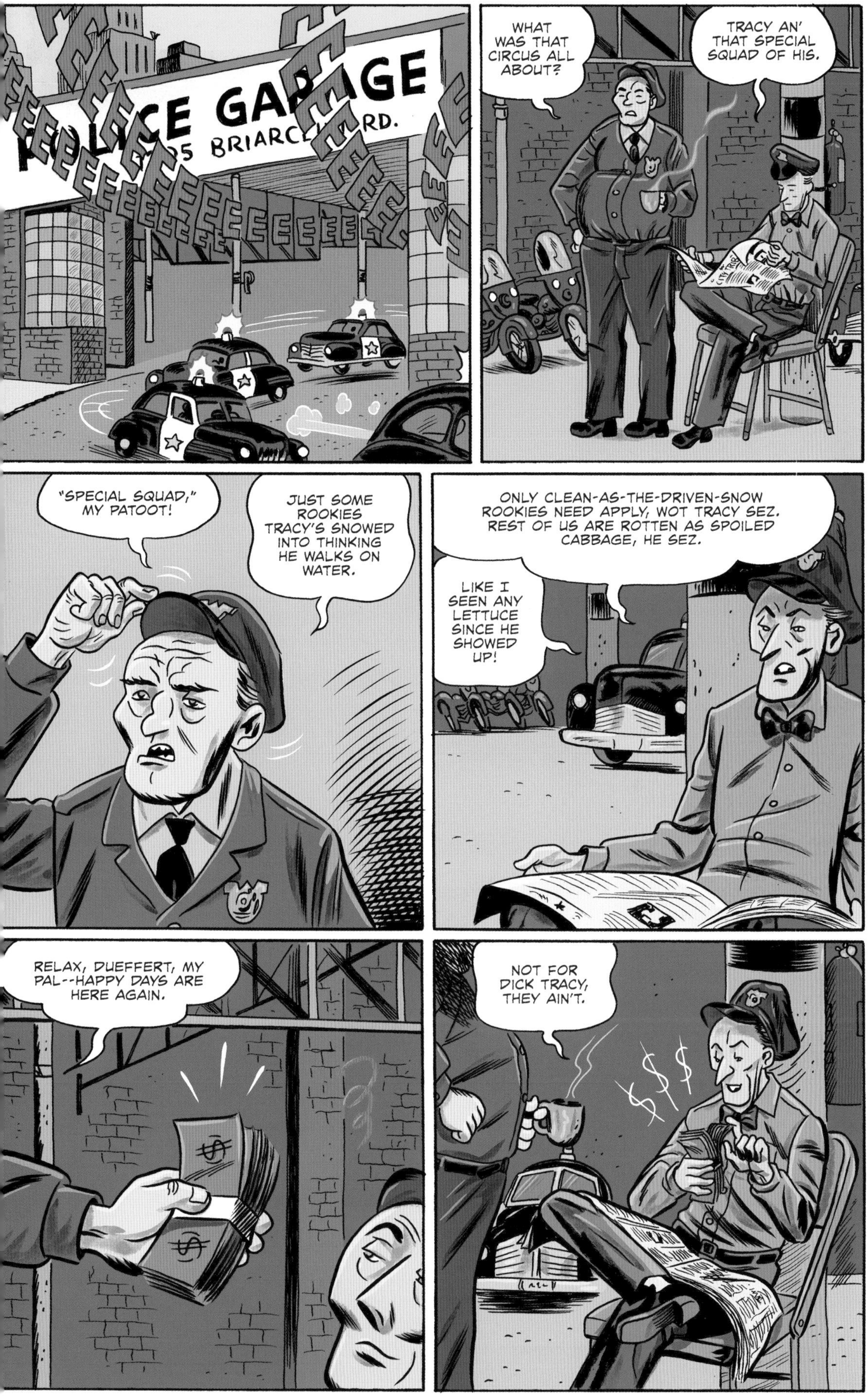

POLICE GARAGE
1205 BRIARCLIFF RD.
EEEEEEEEEEEEEEEEEEEEEEEEEEEE!
WHAT WAS THAT CIRCUS ALL ABOUT?
TRACY AN' THAT SPECIAL SQUAD OF HIS.
"SPECIAL SQUAD," MY PATOOT!
JUST SOME ROOKIES TRACY'S SNOWED INTO THINKING HE WALKS ON WATER.
ONLY CLEAN-AS-THE-DRIVEN-SNOW ROOKIES NEED APPLY, WOT TRACY SEZ. REST OF US ARE ROTTEN AS SPOILED CABBAGE, HE SEZ.
LIKE I SEEN ANY LETTUCE SINCE HE SHOWED UP!
RELAX, DUEFFERT, MY PAL--HAPPY DAYS ARE HERE AGAIN.
NOT FOR DICK TRACY, THEY AIN'T.

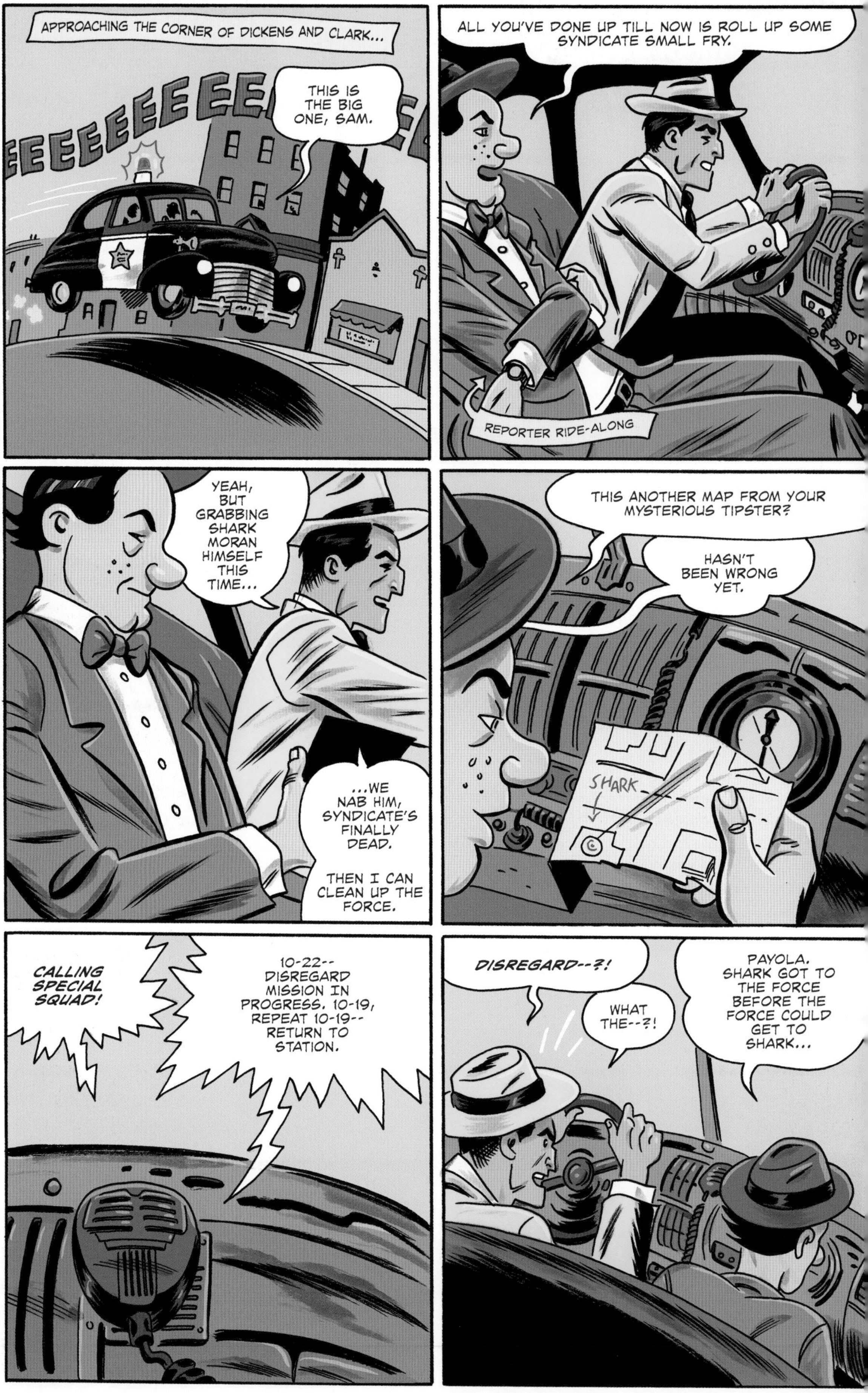
APPROACHING THE CORNER OF DICKENS AND CLARK...
EEEEEEEEEEE
THIS IS THE BIG ONE, SAM.
ALL YOU'VE DONE UP TILL NOW IS ROLL UP SOME SYNDICATE SMALL FRY.
REPORTER RIDE-ALONG
YEAH, BUT GRABBING SHARK MORAN HIMSELF THIS TIME...
...WE NAB HIM, SYNDICATE'S FINALLY DEAD.
THEN I CAN CLEAN UP THE FORCE.
THIS ANOTHER MAP FROM YOUR MYSTERIOUS TIPSTER?
HASN'T BEEN WRONG YET.
SHARK
CALLING SPECIAL SQUAD!
10-22--DISREGARD MISSION IN PROGRESS. 10-19, REPEAT 10-19--RETURN TO STATION.
DISREGARD--?!
WHAT THE--?!
PAYOLA. SHARK GOT TO THE FORCE BEFORE THE FORCE COULD GET TO SHARK...

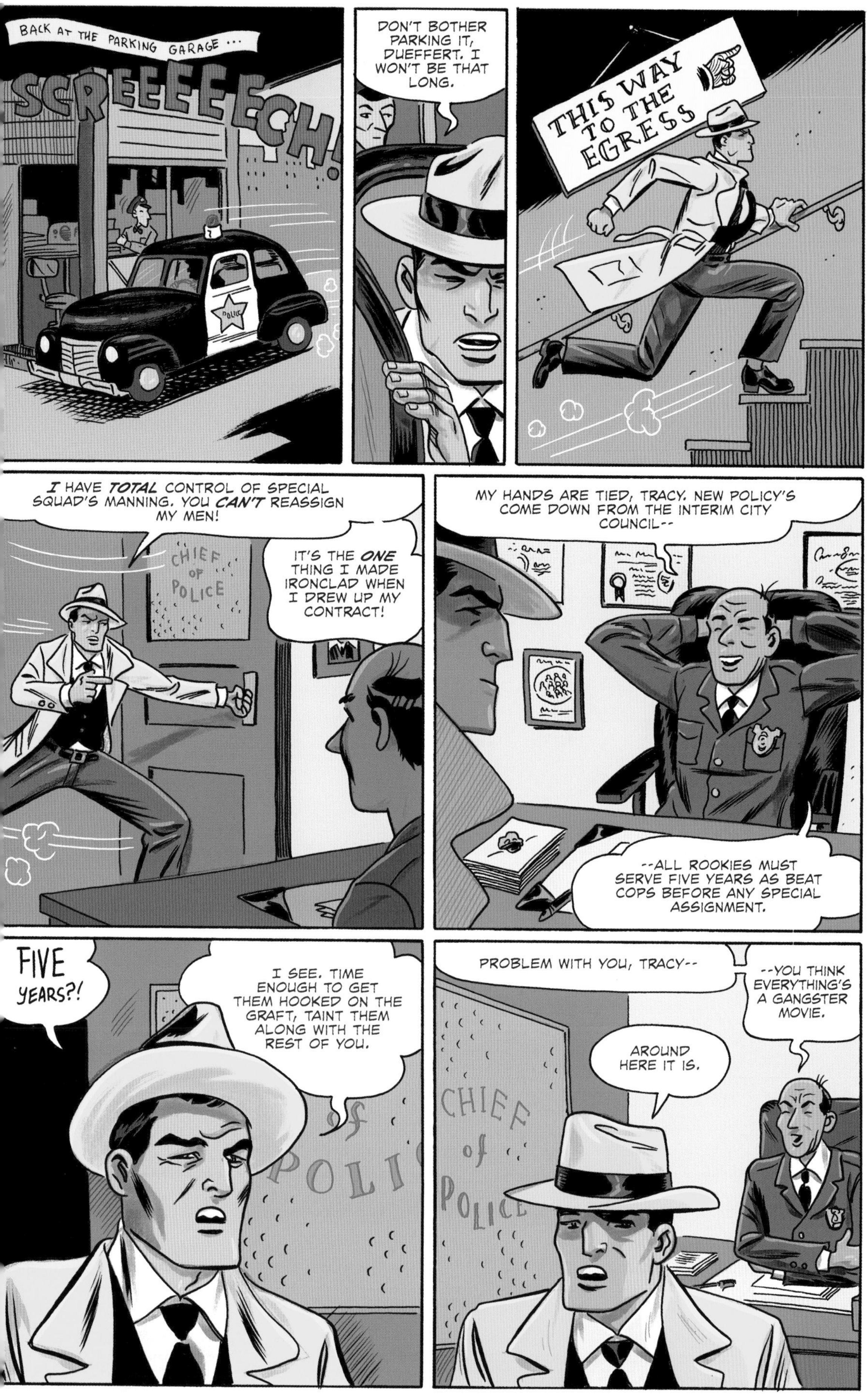

BACK AT THE PARKING GARAGE ...
SCREEEEECH!
DON'T BOTHER PARKING IT, DUEFFERT. I WON'T BE THAT LONG.
THIS WAY TO THE EGRESS
I HAVE TOTAL CONTROL OF SPECIAL SQUAD'S MANNING. YOU CAN'T REASSIGN MY MEN!
CHIEF of POLICE
IT'S THE ONE THING I MADE IRONCLAD WHEN I DREW UP MY CONTRACT!
MY HANDS ARE TIED, TRACY. NEW POLICY'S COME DOWN FROM THE INTERIM CITY COUNCIL--
--ALL ROOKIES MUST SERVE FIVE YEARS AS BEAT COPS BEFORE ANY SPECIAL ASSIGNMENT.
FIVE YEARS?!
I SEE. TIME ENOUGH TO GET THEM HOOKED ON THE GRAFT, TAINT THEM ALONG WITH THE REST OF YOU.
PROBLEM WITH YOU, TRACY--
--YOU THINK EVERYTHING'S A GANGSTER MOVIE.
AROUND HERE IT IS.
CHIEF of POLICE

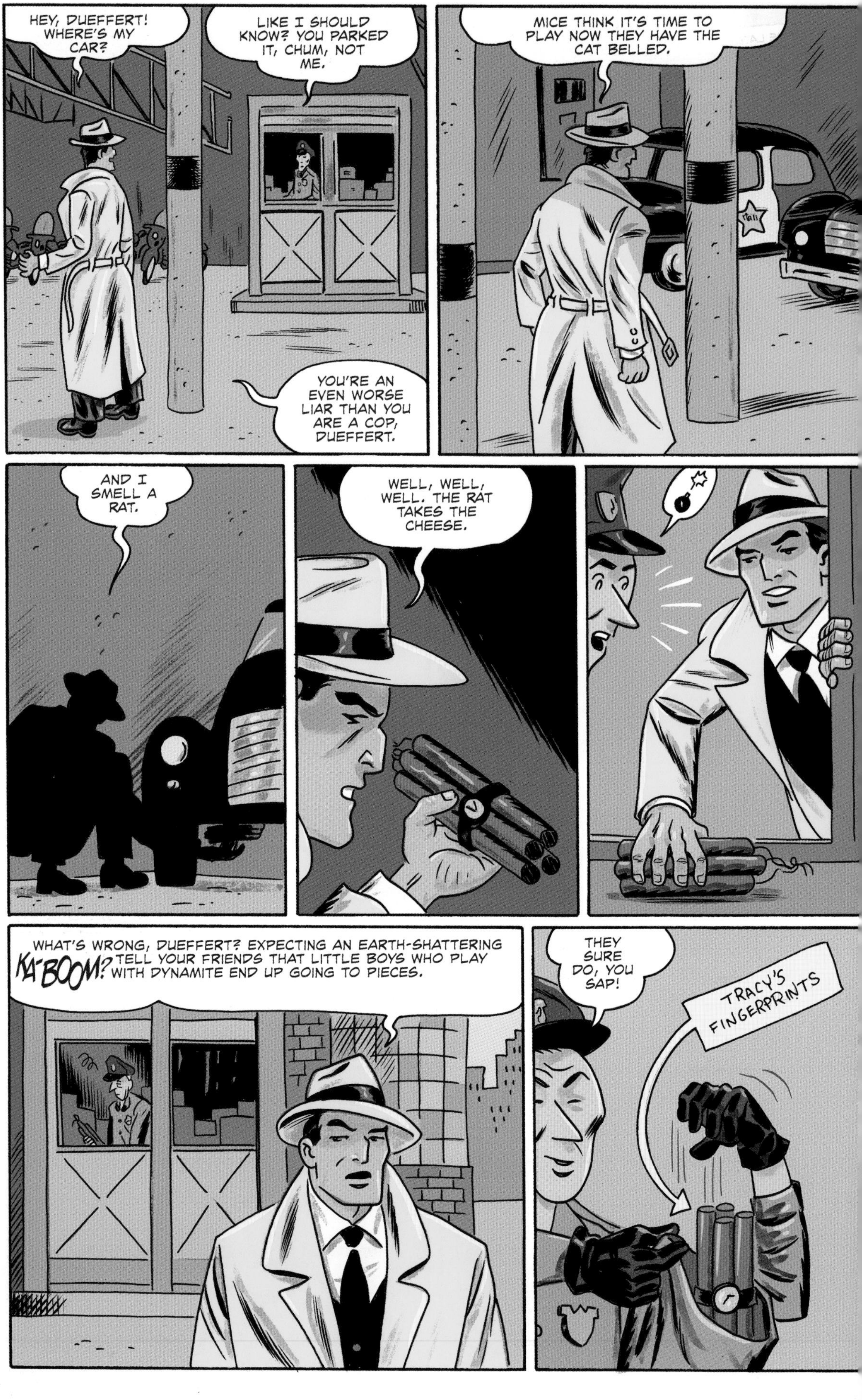
HEY, DUEFFERT! WHERE'S MY CAR?
LIKE I SHOULD KNOW? YOU PARKED IT, CHUM, NOT ME.
YOU'RE AN EVEN WORSE LIAR THAN YOU ARE A COP, DUEFFERT.
MICE THINK IT'S TIME TO PLAY NOW THEY HAVE THE CAT BELLED.
AND I SMELL A RAT.
WELL, WELL, WELL. THE RAT TAKES THE CHEESE.
WHAT'S WRONG, DUEFFERT? EXPECTING AN EARTH-SHATTERING KA-BOOM? TELL YOUR FRIENDS THAT LITTLE BOYS WHO PLAY WITH DYNAMITE END UP GOING TO PIECES.
THEY SURE DO, YOU SAP!
TRACY'S FINGERPRINTS

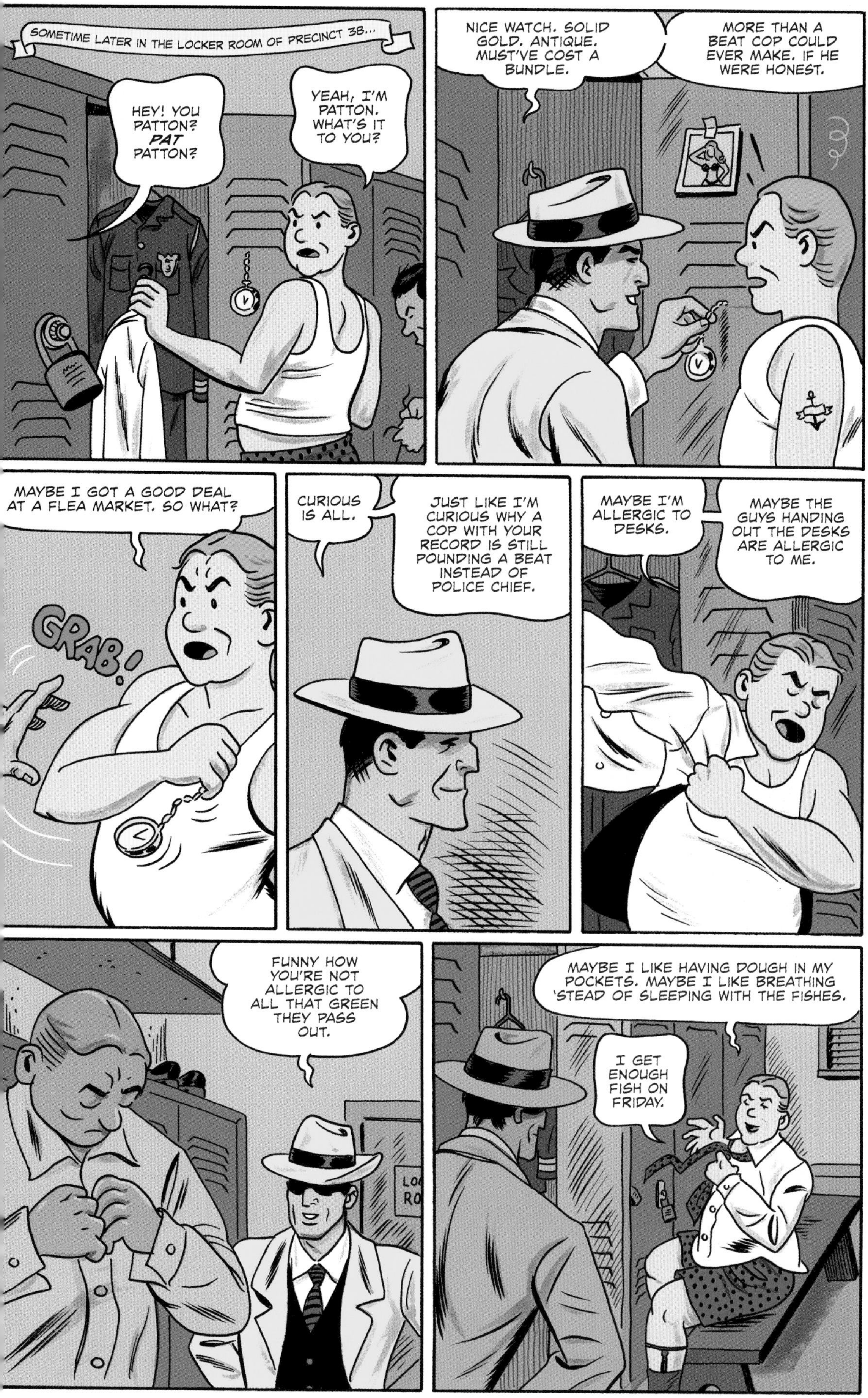
SOMETIME LATER IN THE LOCKER ROOM OF PRECINCT 38...
HEY! YOU PATTON? PAT PATTON?
YEAH, I'M PATTON. WHAT'S IT TO YOU?
NICE WATCH. SOLID GOLD. ANTIQUE. MUST'VE COST A BUNDLE.
MORE THAN A BEAT COP COULD EVER MAKE. IF HE WERE HONEST.
MAYBE I GOT A GOOD DEAL AT A FLEA MARKET. SO WHAT?
GRAB!
CURIOUS IS ALL.
JUST LIKE I'M CURIOUS WHY A COP WITH YOUR RECORD IS STILL POUNDING A BEAT INSTEAD OF POLICE CHIEF.
MAYBE I'M ALLERGIC TO DESKS.
MAYBE THE GUYS HANDING OUT THE DESKS ARE ALLERGIC TO ME.
FUNNY HOW YOU'RE NOT ALLERGIC TO ALL THAT GREEN THEY PASS OUT.
MAYBE I LIKE HAVING DOUGH IN MY POCKETS. MAYBE I LIKE BREATHING 'STEAD OF SLEEPING WITH THE FISHES.
I GET ENOUGH FISH ON FRIDAY.

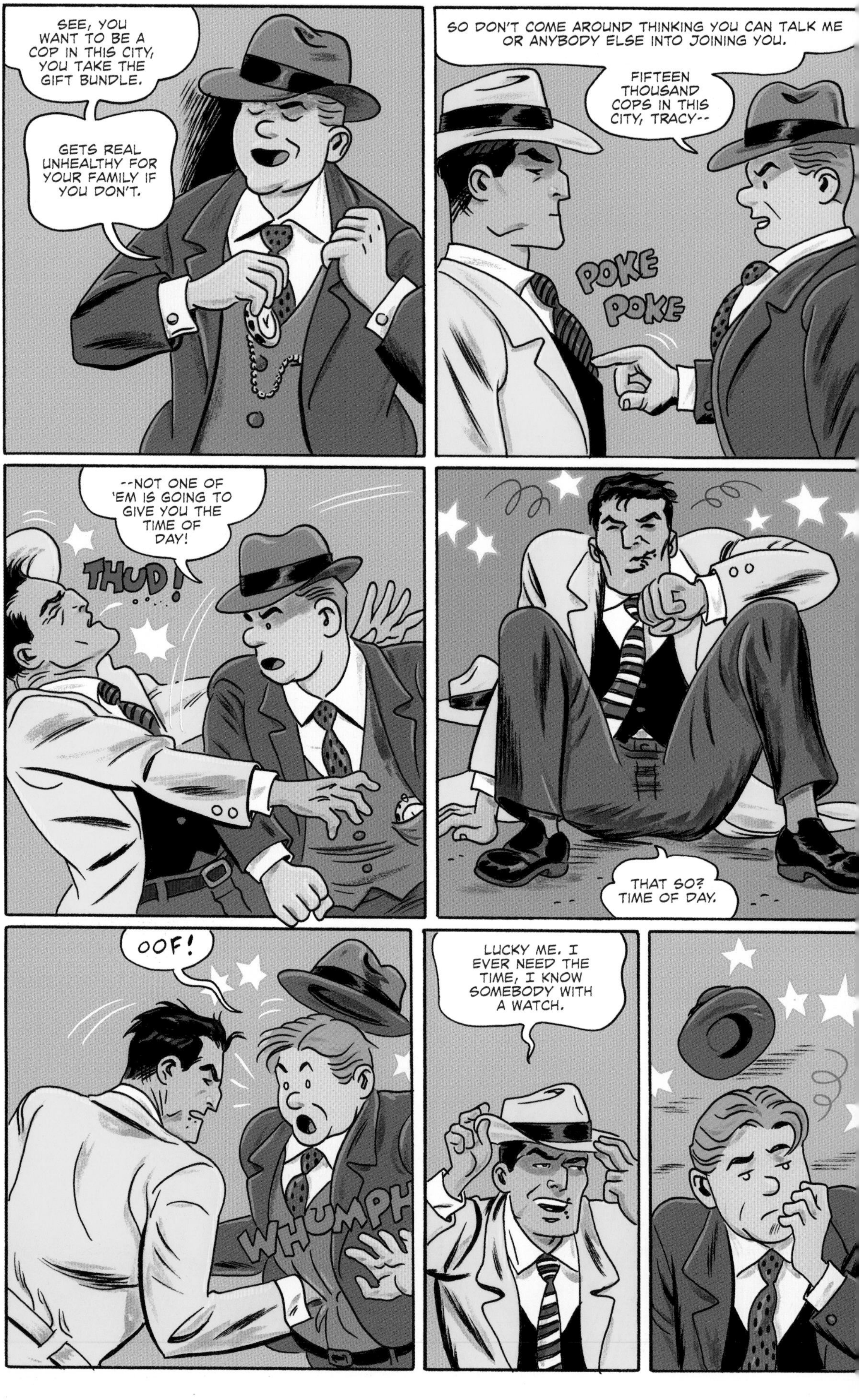
SEE, YOU WANT TO BE A COP IN THIS CITY, YOU TAKE THE GIFT BUNDLE.
GETS REAL UNHEALTHY FOR YOUR FAMILY IF YOU DON'T.
SO DON'T COME AROUND THINKING YOU CAN TALK ME OR ANYBODY ELSE INTO JOINING YOU.
FIFTEEN THOUSAND COPS IN THIS CITY, TRACY--
POKE
POKE
--NOT ONE OF 'EM IS GOING TO GIVE YOU THE TIME OF DAY!
THUD!
THAT SO? TIME OF DAY.
OOF!
WHUMPH
LUCKY ME. I EVER NEED THE TIME, I KNOW SOMEBODY WITH A WATCH.

LATER...

SO MUCH MONEY FOR SO LITTLE A THING, OFFICER PATTON--

ZEITSCHMIDT WATCH and CLOCK

23

REPAIRS FOR WATCHES & CLOCKS

the PEOPLE'S WATCH

--YOUR WATCH, IT RUNS FINE LIKE ALWAYS, JA?

EACH MONTH IT NOT NEED ADJUSTMENT, YET YOU PAY ME ALL THIS.

MY GREAT GRANDFATHER'S WATCH. FOUR GENERATIONS OF PATTONS HAVE CARRIED IT ON THE FORCE.

SO IT'S MONEY WELL SPENT. I NEED YOU TO STAY IN BUSINESS.

SO, DOES SAM THE BUTCHER, HE FIX YOUR WATCH, TOO? THE FLORIST, THE OTHER SHOPS ON YOUR BEAT?

EACH MONTH YOU GIVE US ALL BACK THE MONEY THE SYNDICATE TAKES. FROM YOUR OWN BRIBE MONEY, YET.

SUCH COMPLICATED SHUFFLINGS OF MONEY! FAR EASIER TO HELP THAT NICE MR. TRACY GET RID OF THE CROOKS, JA?

NAW. PEOPLE GET HURT THAT WAY. PEOPLE LIKE YOU.

"AND THEY HURT US HOW IF THEY ALL KAPUT?"

HEY!!! MY WATCH!

COME BACK HERE, KID!

SNATCH!

HA!

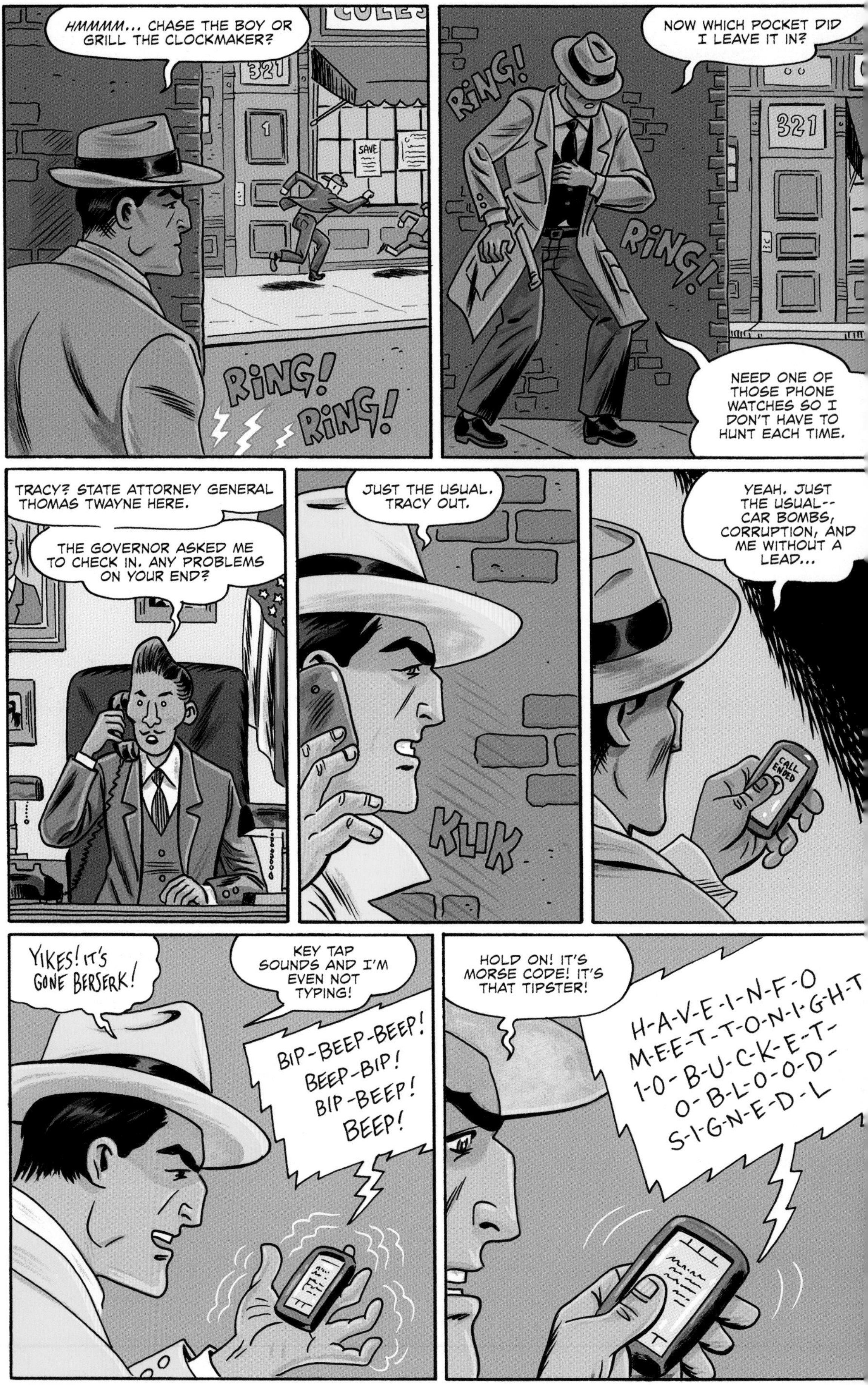
HMMMM... CHASE THE BOY OR GRILL THE CLOCKMAKER?
COLES
321
1
SAVE
RING! RING!
NOW WHICH POCKET DID I LEAVE IT IN?
RING!
RING!
321
NEED ONE OF THOSE PHONE WATCHES SO I DON'T HAVE TO HUNT EACH TIME.
TRACY? STATE ATTORNEY GENERAL THOMAS TWAYNE HERE.
THE GOVERNOR ASKED ME TO CHECK IN. ANY PROBLEMS ON YOUR END?
JUST THE USUAL. TRACY OUT.
KLIK
YEAH. JUST THE USUAL-- CAR BOMBS, CORRUPTION, AND ME WITHOUT A LEAD...
CALL ENDED
YIKES! IT'S GONE BERSERK!
KEY TAP SOUNDS AND I'M EVEN NOT TYPING!
BIP-BEEP-BEEP! BEEP-BIP! BIP-BEEP! BEEP!
HOLD ON! IT'S MORSE CODE! IT'S THAT TIPSTER!
H-A-V-E-I-N-F-O M-E-E-T-T-O-N-I-G-H-T 1-0-B-U-C-K-E-T-O-B-L-O-O-D-S-I-G-N-E-D-L

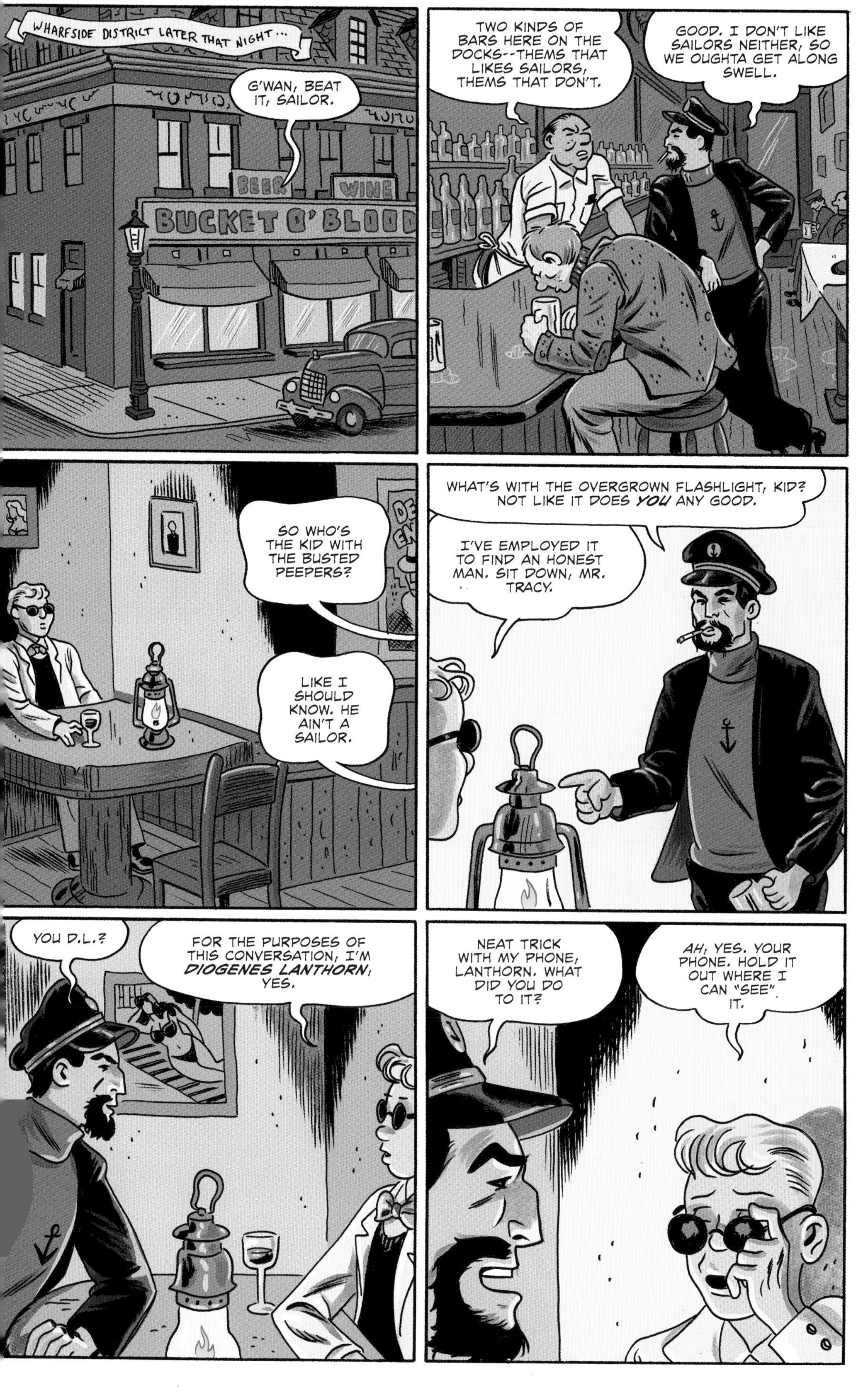

WHARFSIDE DISTRICT LATER THAT NIGHT...
G'WAN, BEAT IT, SAILOR.
BEER
WINE
BUCKET O' BLOOD
TWO KINDS OF BARS HERE ON THE DOCKS--THEMS THAT LIKES SAILORS, THEMS THAT DON'T.
GOOD. I DON'T LIKE SAILORS NEITHER, SO WE OUGHTA GET ALONG SWELL.
SO WHO'S THE KID WITH THE BUSTED PEEPERS?
LIKE I SHOULD KNOW. HE AIN'T A SAILOR.
WHAT'S WITH THE OVERGROWN FLASHLIGHT, KID? NOT LIKE IT DOES *YOU* ANY GOOD.
I'VE EMPLOYED IT TO FIND AN HONEST MAN. SIT DOWN, MR. TRACY.
YOU D.L.?
FOR THE PURPOSES OF THIS CONVERSATION, I'M *DIOGENES LANTHORN*, YES.
NEAT TRICK WITH MY PHONE, LANTHORN. WHAT DID YOU DO TO IT?
AH, YES. YOUR PHONE. HOLD IT OUT WHERE I CAN "SEE" IT.

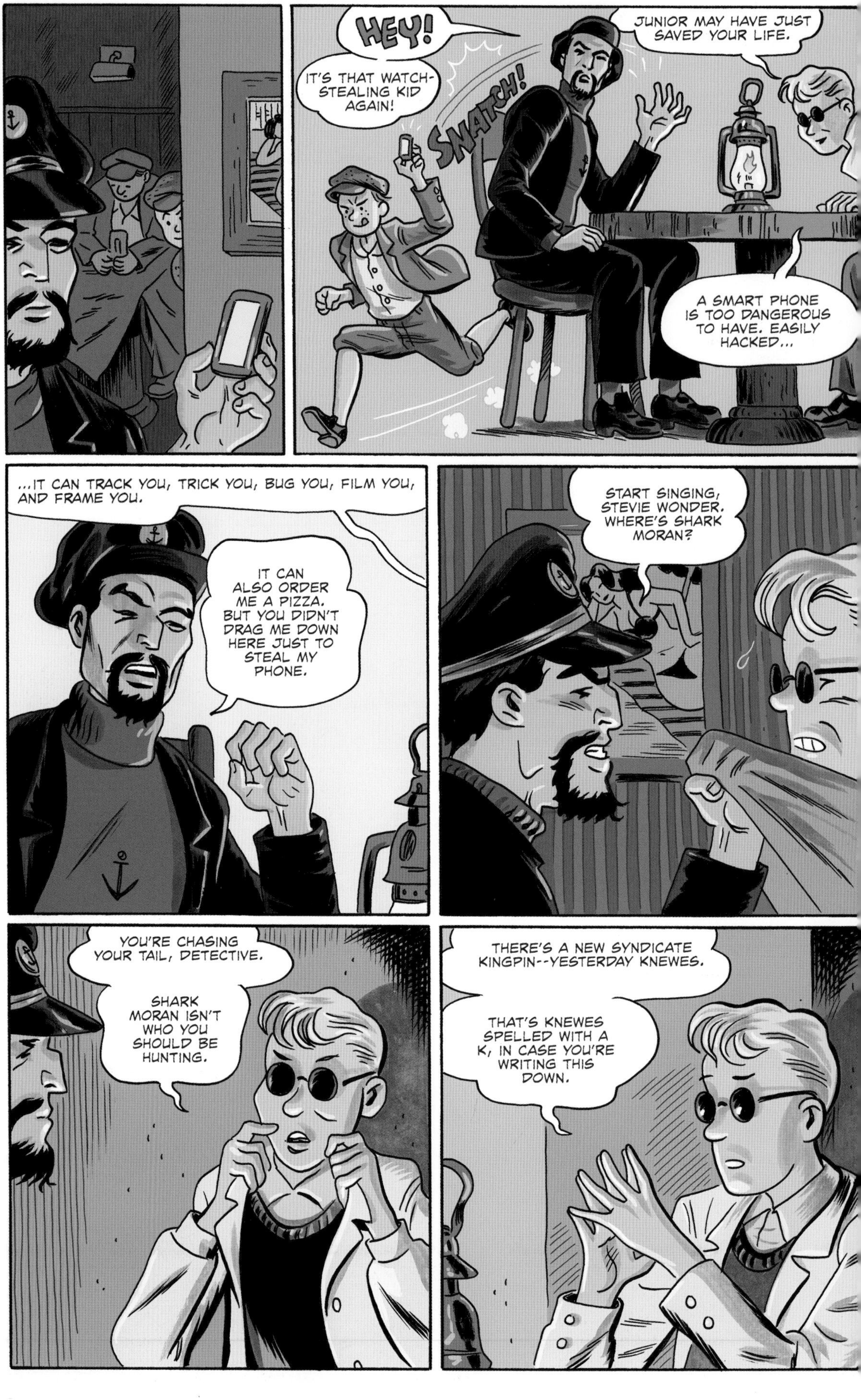
HEY!
IT'S THAT WATCH-STEALING KID AGAIN!
SNATCH!
JUNIOR MAY HAVE JUST SAVED YOUR LIFE.
A SMART PHONE IS TOO DANGEROUS TO HAVE. EASILY HACKED...
...IT CAN TRACK YOU, TRICK YOU, BUG YOU, FILM YOU, AND FRAME YOU.
IT CAN ALSO ORDER ME A PIZZA. BUT YOU DIDN'T DRAG ME DOWN HERE JUST TO STEAL MY PHONE.
START SINGING, STEVIE WONDER. WHERE'S SHARK MORAN?
YOU'RE CHASING YOUR TAIL, DETECTIVE.
SHARK MORAN ISN'T WHO YOU SHOULD BE HUNTING.
THERE'S A NEW SYNDICATE KINGPIN--YESTERDAY KNEWES.
THAT'S KNEWES SPELLED WITH A K, IN CASE YOU'RE WRITING THIS DOWN.

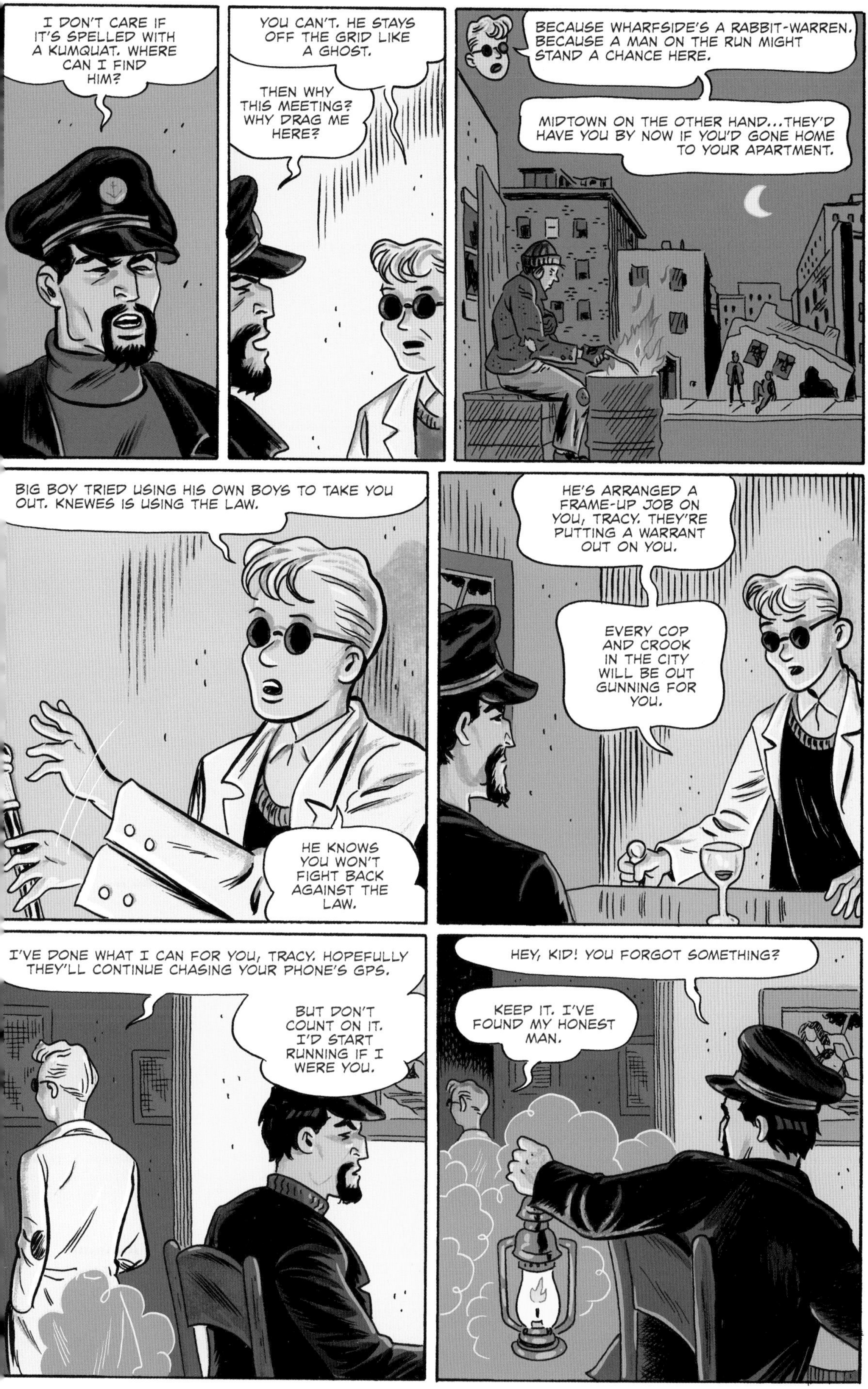

I DON'T CARE IF IT'S SPELLED WITH A KUMQUAT. WHERE CAN I FIND HIM?
YOU CAN'T. HE STAYS OFF THE GRID LIKE A GHOST.
THEN WHY THIS MEETING? WHY DRAG ME HERE?
BECAUSE WHARFSIDE'S A RABBIT-WARREN. BECAUSE A MAN ON THE RUN MIGHT STAND A CHANCE HERE.
MIDTOWN ON THE OTHER HAND...THEY'D HAVE YOU BY NOW IF YOU'D GONE HOME TO YOUR APARTMENT.
BIG BOY TRIED USING HIS OWN BOYS TO TAKE YOU OUT. KNEWES IS USING THE LAW.
HE KNOWS YOU WON'T FIGHT BACK AGAINST THE LAW.
HE'S ARRANGED A FRAME-UP JOB ON YOU, TRACY. THEY'RE PUTTING A WARRANT OUT ON YOU.
EVERY COP AND CROOK IN THE CITY WILL BE OUT GUNNING FOR YOU.
I'VE DONE WHAT I CAN FOR YOU, TRACY. HOPEFULLY THEY'LL CONTINUE CHASING YOUR PHONE'S GPS.
BUT DON'T COUNT ON IT. I'D START RUNNING IF I WERE YOU.
HEY, KID! YOU FORGOT SOMETHING?
KEEP IT. I'VE FOUND MY HONEST MAN.

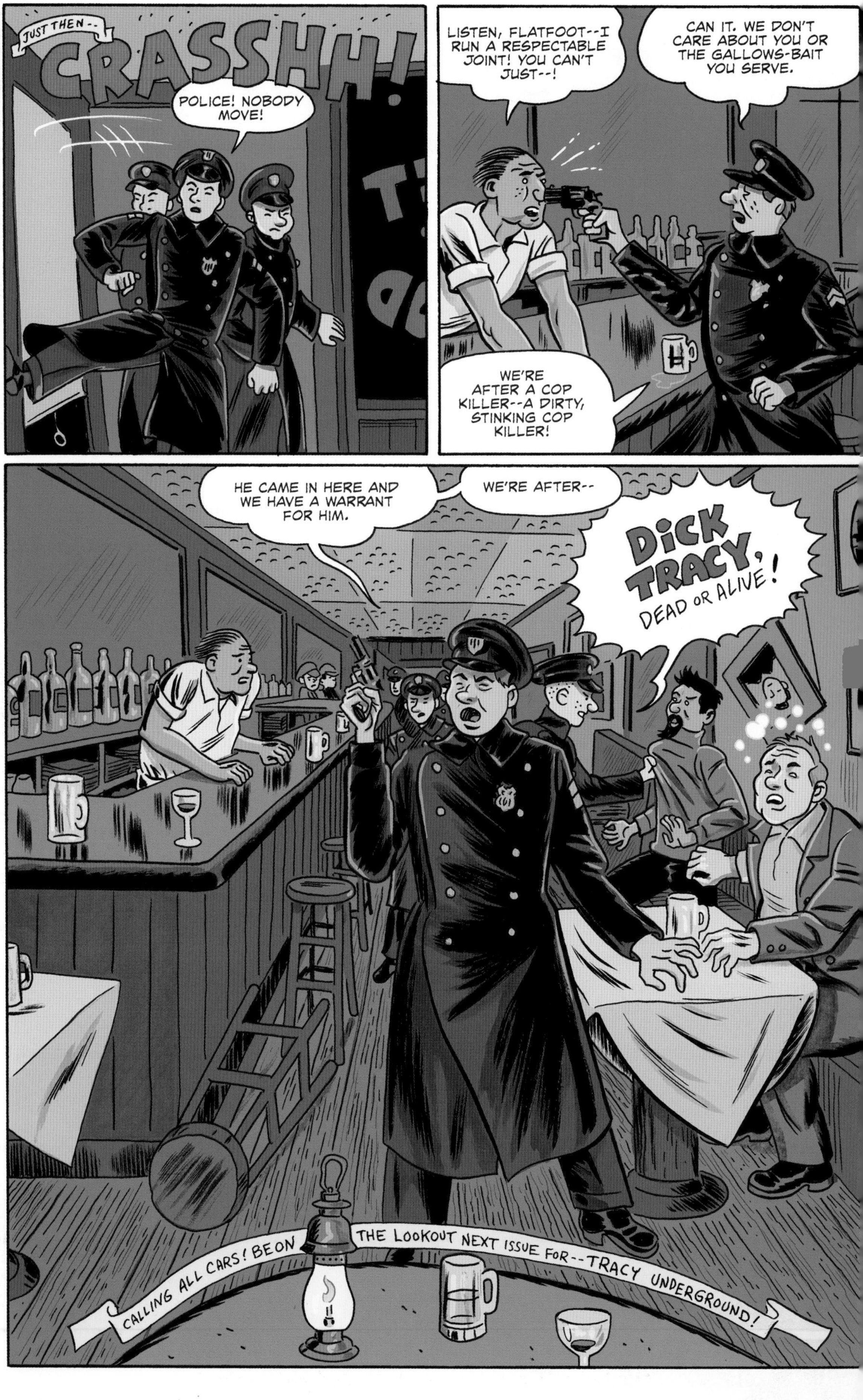
JUST THEN--
CRASSHH!
POLICE! NOBODY MOVE!
LISTEN, FLATFOOT--I RUN A RESPECTABLE JOINT! YOU CAN'T JUST--!
CAN IT. WE DON'T CARE ABOUT YOU OR THE GALLOWS-BAIT YOU SERVE.
WE'RE AFTER A COP KILLER--A DIRTY, STINKING COP KILLER!
HE CAME IN HERE AND WE HAVE A WARRANT FOR HIM.
WE'RE AFTER--
DICK TRACY, DEAD OR ALIVE!
CALLING ALL CARS! BE ON THE LOOKOUT NEXT ISSUE FOR--TRACY UNDERGROUND!

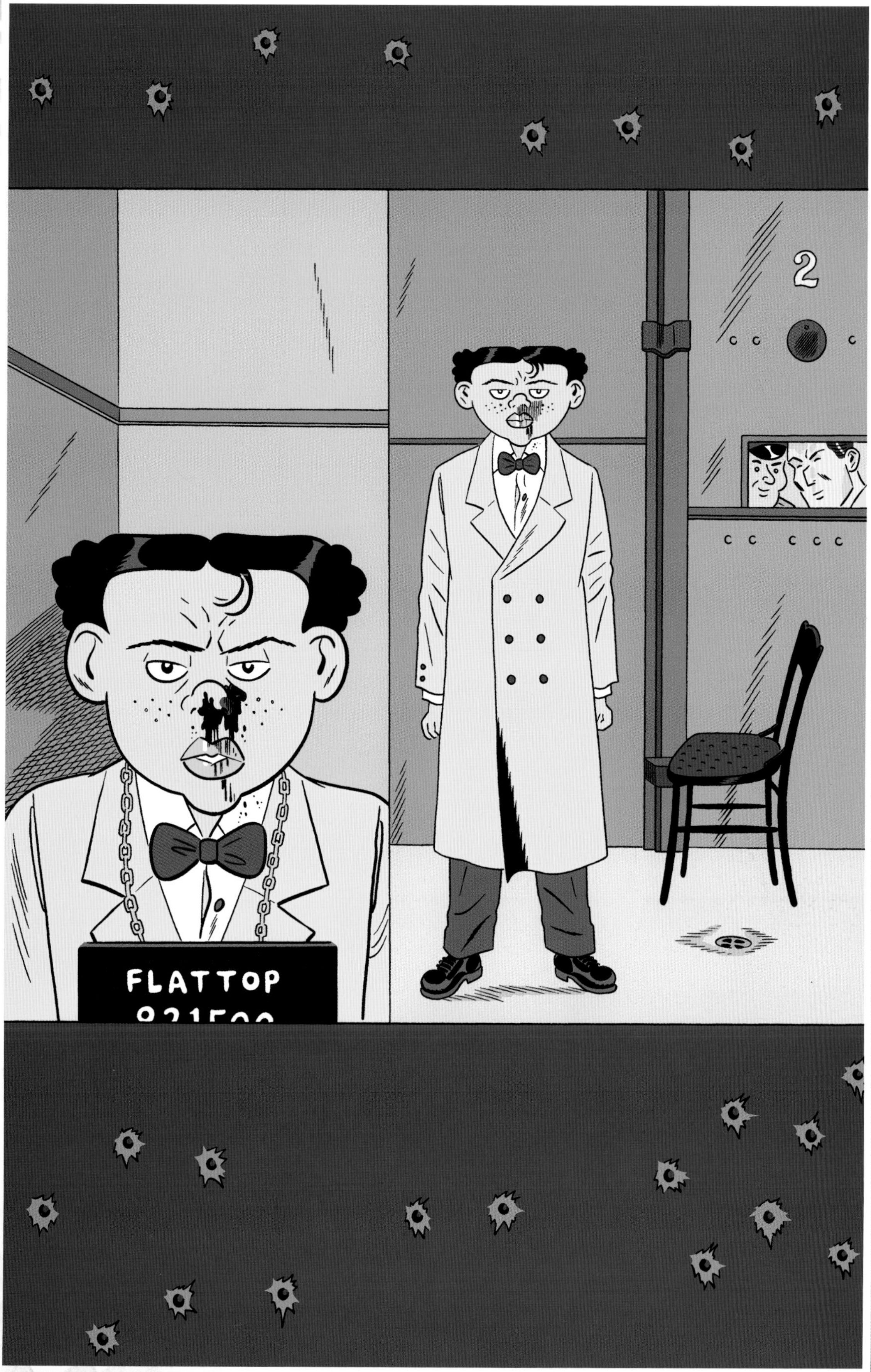
2
FLATTOP

ART BY RICH TOMMASO | COLORS BY AMY PLASMAN

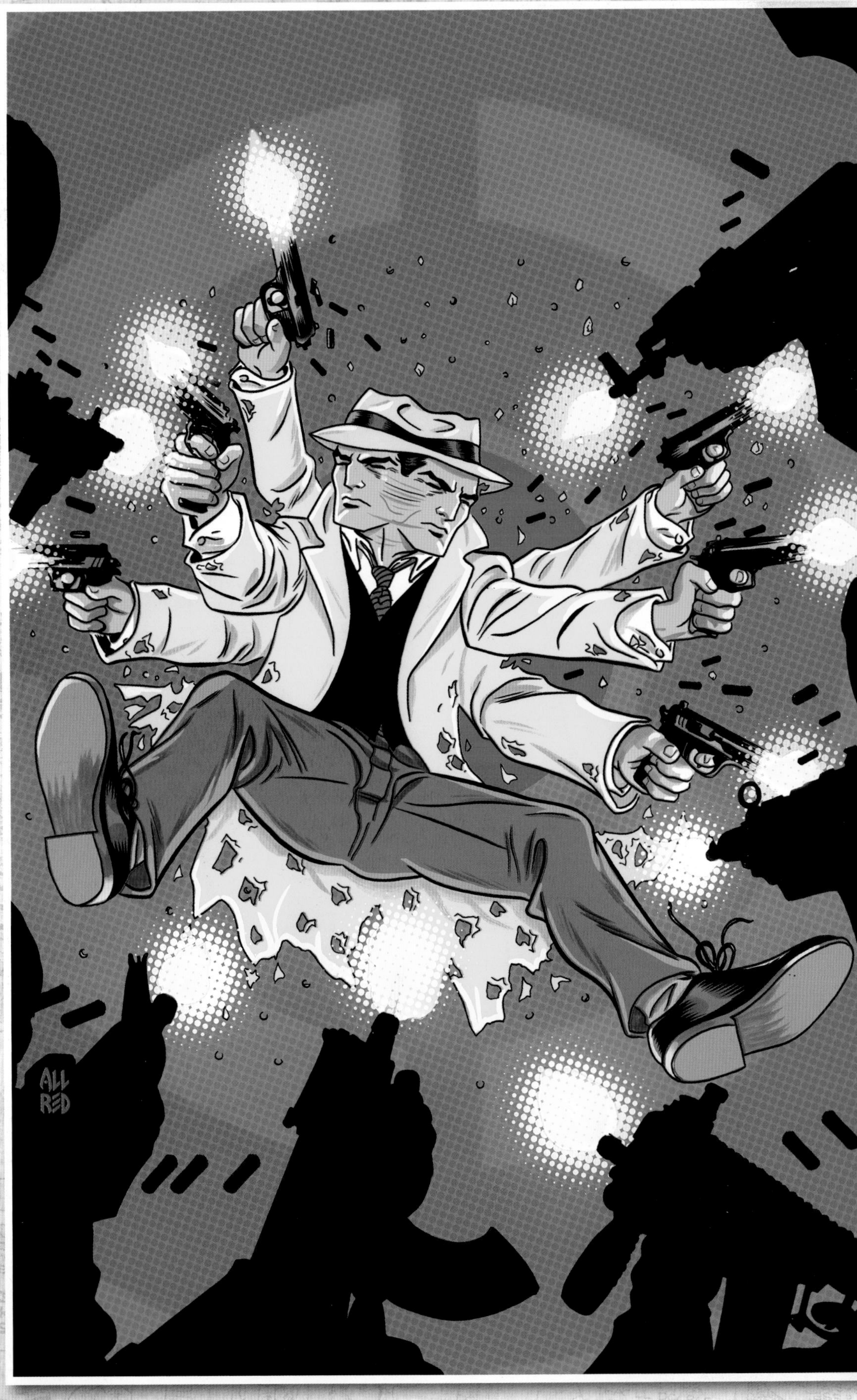
ALL RED

ART BY **MICHAEL ALLRED** | COLORS BY **LAURA ALLRED**

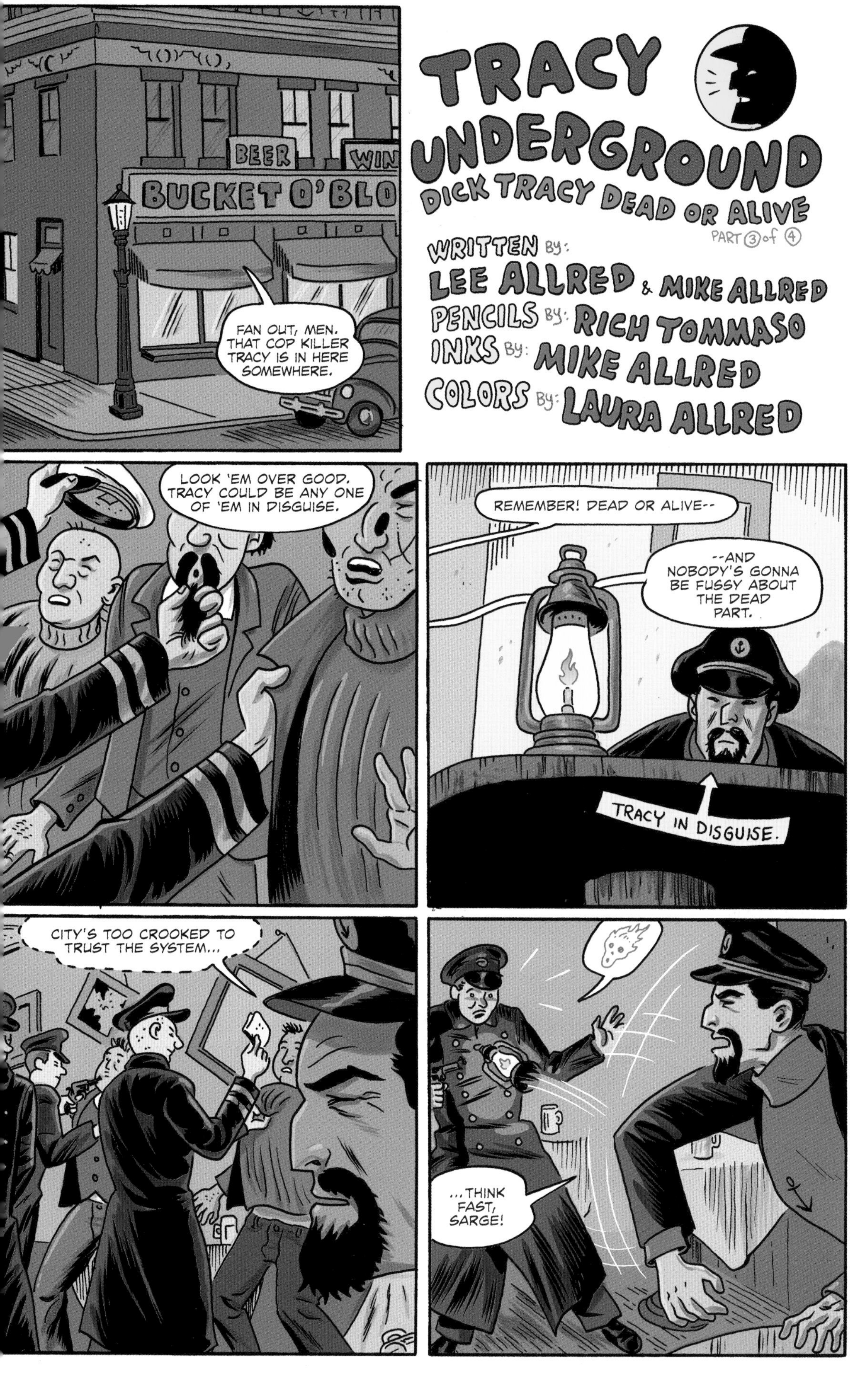
BEER
WIN
BUCKET O' BLO
FAN OUT, MEN. THAT COP KILLER TRACY IS IN HERE SOMEWHERE.
TRACY UNDERGROUND
DICK TRACY DEAD OR ALIVE
PART 3 of 4
WRITTEN BY: LEE ALLRED & MIKE ALLRED
PENCILS BY: RICH TOMMASO
INKS BY: MIKE ALLRED
COLORS BY: LAURA ALLRED
LOOK 'EM OVER GOOD. TRACY COULD BE ANY ONE OF 'EM IN DISGUISE.
REMEMBER! DEAD OR ALIVE--
--AND NOBODY'S GONNA BE FUSSY ABOUT THE DEAD PART.
TRACY IN DISGUISE.
CITY'S TOO CROOKED TO TRUST THE SYSTEM...
...THINK FAST, SARGE!

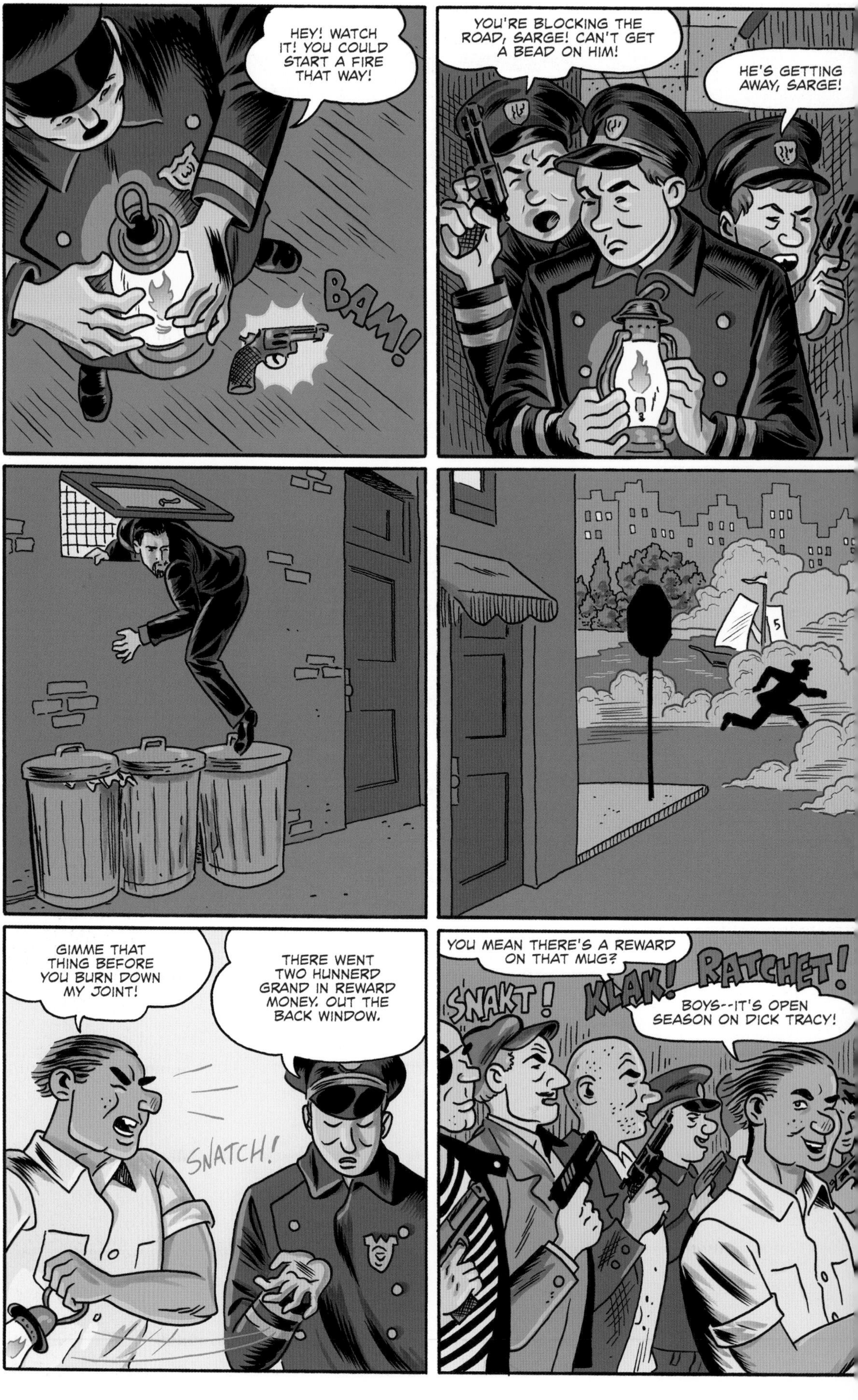
HEY! WATCH IT! YOU COULD START A FIRE THAT WAY!
BAM!
YOU'RE BLOCKING THE ROAD, SARGE! CAN'T GET A BEAD ON HIM!
HE'S GETTING AWAY, SARGE!
GIMME THAT THING BEFORE YOU BURN DOWN MY JOINT!
THERE WENT TWO HUNNERD GRAND IN REWARD MONEY. OUT THE BACK WINDOW.
SNATCH!
YOU MEAN THERE'S A REWARD ON THAT MUG?
SNAKT!
KLAK!
RATCHET!
BOYS--IT'S OPEN SEASON ON DICK TRACY!

THE DRAGNET TIGHTENS...

WEEOOOO WEEOOOO

FWEET! FWEET!

THERE HE IS!

BLIND ALLEY! NOWHERE TO RUN!

CAN'T SHOOT A FELLOW COP--

BANG! BANG!

SPING!

SPANG!

SUDDEN DROP

THONK!

UNNGGGH!

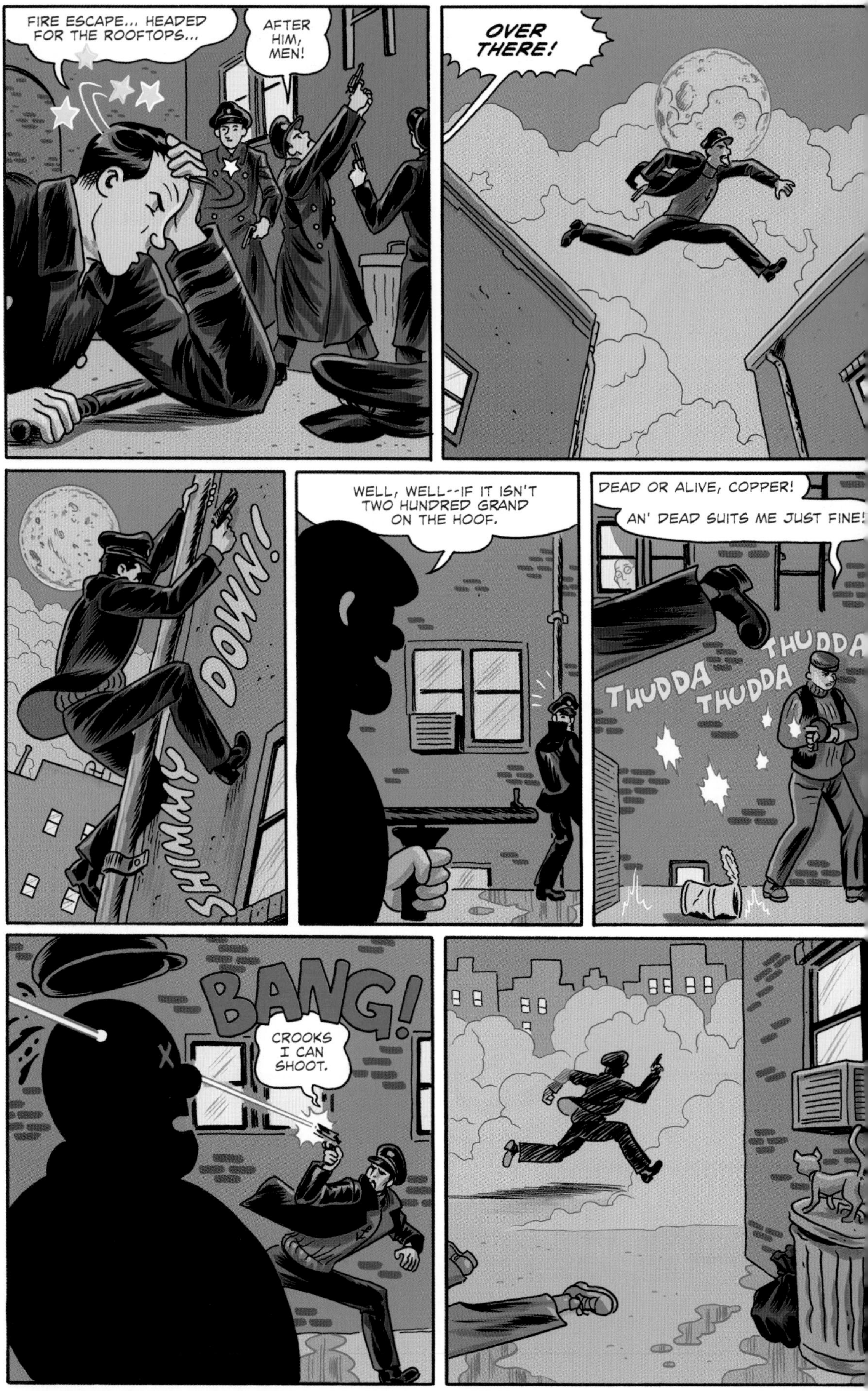

FIRE ESCAPE... HEADED FOR THE ROOFTOPS...
AFTER HIM, MEN!
OVER THERE!
SHIMMY DOWN!
WELL, WELL--IF IT ISN'T TWO HUNDRED GRAND ON THE HOOF.
DEAD OR ALIVE, COPPER!
AN' DEAD SUITS ME JUST FINE!
THUDDA THUDDA THUDDA
BANG!
CROOKS I CAN SHOOT.

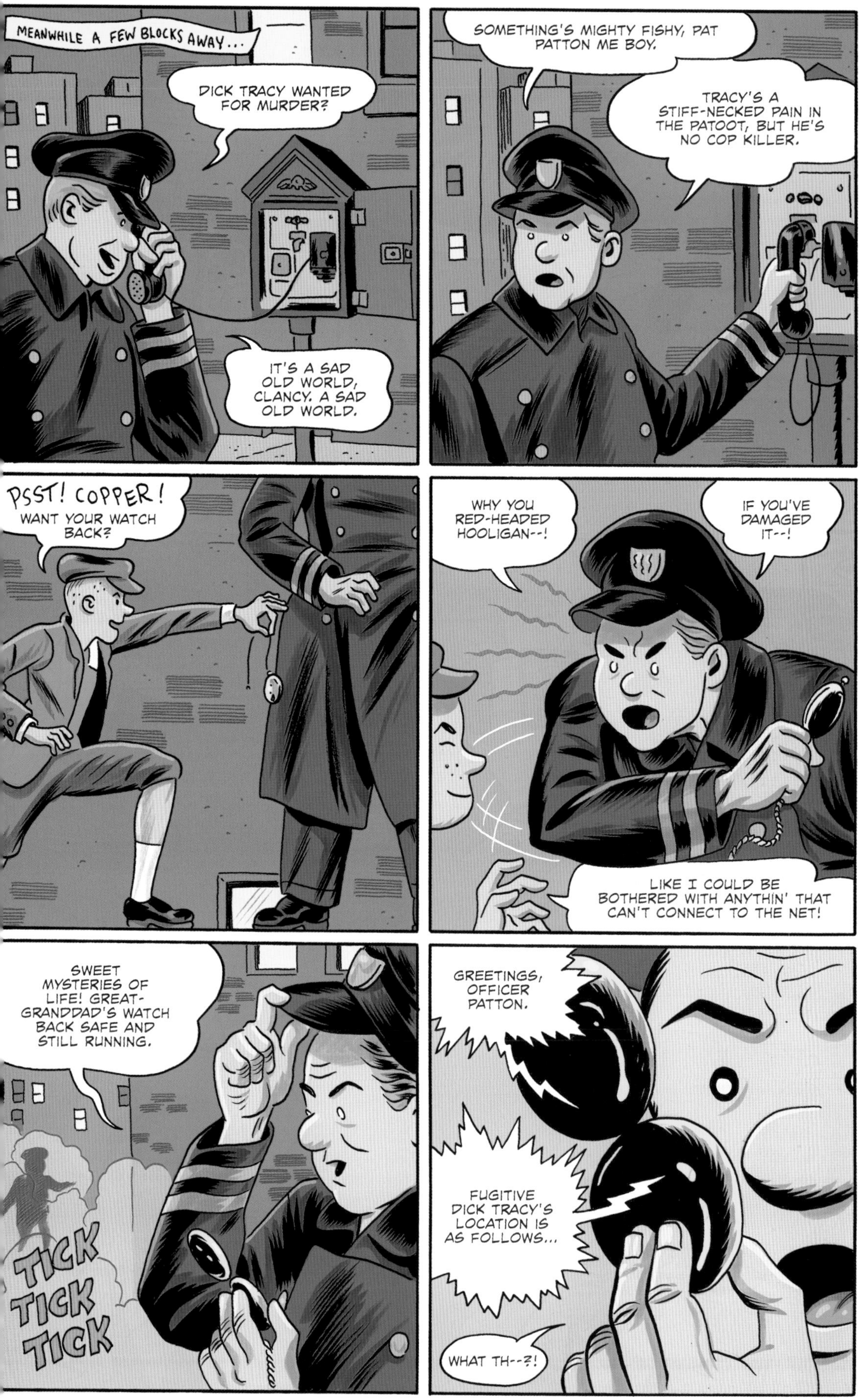
MEANWHILE A FEW BLOCKS AWAY...
DICK TRACY WANTED FOR MURDER?
IT'S A SAD OLD WORLD, CLANCY. A SAD OLD WORLD.
SOMETHING'S MIGHTY FISHY, PAT PATTON ME BOY.
TRACY'S A STIFF-NECKED PAIN IN THE PATOOT, BUT HE'S NO COP KILLER.
PSST! COPPER! WANT YOUR WATCH BACK?
WHY YOU RED-HEADED HOOLIGAN--!
IF YOU'VE DAMAGED IT--!
LIKE I COULD BE BOTHERED WITH ANYTHIN' THAT CAN'T CONNECT TO THE NET!
SWEET MYSTERIES OF LIFE! GREAT-GRANDDAD'S WATCH BACK SAFE AND STILL RUNNING.
TICK
TICK
TICK
GREETINGS, OFFICER PATTON.
FUGITIVE DICK TRACY'S LOCATION IS AS FOLLOWS...
WHAT TH--?!

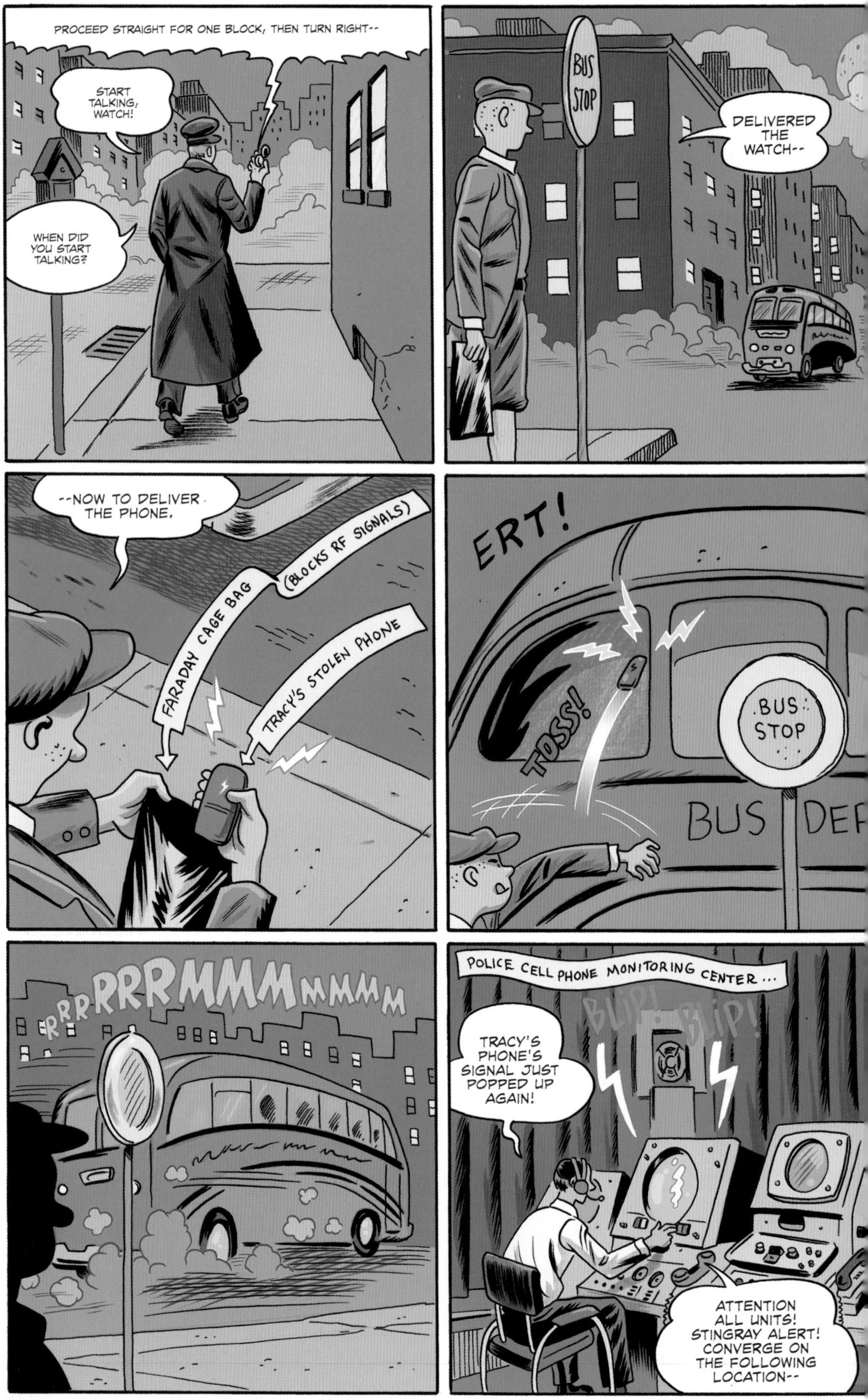
PROCEED STRAIGHT FOR ONE BLOCK, THEN TURN RIGHT--
START TALKING, WATCH!
WHEN DID YOU START TALKING?
BUS STOP
DELIVERED THE WATCH--
--NOW TO DELIVER THE PHONE.
FARADAY CAGE BAG
(BLOCKS RF SIGNALS)
TRACY'S STOLEN PHONE
ERT!
TOSS!
BUS STOP
BUS DEP
RRRRRRMMMMMMMMM
POLICE CELL PHONE MONITORING CENTER...
BLIP! BLIP!
TRACY'S PHONE'S SIGNAL JUST POPPED UP AGAIN!
ATTENTION ALL UNITS! STINGRAY ALERT! CONVERGE ON THE FOLLOWING LOCATION--

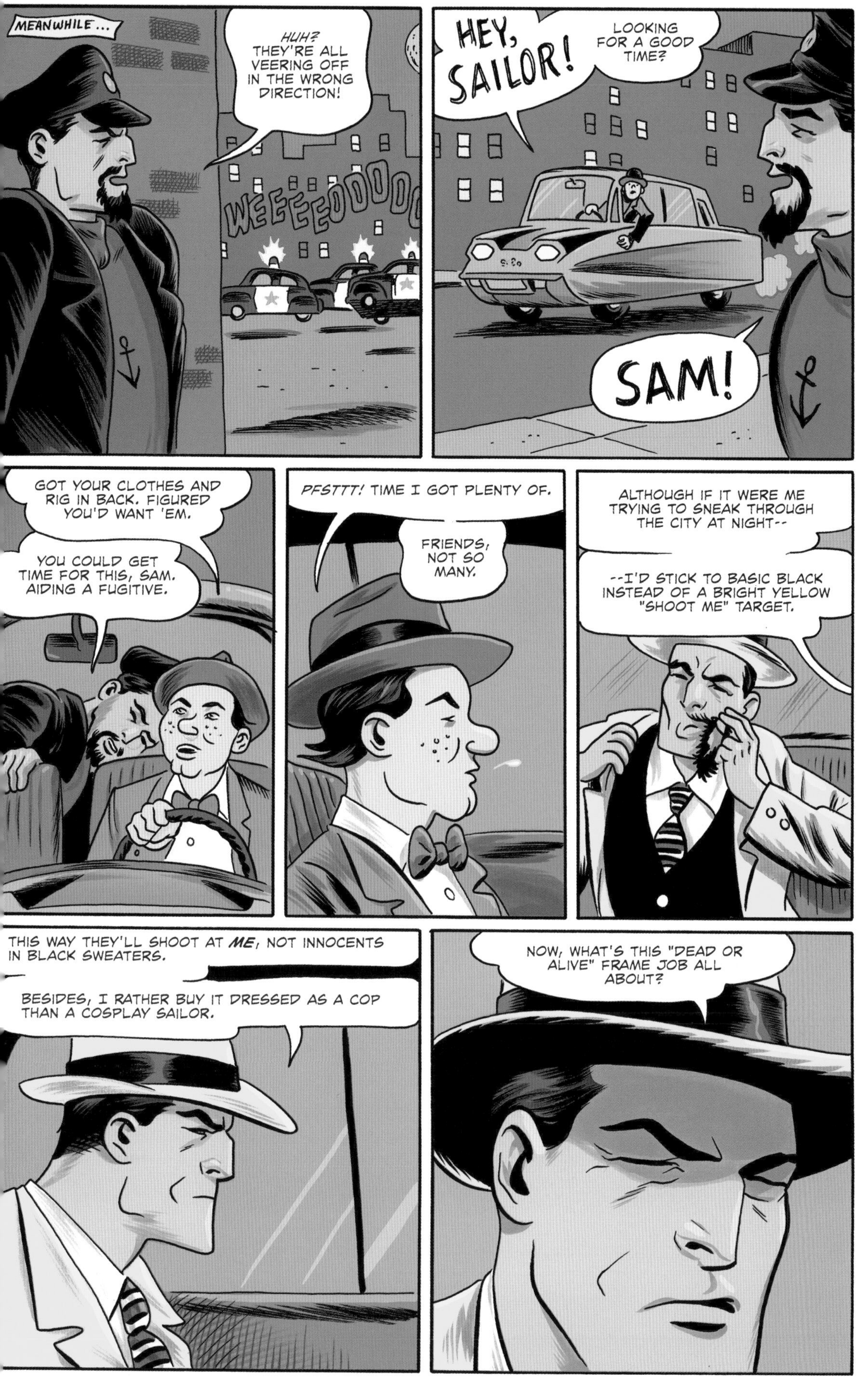
MEANWHILE...
HUH? THEY'RE ALL VEERING OFF IN THE WRONG DIRECTION!
WEEEEOOOOO
HEY, SAILOR!
LOOKING FOR A GOOD TIME?
SAM!
GOT YOUR CLOTHES AND RIG IN BACK. FIGURED YOU'D WANT 'EM.
YOU COULD GET TIME FOR THIS, SAM. AIDING A FUGITIVE.
PFSTTT! TIME I GOT PLENTY OF.
FRIENDS, NOT SO MANY.
ALTHOUGH IF IT WERE ME TRYING TO SNEAK THROUGH THE CITY AT NIGHT--
--I'D STICK TO BASIC BLACK INSTEAD OF A BRIGHT YELLOW "SHOOT ME" TARGET.
THIS WAY THEY'LL SHOOT AT ME, NOT INNOCENTS IN BLACK SWEATERS.
BESIDES, I RATHER BUY IT DRESSED AS A COP THAN A COSPLAY SAILOR.
NOW, WHAT'S THIS "DEAD OR ALIVE" FRAME JOB ALL ABOUT?

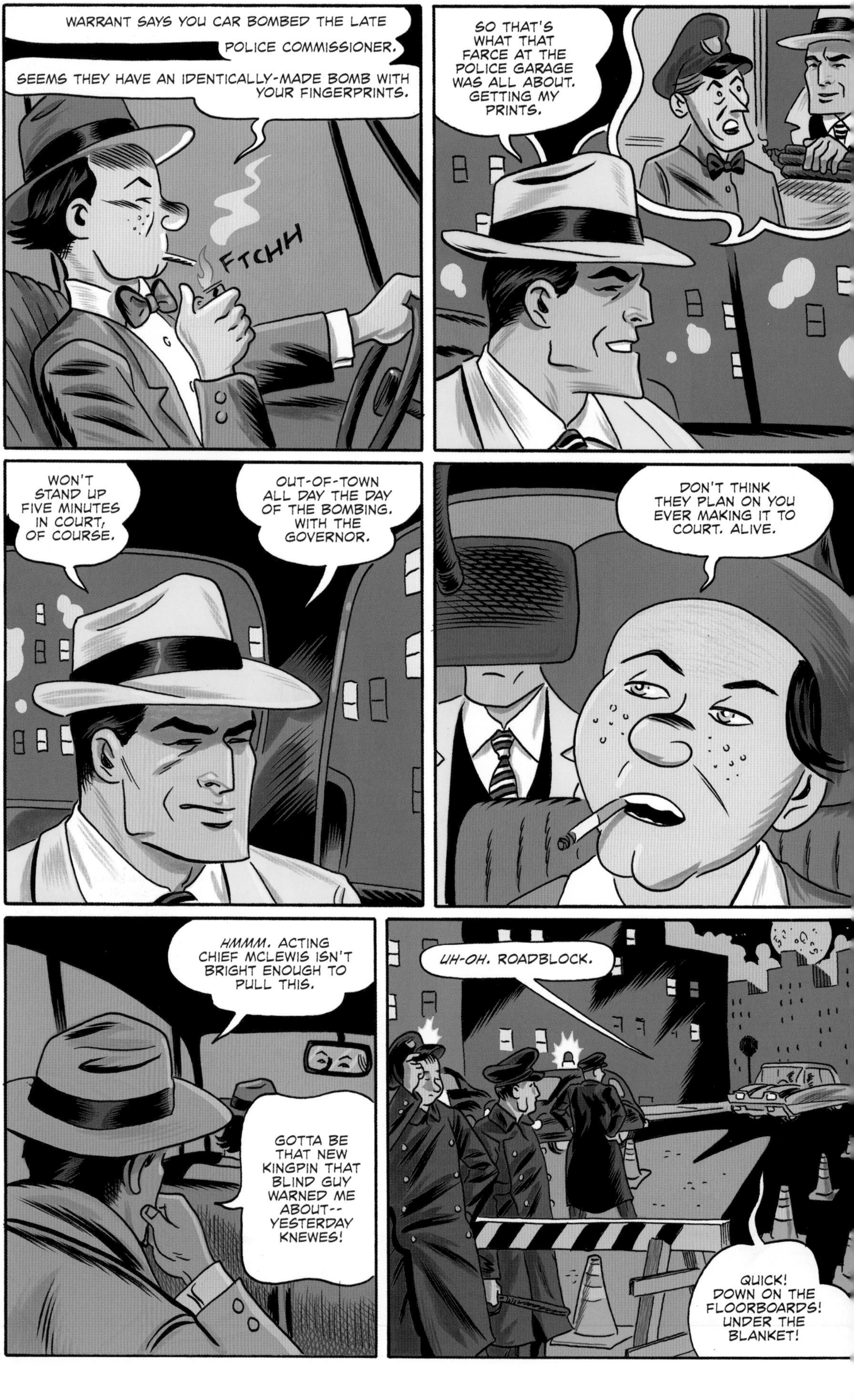
WARRANT SAYS YOU CAR BOMBED THE LATE
POLICE COMMISSIONER.
SEEMS THEY HAVE AN IDENTICALLY-MADE BOMB WITH YOUR FINGERPRINTS.
FTCHH
SO THAT'S WHAT THAT FARCE AT THE POLICE GARAGE WAS ALL ABOUT. GETTING MY PRINTS.
WON'T STAND UP FIVE MINUTES IN COURT, OF COURSE.
OUT-OF-TOWN ALL DAY THE DAY OF THE BOMBING. WITH THE GOVERNOR.
DON'T THINK THEY PLAN ON YOU EVER MAKING IT TO COURT. ALIVE.
HMMM. ACTING CHIEF MCLEWIS ISN'T BRIGHT ENOUGH TO PULL THIS.
GOTTA BE THAT NEW KINGPIN THAT BLIND GUY WARNED ME ABOUT-- YESTERDAY KNEWES!
UH-OH. ROADBLOCK.
QUICK! DOWN ON THE FLOORBOARDS! UNDER THE BLANKET!

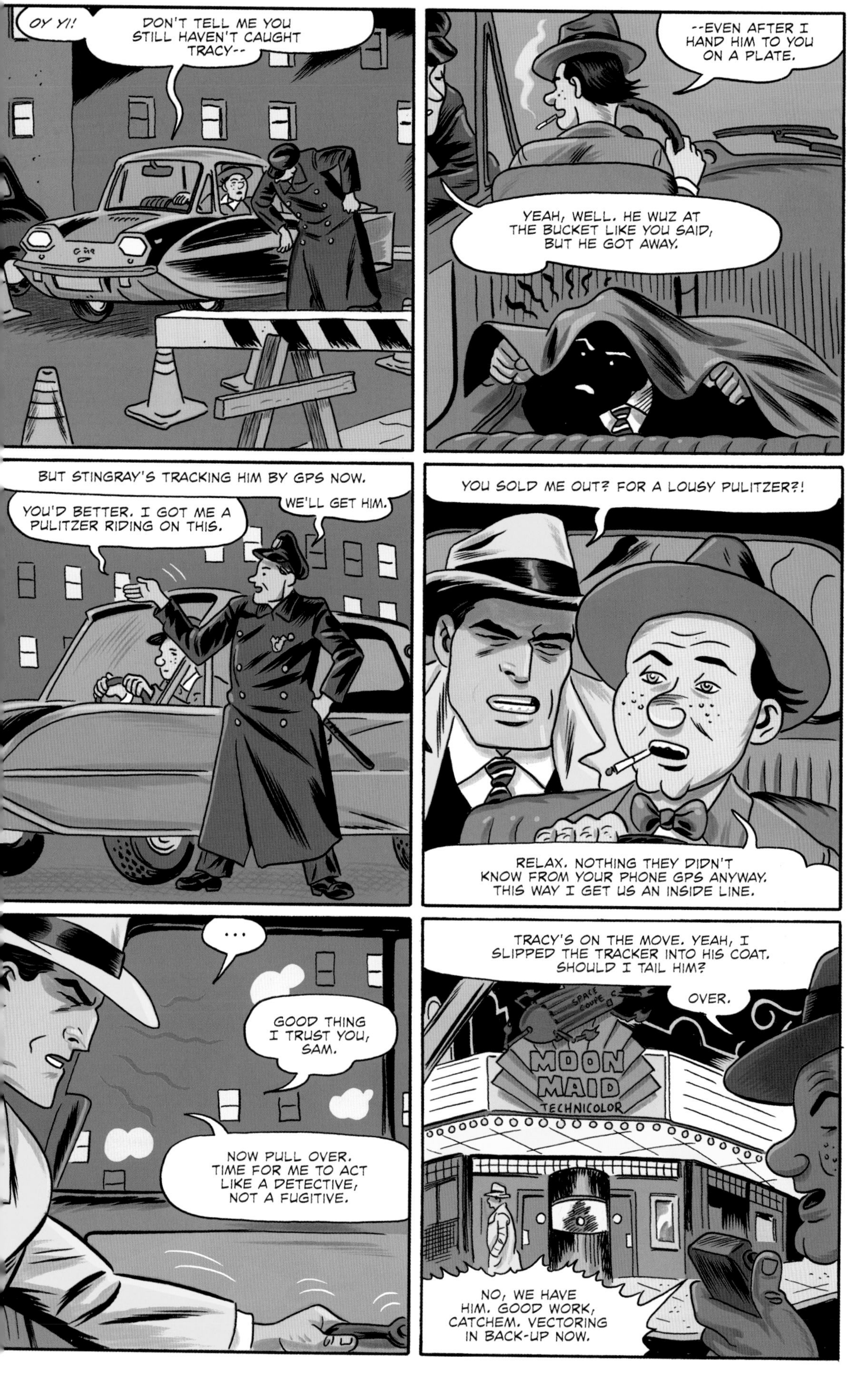

OY YI!
DON'T TELL ME YOU STILL HAVEN'T CAUGHT TRACY--
--EVEN AFTER I HAND HIM TO YOU ON A PLATE.
YEAH, WELL. HE WUZ AT THE BUCKET LIKE YOU SAID, BUT HE GOT AWAY.
BUT STINGRAY'S TRACKING HIM BY GPS NOW.
YOU'D BETTER. I GOT ME A PULITZER RIDING ON THIS.
WE'LL GET HIM.
YOU SOLD ME OUT? FOR A LOUSY PULITZER?!
RELAX. NOTHING THEY DIDN'T KNOW FROM YOUR PHONE GPS ANYWAY. THIS WAY I GET US AN INSIDE LINE.
...
GOOD THING I TRUST YOU, SAM.
NOW PULL OVER. TIME FOR ME TO ACT LIKE A DETECTIVE, NOT A FUGITIVE.
TRACY'S ON THE MOVE. YEAH, I SLIPPED THE TRACKER INTO HIS COAT. SHOULD I TAIL HIM?
OVER.
MOON MAID
TECHNICOLOR
NO, WE HAVE HIM. GOOD WORK, CATCHEM. VECTORING IN BACK-UP NOW.

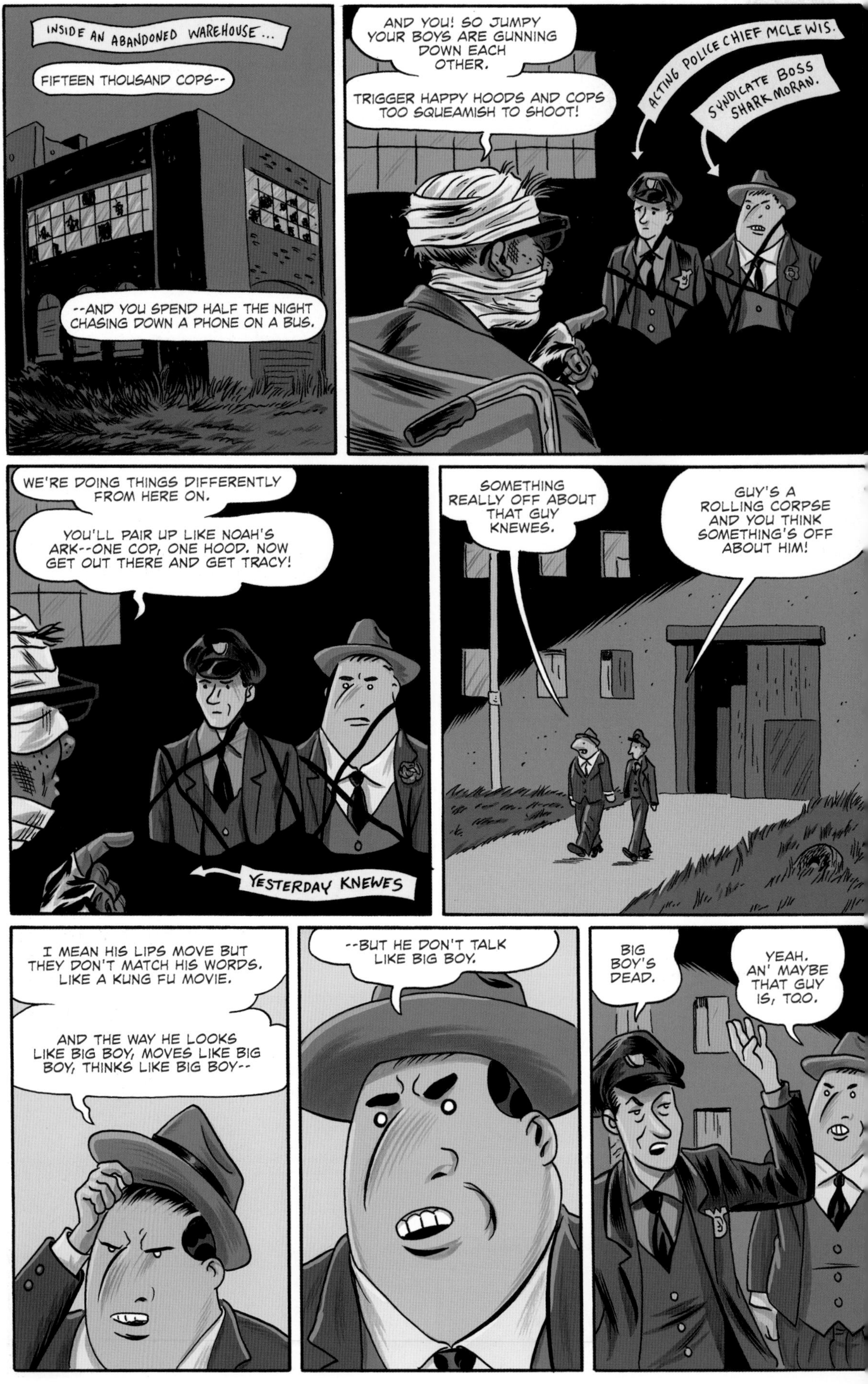

INSIDE AN ABANDONED WAREHOUSE...
FIFTEEN THOUSAND COPS--
--AND YOU SPEND HALF THE NIGHT CHASING DOWN A PHONE ON A BUS.
AND YOU! SO JUMPY YOUR BOYS ARE GUNNING DOWN EACH OTHER.
TRIGGER HAPPY HOODS AND COPS TOO SQUEAMISH TO SHOOT!
ACTING POLICE CHIEF MCLEWIS.
SYNDICATE BOSS SHARK MORAN.
WE'RE DOING THINGS DIFFERENTLY FROM HERE ON.
YOU'LL PAIR UP LIKE NOAH'S ARK--ONE COP, ONE HOOD. NOW GET OUT THERE AND GET TRACY!
YESTERDAY KNEWES
SOMETHING REALLY OFF ABOUT THAT GUY KNEWES.
GUY'S A ROLLING CORPSE AND YOU THINK SOMETHING'S OFF ABOUT HIM!
I MEAN HIS LIPS MOVE BUT THEY DON'T MATCH HIS WORDS. LIKE A KUNG FU MOVIE.
AND THE WAY HE LOOKS LIKE BIG BOY, MOVES LIKE BIG BOY, THINKS LIKE BIG BOY--
--BUT HE DON'T TALK LIKE BIG BOY.
BIG BOY'S DEAD.
YEAH. AN' MAYBE THAT GUY IS, TOO.

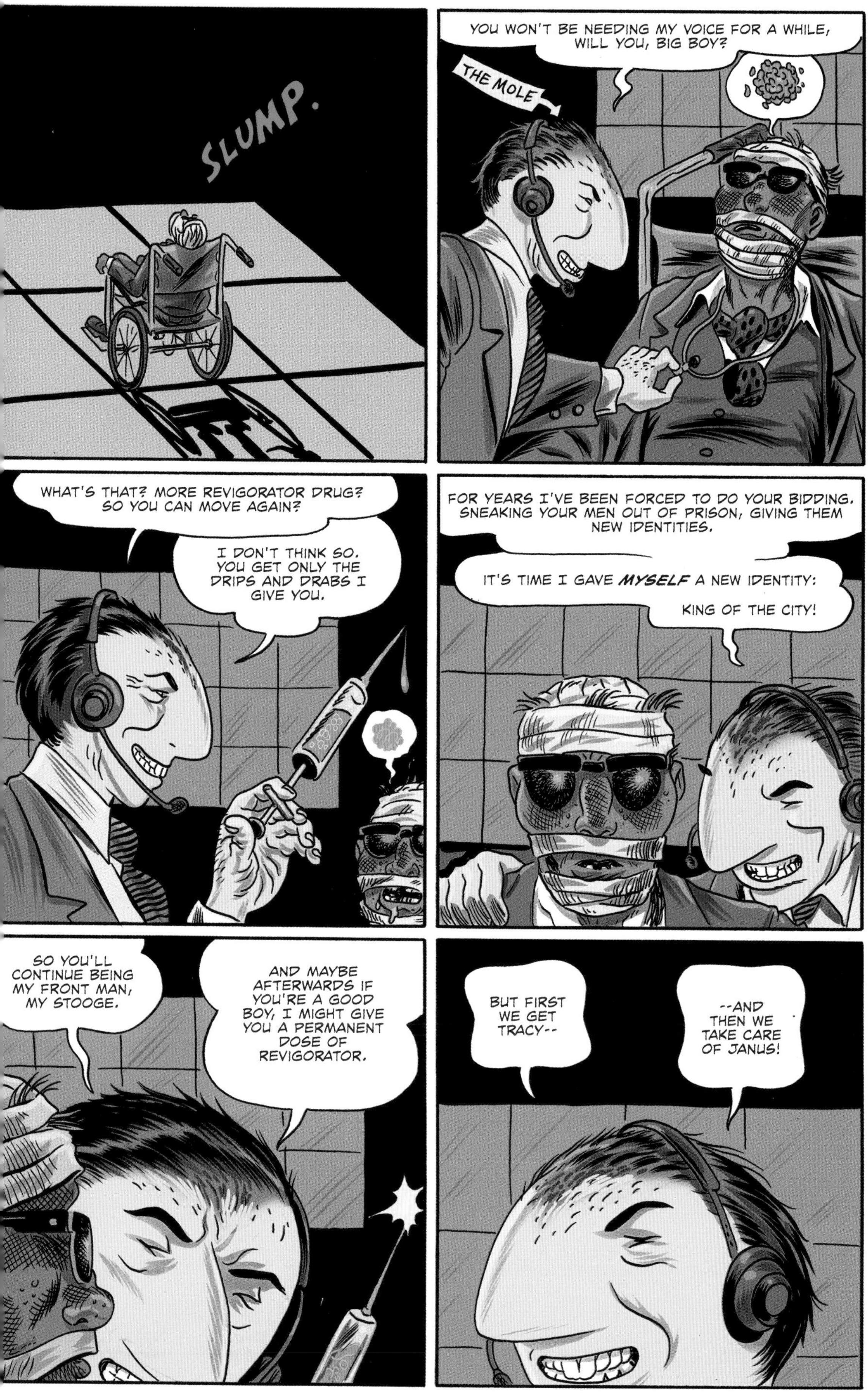
SLUMP.
YOU WON'T BE NEEDING MY VOICE FOR A WHILE, WILL YOU, BIG BOY?
THE MOLE
WHAT'S THAT? MORE REVIGORATOR DRUG? SO YOU CAN MOVE AGAIN?
I DON'T THINK SO. YOU GET ONLY THE DRIPS AND DRABS I GIVE YOU.
FOR YEARS I'VE BEEN FORCED TO DO YOUR BIDDING. SNEAKING YOUR MEN OUT OF PRISON, GIVING THEM NEW IDENTITIES.
IT'S TIME I GAVE *MYSELF* A NEW IDENTITY:
KING OF THE CITY!
SO YOU'LL CONTINUE BEING MY FRONT MAN, MY STOOGE.
AND MAYBE AFTERWARDS IF YOU'RE A GOOD BOY, I MIGHT GIVE YOU A PERMANENT DOSE OF REVIGORATOR.
BUT FIRST WE GET TRACY--
--AND THEN WE TAKE CARE OF JANUS!

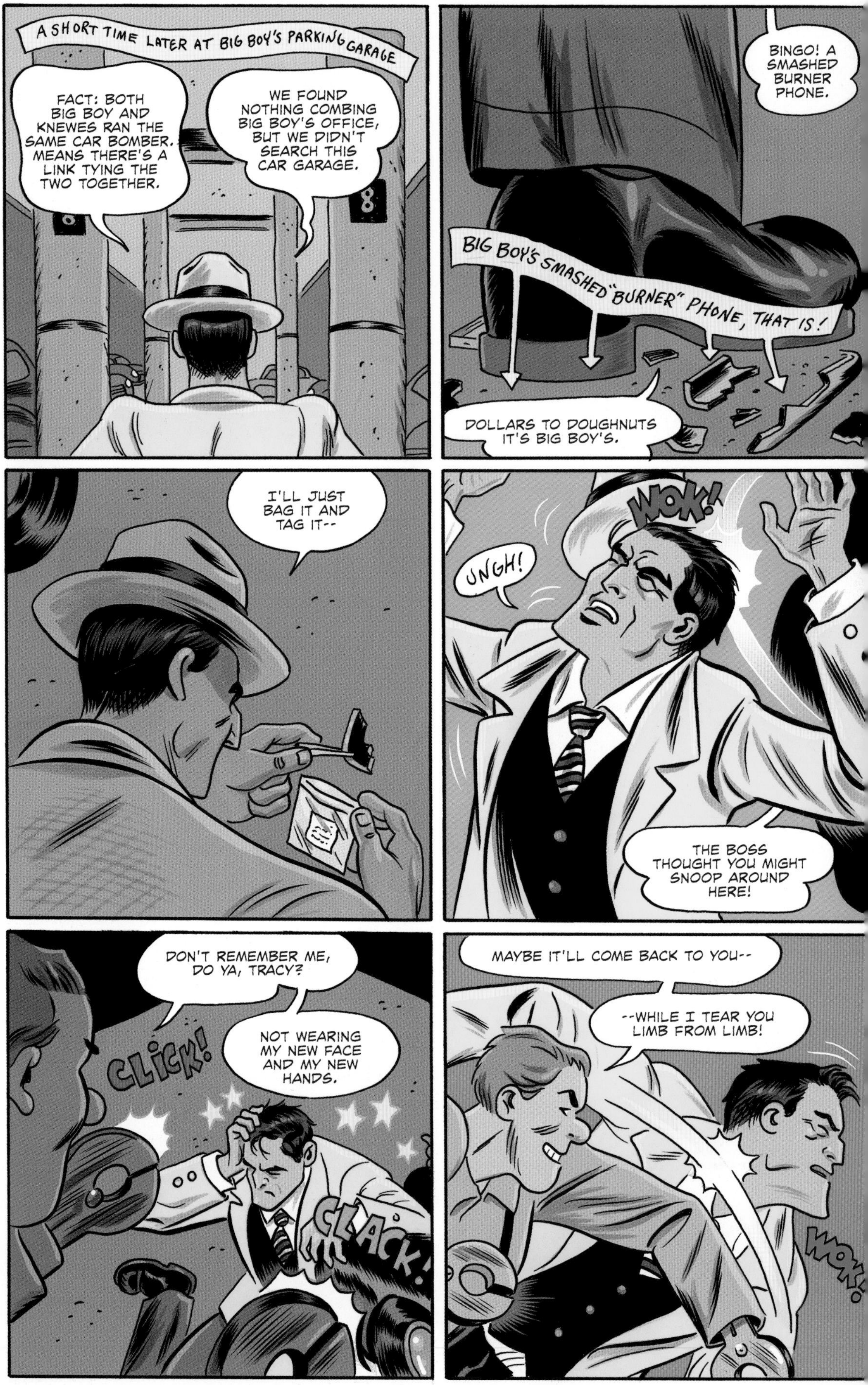
A SHORT TIME LATER AT BIG BOY'S PARKING GARAGE
FACT: BOTH BIG BOY AND KNEWES RAN THE SAME CAR BOMBER. MEANS THERE'S A LINK TYING THE TWO TOGETHER.
WE FOUND NOTHING COMBING BIG BOY'S OFFICE, BUT WE DIDN'T SEARCH THIS CAR GARAGE.
BINGO! A SMASHED BURNER PHONE.
BIG BOY'S SMASHED "BURNER" PHONE, THAT IS!
DOLLARS TO DOUGHNUTS IT'S BIG BOY'S.
I'LL JUST BAG IT AND TAG IT--
WOK!
UNGH!
THE BOSS THOUGHT YOU MIGHT SNOOP AROUND HERE!
DON'T REMEMBER ME, DO YA, TRACY?
CLICK!
NOT WEARING MY NEW FACE AND MY NEW HANDS.
CLACK!
MAYBE IT'LL COME BACK TO YOU--
--WHILE I TEAR YOU LIMB FROM LIMB!
WOK!

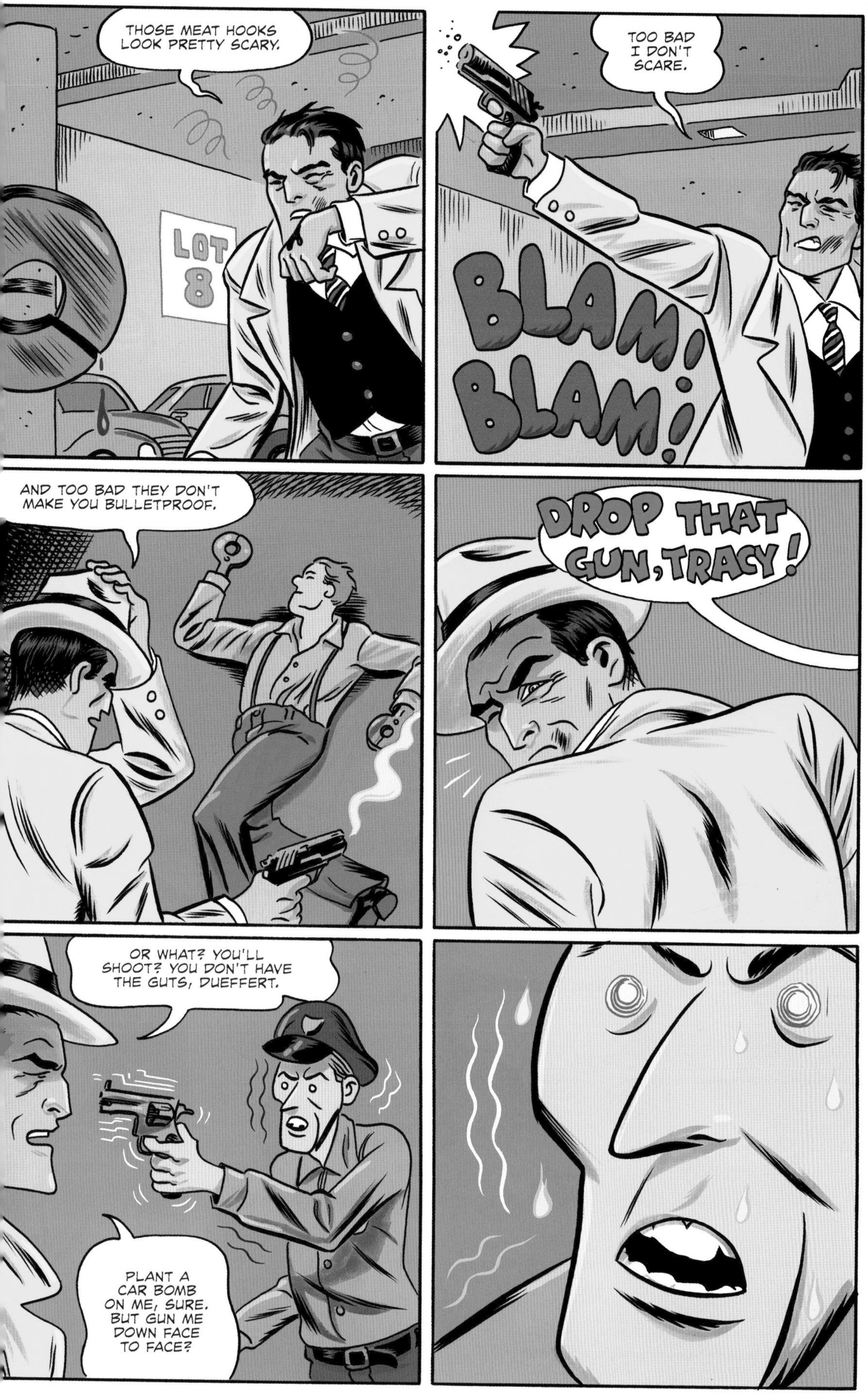
THOSE MEAT HOOKS LOOK PRETTY SCARY.
LOT 8
TOO BAD I DON'T SCARE.
BLAM! BLAM!
AND TOO BAD THEY DON'T MAKE YOU BULLETPROOF.
DROP THAT GUN, TRACY!
OR WHAT? YOU'LL SHOOT? YOU DON'T HAVE THE GUTS, DUEFFERT.
PLANT A CAR BOMB ON ME, SURE. BUT GUN ME DOWN FACE TO FACE?

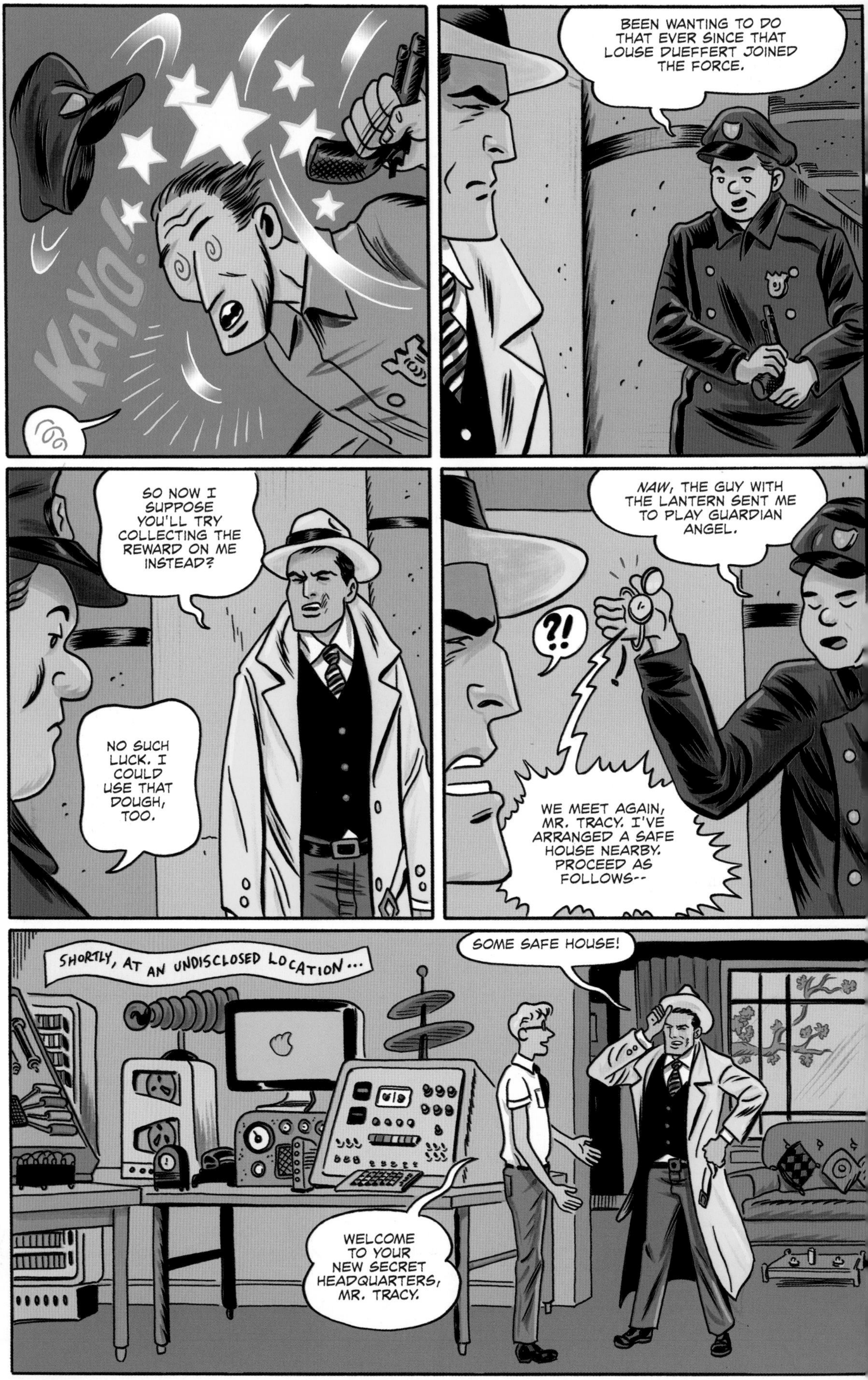
KAYO!
BEEN WANTING TO DO THAT EVER SINCE THAT LOUSE DUEFFERT JOINED THE FORCE.
SO NOW I SUPPOSE YOU'LL TRY COLLECTING THE REWARD ON ME INSTEAD?
NO SUCH LUCK. I COULD USE THAT DOUGH, TOO.
NAW, THE GUY WITH THE LANTERN SENT ME TO PLAY GUARDIAN ANGEL.
?!
WE MEET AGAIN, MR. TRACY. I'VE ARRANGED A SAFE HOUSE NEARBY. PROCEED AS FOLLOWS--
SHORTLY, AT AN UNDISCLOSED LOCATION...
SOME SAFE HOUSE!
WELCOME TO YOUR NEW SECRET HEADQUARTERS, MR. TRACY.

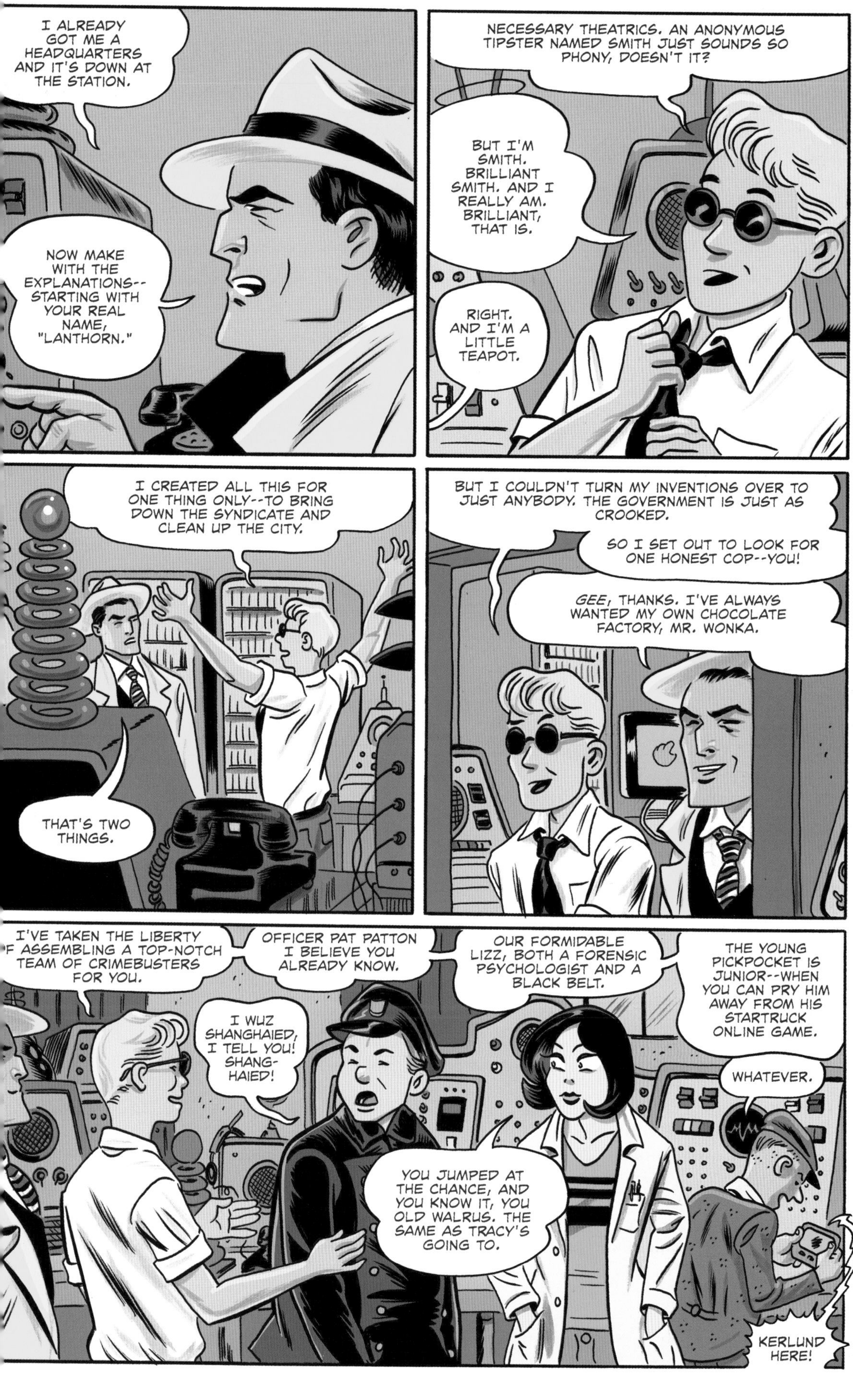

I ALREADY GOT ME A HEADQUARTERS AND IT'S DOWN AT THE STATION.
NOW MAKE WITH THE EXPLANATIONS--STARTING WITH YOUR REAL NAME, "LANTHORN."
NECESSARY THEATRICS. AN ANONYMOUS TIPSTER NAMED SMITH JUST SOUNDS SO PHONY, DOESN'T IT?
BUT I'M SMITH. BRILLIANT SMITH. AND I REALLY AM. BRILLIANT, THAT IS.
RIGHT. AND I'M A LITTLE TEAPOT.
I CREATED ALL THIS FOR ONE THING ONLY--TO BRING DOWN THE SYNDICATE AND CLEAN UP THE CITY.
THAT'S TWO THINGS.
BUT I COULDN'T TURN MY INVENTIONS OVER TO JUST ANYBODY. THE GOVERNMENT IS JUST AS CROOKED.
SO I SET OUT TO LOOK FOR ONE HONEST COP--YOU!
GEE, THANKS. I'VE ALWAYS WANTED MY OWN CHOCOLATE FACTORY, MR. WONKA.
I'VE TAKEN THE LIBERTY OF ASSEMBLING A TOP-NOTCH TEAM OF CRIMEBUSTERS FOR YOU.
OFFICER PAT PATTON I BELIEVE YOU ALREADY KNOW.
I WUZ SHANGHAIED, I TELL YOU! SHANG-HAIED!
OUR FORMIDABLE LIZZ, BOTH A FORENSIC PSYCHOLOGIST AND A BLACK BELT.
THE YOUNG PICKPOCKET IS JUNIOR--WHEN YOU CAN PRY HIM AWAY FROM HIS STARTRUCK ONLINE GAME.
WHATEVER.
YOU JUMPED AT THE CHANCE, AND YOU KNOW IT, YOU OLD WALRUS. THE SAME AS TRACY'S GOING TO.
KERLUND HERE!

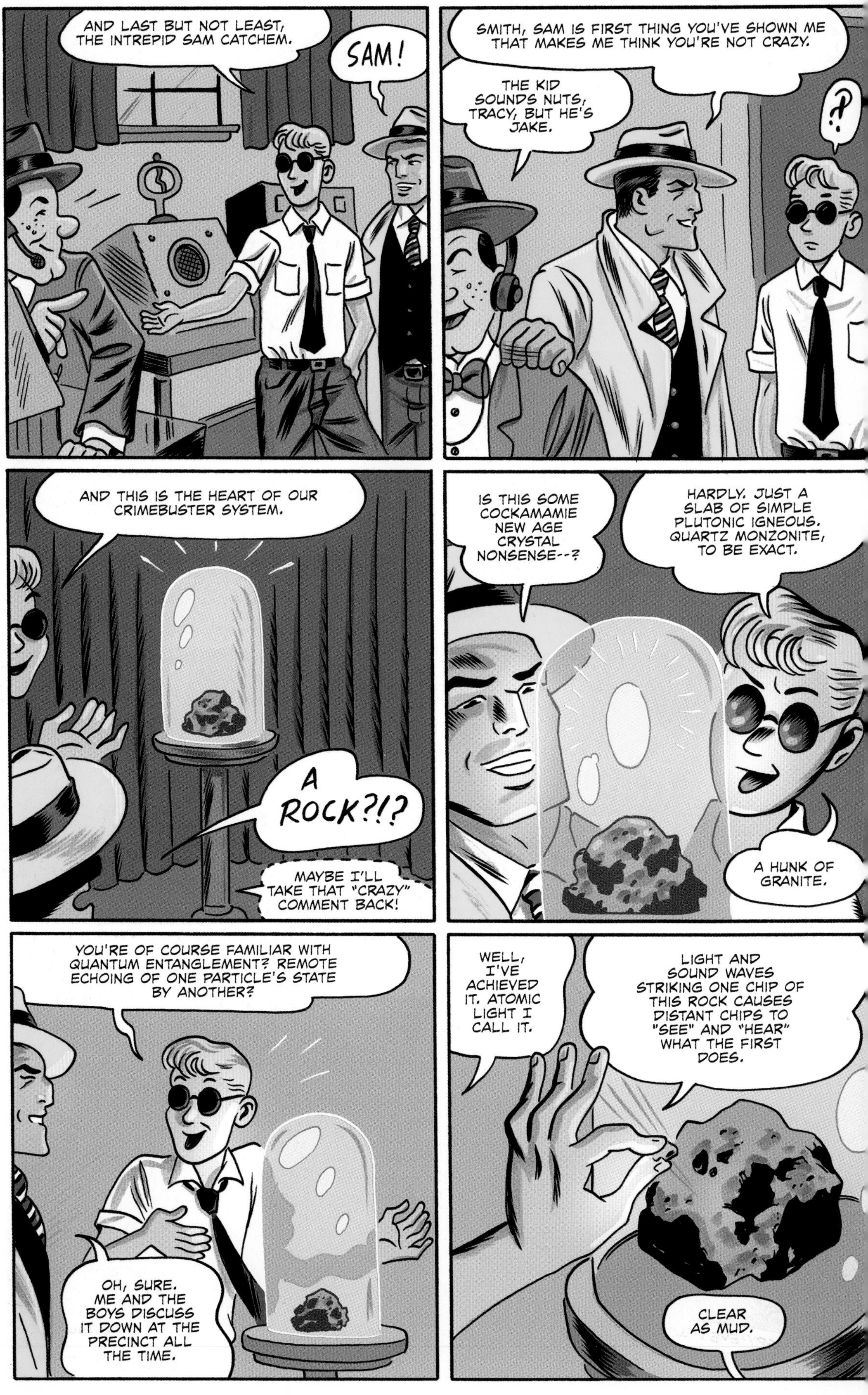
AND LAST BUT NOT LEAST, THE INTREPID SAM CATCHEM.
SAM!
SMITH, SAM IS FIRST THING YOU'VE SHOWN ME THAT MAKES ME THINK YOU'RE NOT CRAZY.
THE KID SOUNDS NUTS, TRACY, BUT HE'S JAKE.
?
AND THIS IS THE HEART OF OUR CRIMEBUSTER SYSTEM.
A ROCK?!?
MAYBE I'LL TAKE THAT "CRAZY" COMMENT BACK!
IS THIS SOME COCKAMAMIE NEW AGE CRYSTAL NONSENSE--?
HARDLY. JUST A SLAB OF SIMPLE PLUTONIC IGNEOUS. QUARTZ MONZONITE, TO BE EXACT.
A HUNK OF GRANITE.
YOU'RE OF COURSE FAMILIAR WITH QUANTUM ENTANGLEMENT? REMOTE ECHOING OF ONE PARTICLE'S STATE BY ANOTHER?
OH, SURE. ME AND THE BOYS DISCUSS IT DOWN AT THE PRECINCT ALL THE TIME.
WELL, I'VE ACHIEVED IT. ATOMIC LIGHT I CALL IT.
LIGHT AND SOUND WAVES STRIKING ONE CHIP OF THIS ROCK CAUSES DISTANT CHIPS TO "SEE" AND "HEAR" WHAT THE FIRST DOES.
CLEAR AS MUD.

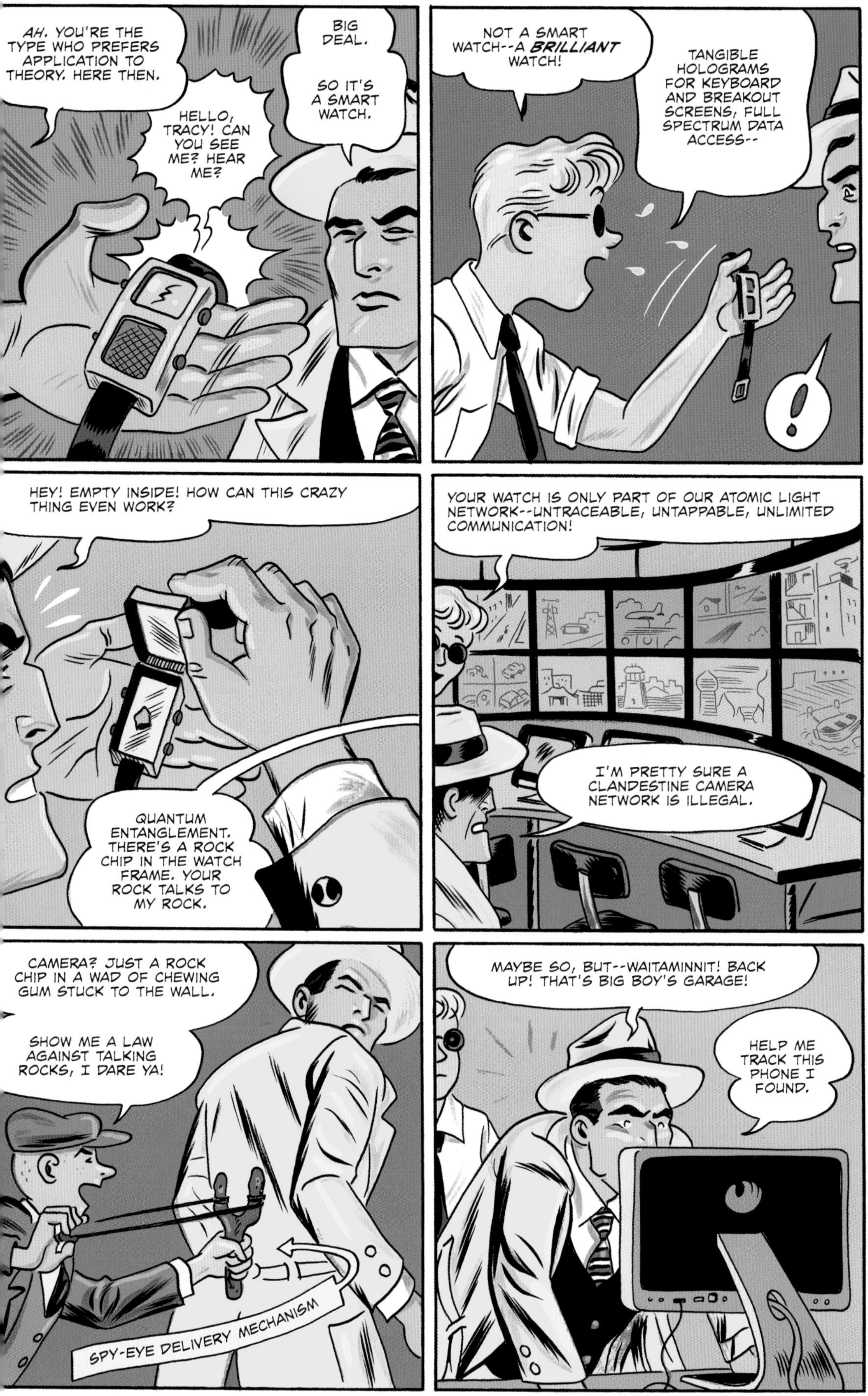
AH. YOU'RE THE TYPE WHO PREFERS APPLICATION TO THEORY. HERE THEN.
HELLO, TRACY! CAN YOU SEE ME? HEAR ME?
BIG DEAL.
SO IT'S A SMART WATCH.
NOT A SMART WATCH--A BRILLIANT WATCH!
TANGIBLE HOLOGRAMS FOR KEYBOARD AND BREAKOUT SCREENS, FULL SPECTRUM DATA ACCESS--
!
HEY! EMPTY INSIDE! HOW CAN THIS CRAZY THING EVEN WORK?
QUANTUM ENTANGLEMENT. THERE'S A ROCK CHIP IN THE WATCH FRAME. YOUR ROCK TALKS TO MY ROCK.
YOUR WATCH IS ONLY PART OF OUR ATOMIC LIGHT NETWORK--UNTRACEABLE, UNTAPPABLE, UNLIMITED COMMUNICATION!
I'M PRETTY SURE A CLANDESTINE CAMERA NETWORK IS ILLEGAL.
CAMERA? JUST A ROCK CHIP IN A WAD OF CHEWING GUM STUCK TO THE WALL.
SHOW ME A LAW AGAINST TALKING ROCKS, I DARE YA!
SPY-EYE DELIVERY MECHANISM
MAYBE SO, BUT--WAITAMINNIT! BACK UP! THAT'S BIG BOY'S GARAGE!
HELP ME TRACK THIS PHONE I FOUND.

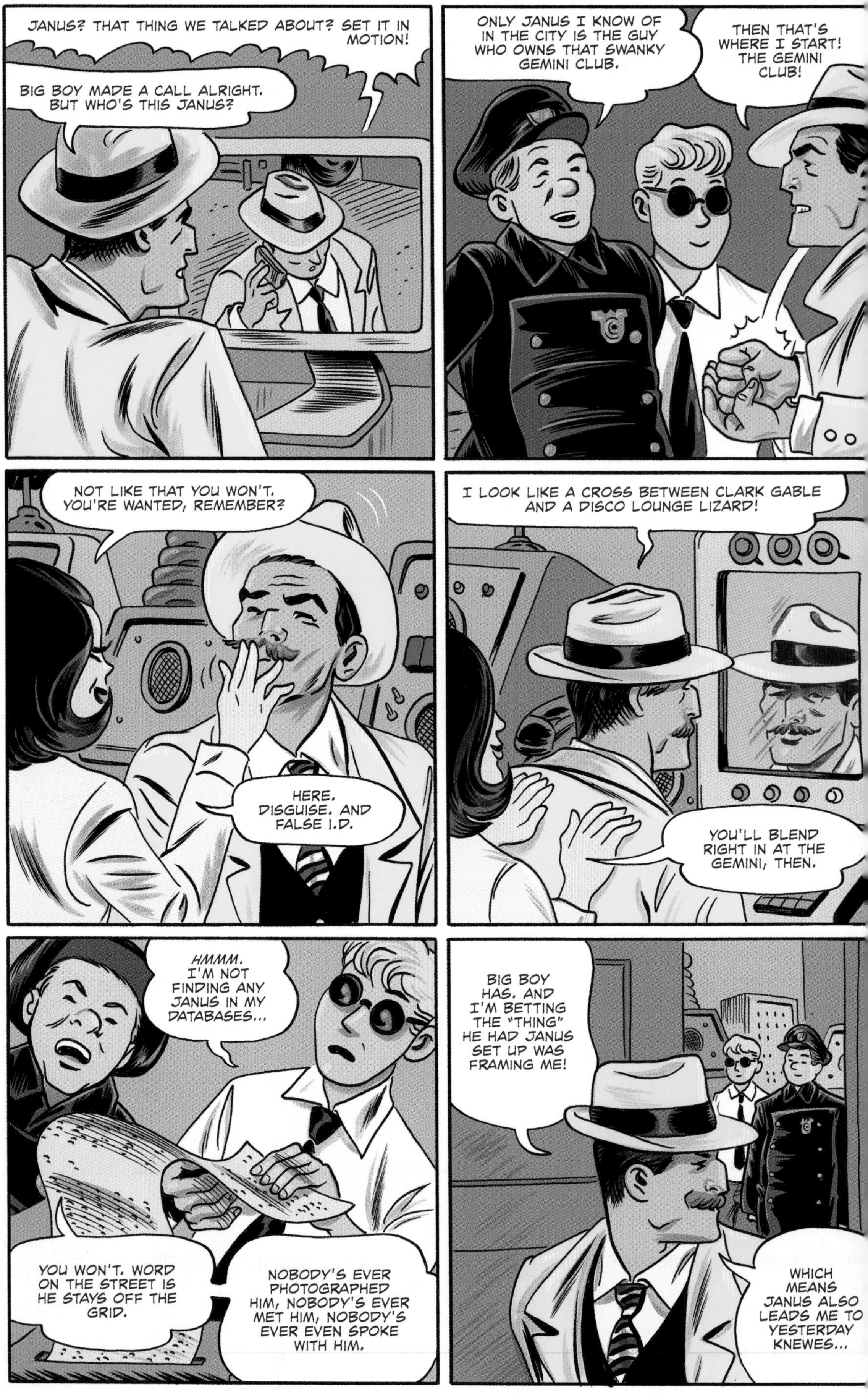
JANUS? THAT THING WE TALKED ABOUT? SET IT IN MOTION!
BIG BOY MADE A CALL ALRIGHT. BUT WHO'S THIS JANUS?
ONLY JANUS I KNOW OF IN THE CITY IS THE GUY WHO OWNS THAT SWANKY GEMINI CLUB.
THEN THAT'S WHERE I START! THE GEMINI CLUB!
NOT LIKE THAT YOU WON'T. YOU'RE WANTED, REMEMBER?
HERE. DISGUISE. AND FALSE I.D.
I LOOK LIKE A CROSS BETWEEN CLARK GABLE AND A DISCO LOUNGE LIZARD!
YOU'LL BLEND RIGHT IN AT THE GEMINI, THEN.
HMMM. I'M NOT FINDING ANY JANUS IN MY DATABASES...
YOU WON'T. WORD ON THE STREET IS HE STAYS OFF THE GRID.
NOBODY'S EVER PHOTOGRAPHED HIM, NOBODY'S EVER MET HIM, NOBODY'S EVER EVEN SPOKE WITH HIM.
BIG BOY HAS. AND I'M BETTING THE "THING" HE HAD JANUS SET UP WAS FRAMING ME!
WHICH MEANS JANUS ALSO LEADS ME TO YESTERDAY KNEWES...

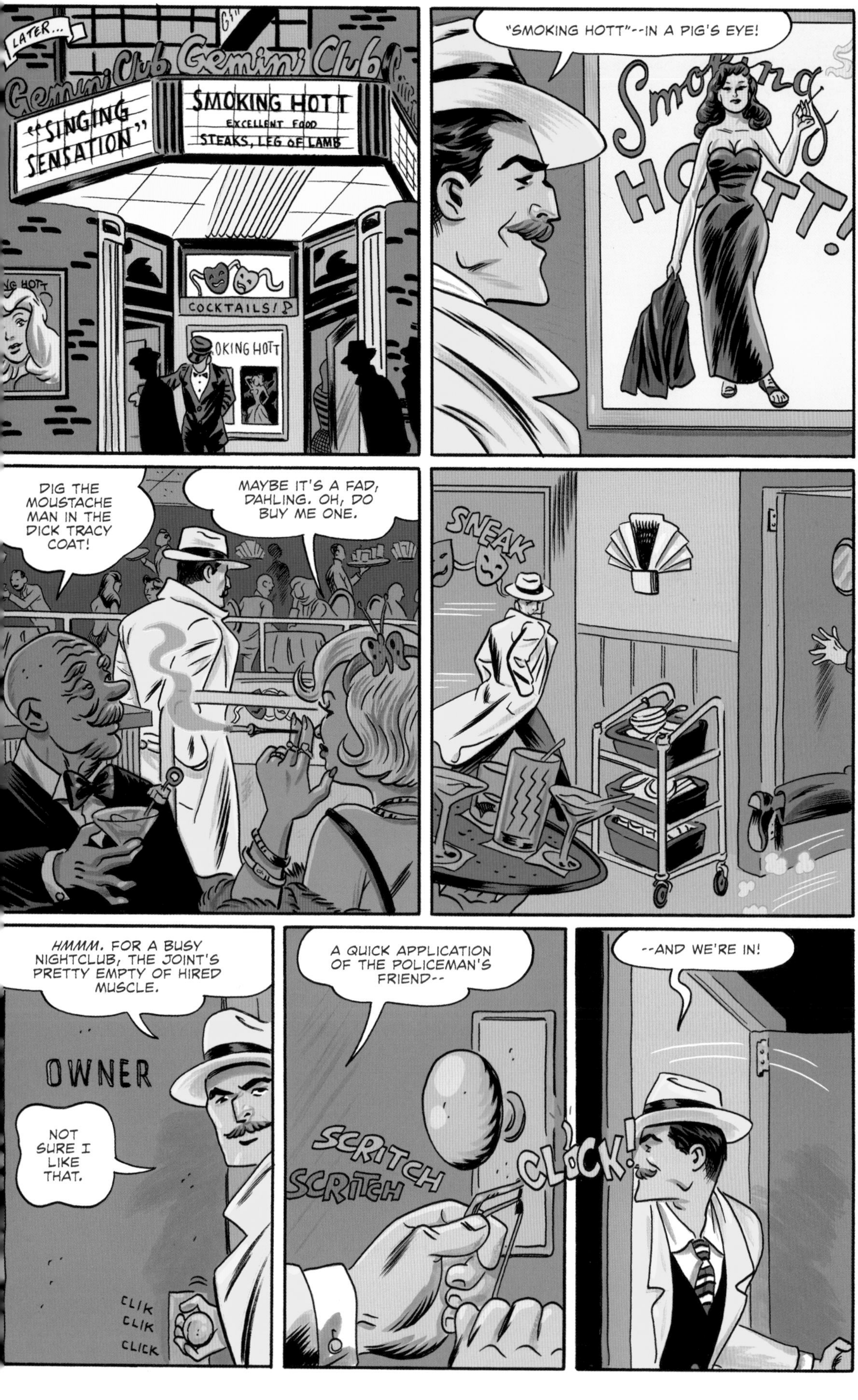
LATER...
Gemini Club Gemini Club
"SINGING SENSATION"
SMOKING HOTT
EXCELLENT FOOD
STEAKS, LEG OF LAMB
COCKTAILS!
OKING HOTT
"SMOKING HOTT"--IN A PIG'S EYE!
Smoking HOTT!
DIG THE MOUSTACHE MAN IN THE DICK TRACY COAT!
MAYBE IT'S A FAD, DAHLING. OH, DO BUY ME ONE.
SNEAK
HMMM. FOR A BUSY NIGHTCLUB, THE JOINT'S PRETTY EMPTY OF HIRED MUSCLE.
OWNER
NOT SURE I LIKE THAT.
CLIK
CLIK
CLICK
A QUICK APPLICATION OF THE POLICEMAN'S FRIEND--
SCRITCH
SCRITCH
CLICK!
--AND WE'RE IN!

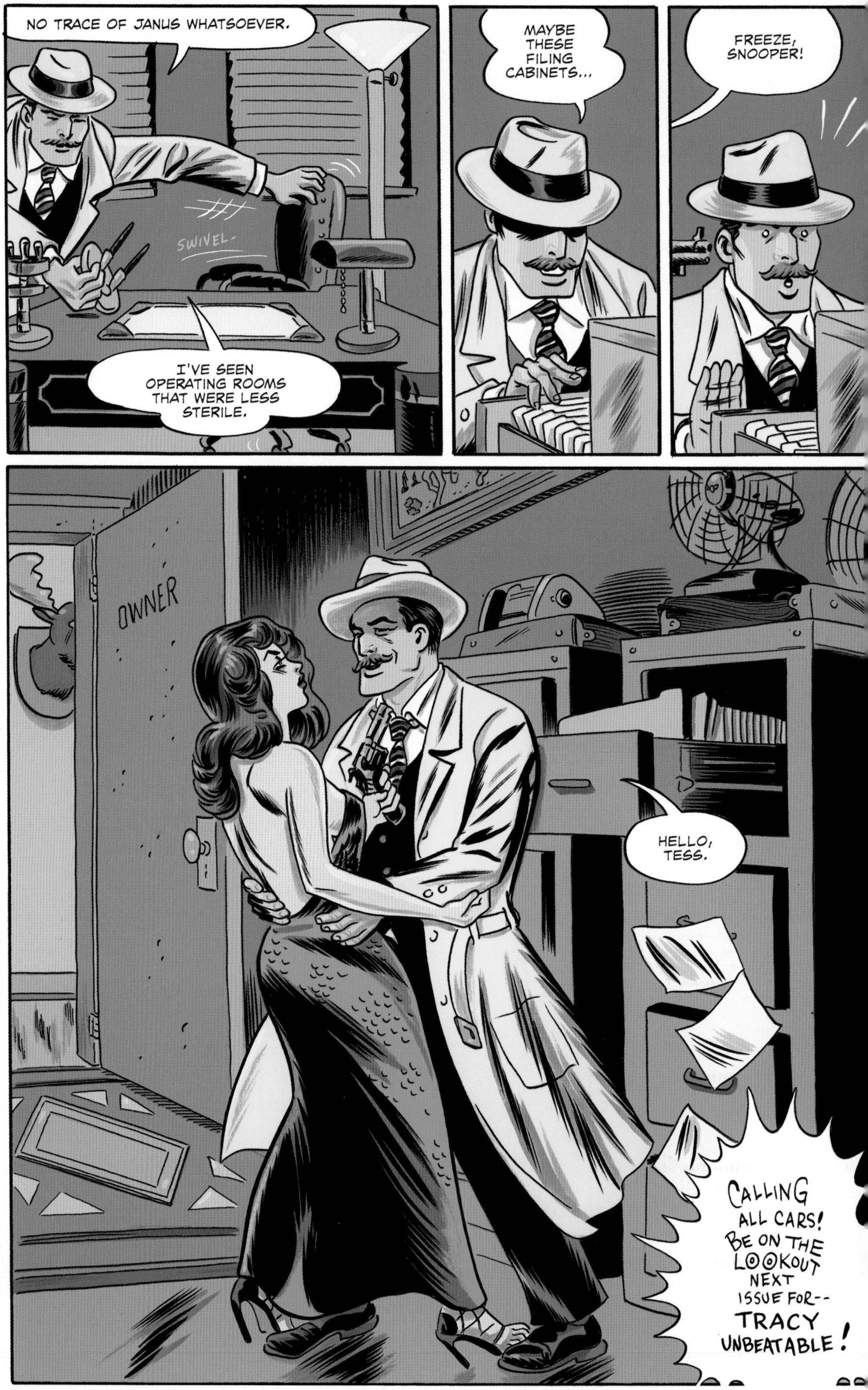
NO TRACE OF JANUS WHATSOEVER.
SWIVEL.
I'VE SEEN OPERATING ROOMS THAT WERE LESS STERILE.
MAYBE THESE FILING CABINETS...
FREEZE, SNOOPER!
OWNER
HELLO, TESS.
CALLING ALL CARS! BE ON THE LOOKOUT NEXT ISSUE FOR-- TRACY UNBEATABLE!

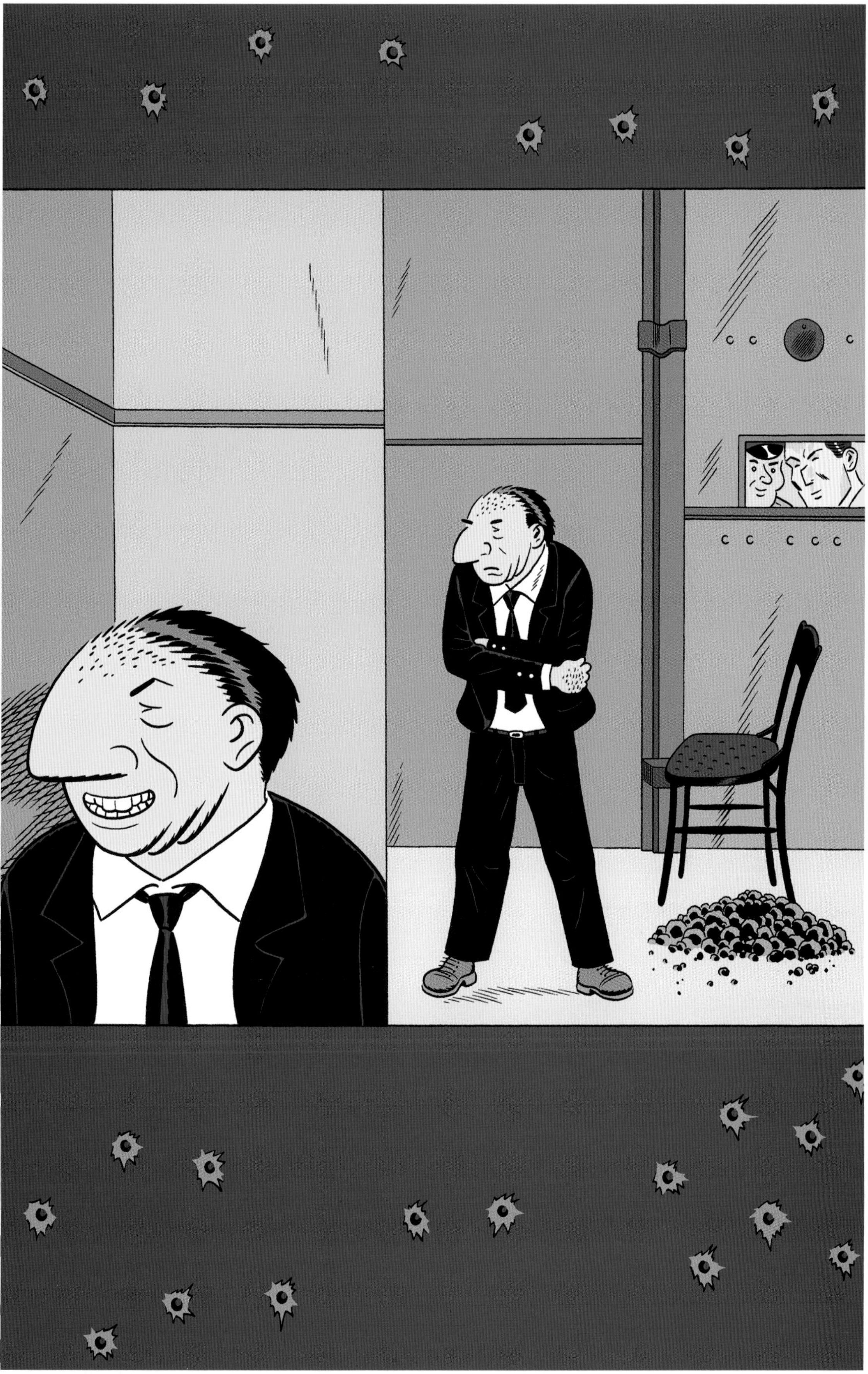

ART BY **RICH TOMMASO** | COLORS BY **AMY PLASMAN**

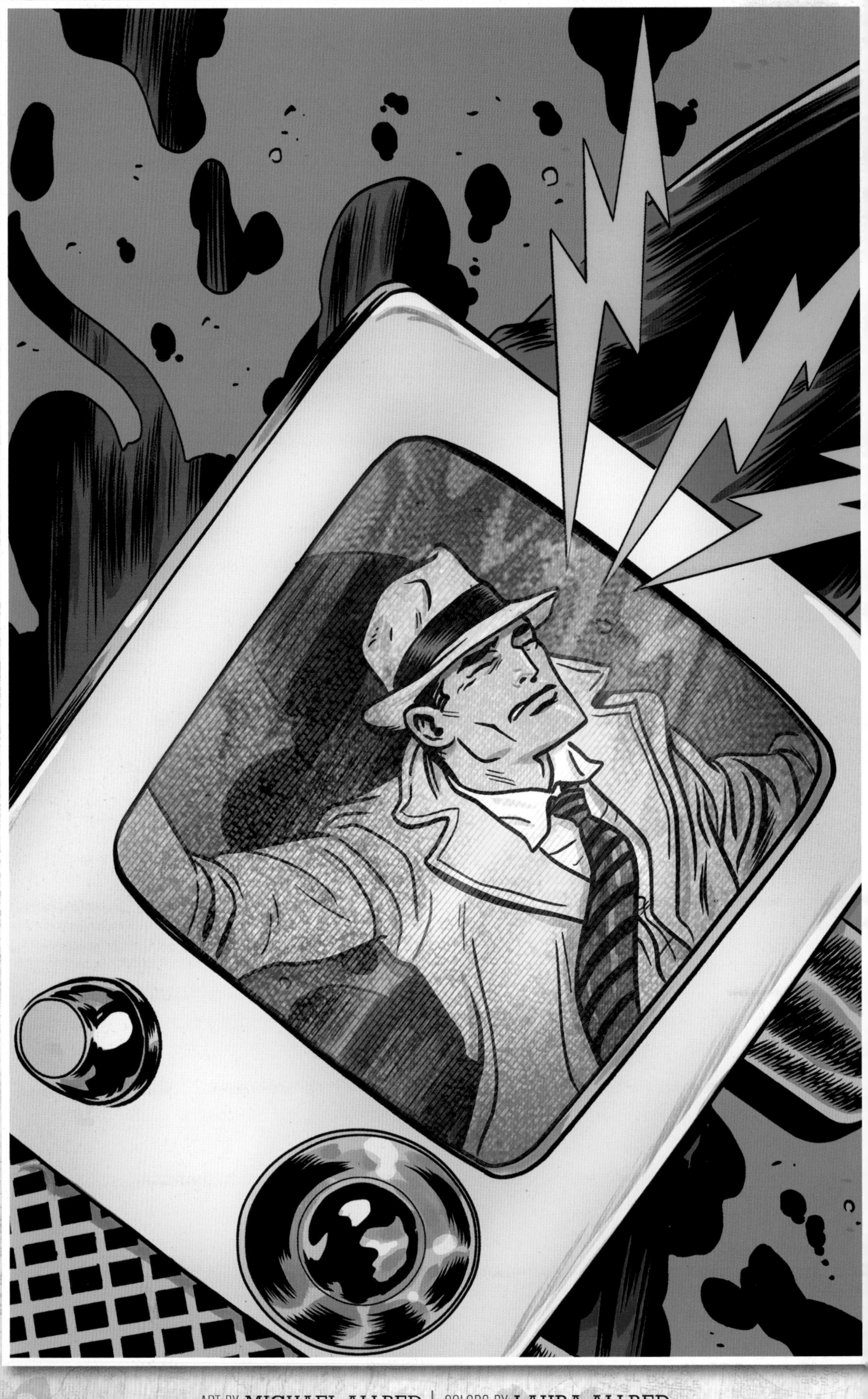

ART BY **MICHAEL ALLRED** | COLORS BY **LAURA ALLRED**

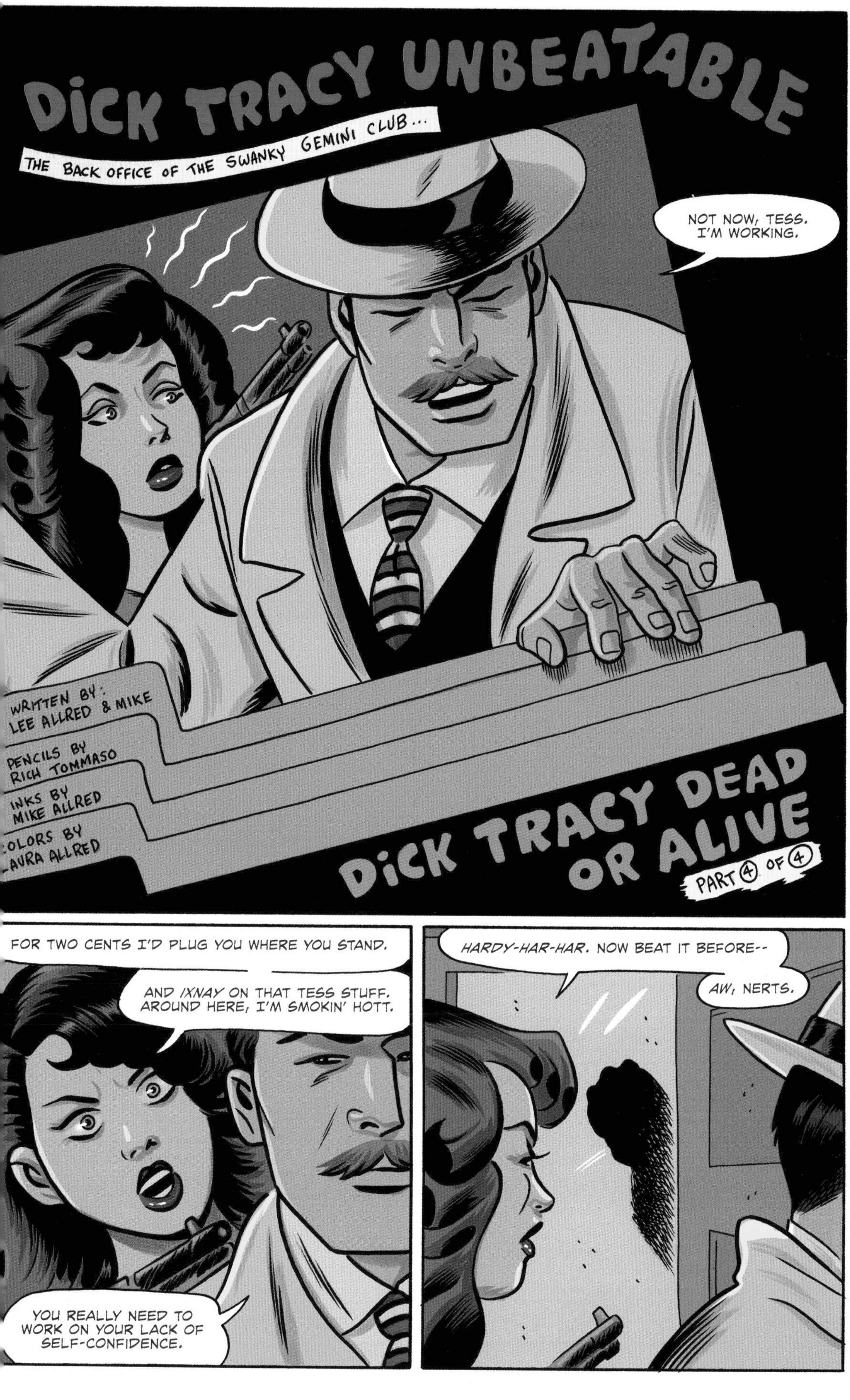

DICK TRACY UNBEATABLE
THE BACK OFFICE OF THE SWANKY GEMINI CLUB...
NOT NOW, TESS. I'M WORKING.
WRITTEN BY: LEE ALLRED & MIKE
PENCILS BY RICH TOMMASO
INKS BY MIKE ALLRED
COLORS BY LAURA ALLRED
DICK TRACY DEAD OR ALIVE
PART 4 OF 4
FOR TWO CENTS I'D PLUG YOU WHERE YOU STAND.
AND *IXNAY* ON THAT TESS STUFF. AROUND HERE, I'M SMOKIN' HOTT.
YOU REALLY NEED TO WORK ON YOUR LACK OF SELF-CONFIDENCE.
HARDY-HAR-HAR. NOW BEAT IT BEFORE--
AW, NERTS.

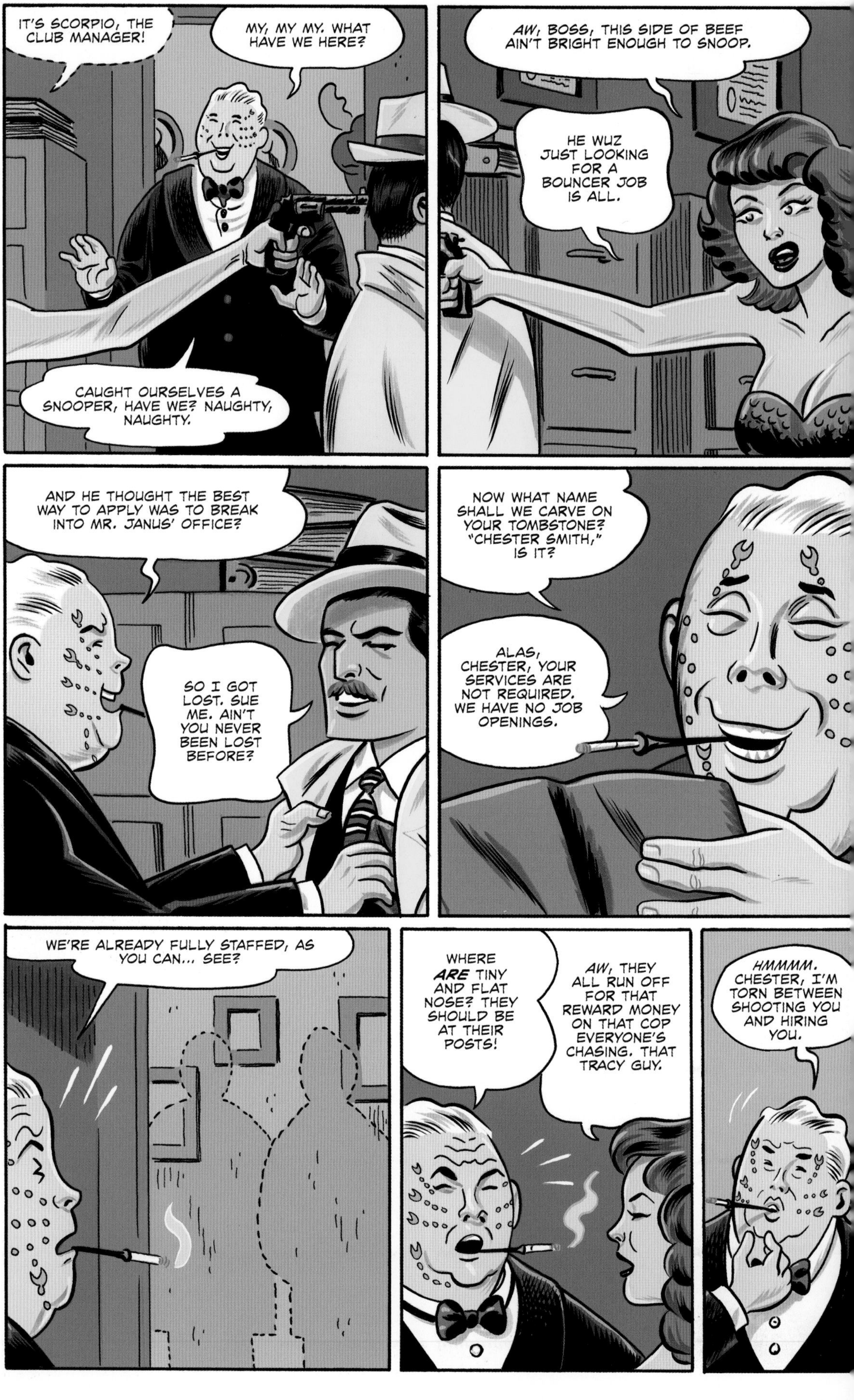
IT'S SCORPIO, THE CLUB MANAGER!
MY, MY MY. WHAT HAVE WE HERE?
CAUGHT OURSELVES A SNOOPER, HAVE WE? NAUGHTY, NAUGHTY.
AW, BOSS, THIS SIDE OF BEEF AIN'T BRIGHT ENOUGH TO SNOOP.
HE WUZ JUST LOOKING FOR A BOUNCER JOB IS ALL.
AND HE THOUGHT THE BEST WAY TO APPLY WAS TO BREAK INTO MR. JANUS' OFFICE?
SO I GOT LOST. SUE ME. AIN'T YOU NEVER BEEN LOST BEFORE?
NOW WHAT NAME SHALL WE CARVE ON YOUR TOMBSTONE? "CHESTER SMITH," IS IT?
ALAS, CHESTER, YOUR SERVICES ARE NOT REQUIRED. WE HAVE NO JOB OPENINGS.
WE'RE ALREADY FULLY STAFFED, AS YOU CAN... SEE?
WHERE ARE TINY AND FLAT NOSE? THEY SHOULD BE AT THEIR POSTS!
AW, THEY ALL RUN OFF FOR THAT REWARD MONEY ON THAT COP EVERYONE'S CHASING. THAT TRACY GUY.
HMMMM. CHESTER, I'M TORN BETWEEN SHOOTING YOU AND HIRING YOU.

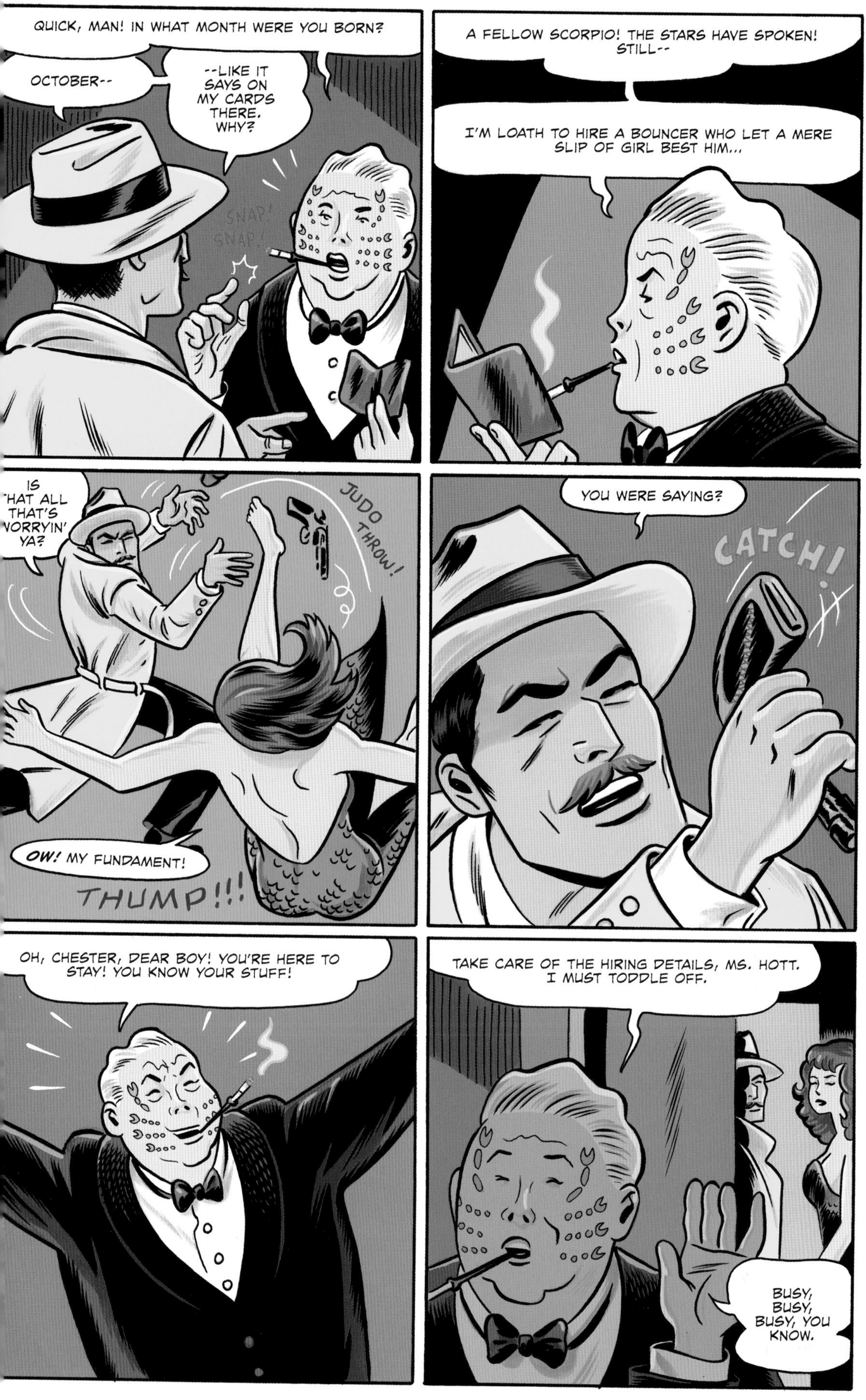

QUICK, MAN! IN WHAT MONTH WERE YOU BORN?
OCTOBER--
--LIKE IT SAYS ON MY CARDS THERE. WHY?
SNAP! SNAP!
A FELLOW SCORPIO! THE STARS HAVE SPOKEN! STILL--
I'M LOATH TO HIRE A BOUNCER WHO LET A MERE SLIP OF GIRL BEST HIM...
IS 'HAT ALL THAT'S VORRYIN' YA?
JUDO THROW!
OW! MY FUNDAMENT!
THUMP!!!
YOU WERE SAYING?
CATCH!
OH, CHESTER, DEAR BOY! YOU'RE HERE TO STAY! YOU KNOW YOUR STUFF!
TAKE CARE OF THE HIRING DETAILS, MS. HOTT. I MUST TODDLE OFF.
BUSY, BUSY, BUSY, YOU KNOW.

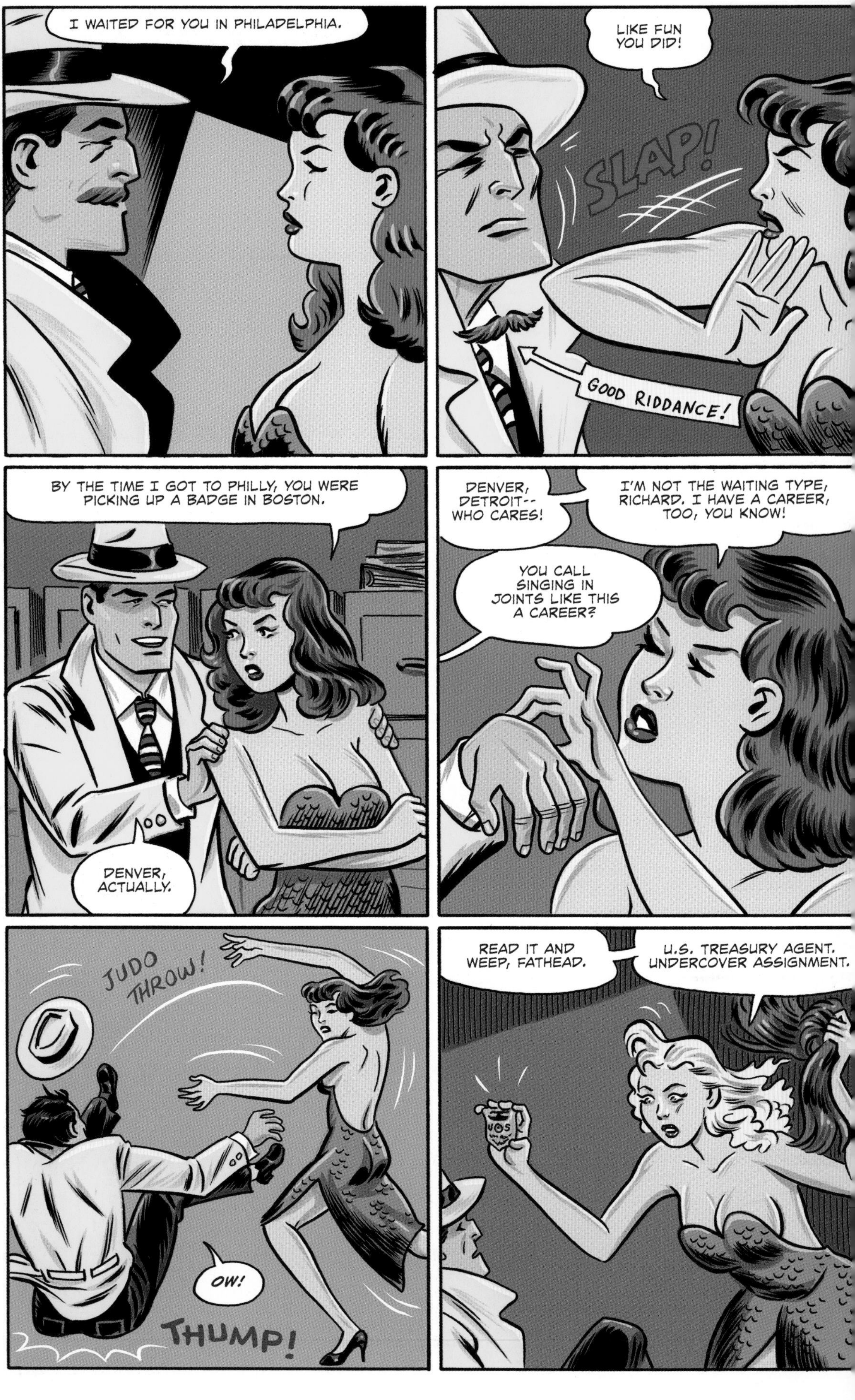
I WAITED FOR YOU IN PHILADELPHIA.
LIKE FUN YOU DID!
SLAP!
GOOD RIDDANCE!
BY THE TIME I GOT TO PHILLY, YOU WERE PICKING UP A BADGE IN BOSTON.
DENVER, ACTUALLY.
DENVER, DETROIT-- WHO CARES!
I'M NOT THE WAITING TYPE, RICHARD. I HAVE A CAREER, TOO, YOU KNOW!
YOU CALL SINGING IN JOINTS LIKE THIS A CAREER?
JUDO THROW!
OW!
THUMP!
READ IT AND WEEP, FATHEAD.
U.S. TREASURY AGENT. UNDERCOVER ASSIGNMENT.

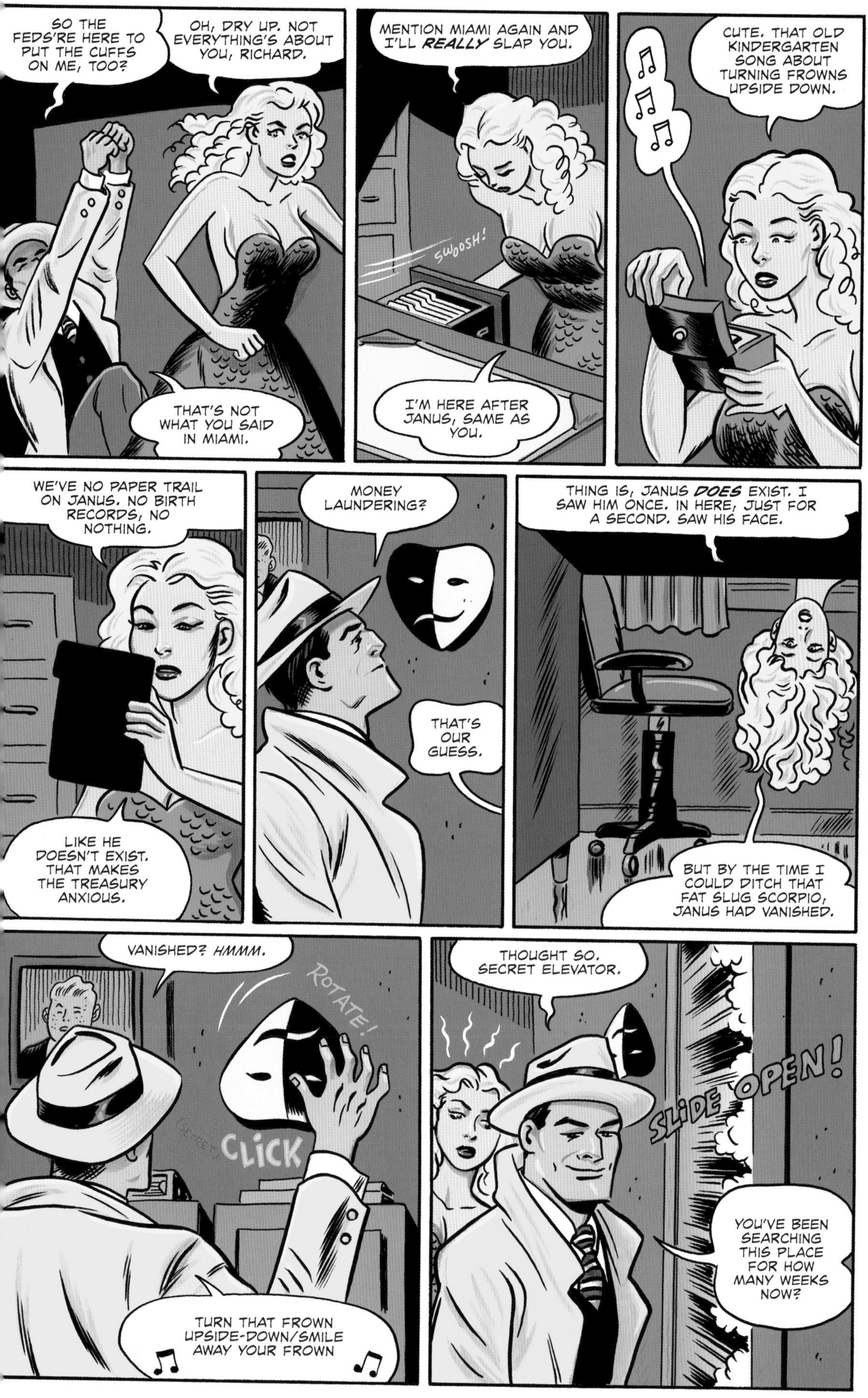

SO THE FEDS'RE HERE TO PUT THE CUFFS ON ME, TOO?
OH, DRY UP. NOT EVERYTHING'S ABOUT YOU, RICHARD.
THAT'S NOT WHAT YOU SAID IN MIAMI.
MENTION MIAMI AGAIN AND I'LL *REALLY* SLAP YOU.
SWOOSH!
I'M HERE AFTER JANUS, SAME AS YOU.
CUTE. THAT OLD KINDERGARTEN SONG ABOUT TURNING FROWNS UPSIDE DOWN.
WE'VE NO PAPER TRAIL ON JANUS. NO BIRTH RECORDS, NO NOTHING.
LIKE HE DOESN'T EXIST. THAT MAKES THE TREASURY ANXIOUS.
MONEY LAUNDERING?
THAT'S OUR GUESS.
THING IS, JANUS *DOES* EXIST. I SAW HIM ONCE. IN HERE, JUST FOR A SECOND. SAW HIS FACE.
BUT BY THE TIME I COULD DITCH THAT FAT SLUG SCORPIO, JANUS HAD VANISHED.
VANISHED? *HMMM.*
ROTATE!
(SECRET) CLICK
TURN THAT FROWN UPSIDE-DOWN/SMILE AWAY YOUR FROWN
THOUGHT SO. SECRET ELEVATOR.
SLIDE OPEN!
YOU'VE BEEN SEARCHING THIS PLACE FOR HOW MANY WEEKS NOW?

A FAST TRIP DOWN A *SLOW* ELEVATOR...

A COMBINATION HOTEL-AND-HOSPITAL.

NOT QUITE WHAT I WAS EXPECTING.

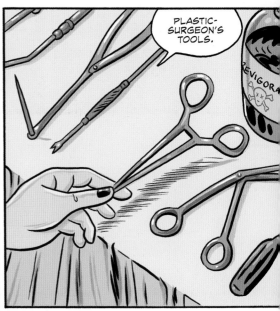

PLASTIC-SURGEON'S TOOLS.

ROTARY SANDER, DERMATOLOGICAL ACID, FINGERPRINT MOLDS.

SANDING OFF FINGERPRINTS TO ETCH ON NEW ONES. GOOD WAY TO END UP WITH GANGRENE.

WHAT THE--?!

"DON'T KNOW ME WITH MY NEW FACE AND HANDS, DO YA?"

SNAP!

OF COURSE! CLAMPS COULDN'T KEEP HIS TRAP SHUT. GAVE AWAY THE GAME.

THIS HERE'S A NEW IDENTITY FACTORY. CROOKS ON THE LAM MUST PAY JANUS BIG BUCKS, TOO.

THERE GOES MY MONEY LAUNDERING ANGLE.

WISH I'D BROUGHT MY KIT SO I COULD DUST FOR PRINTS.

GOT IT COVERED. THEY TELL ME I HAVE A FULL CRIME LAB RIGHT HERE!

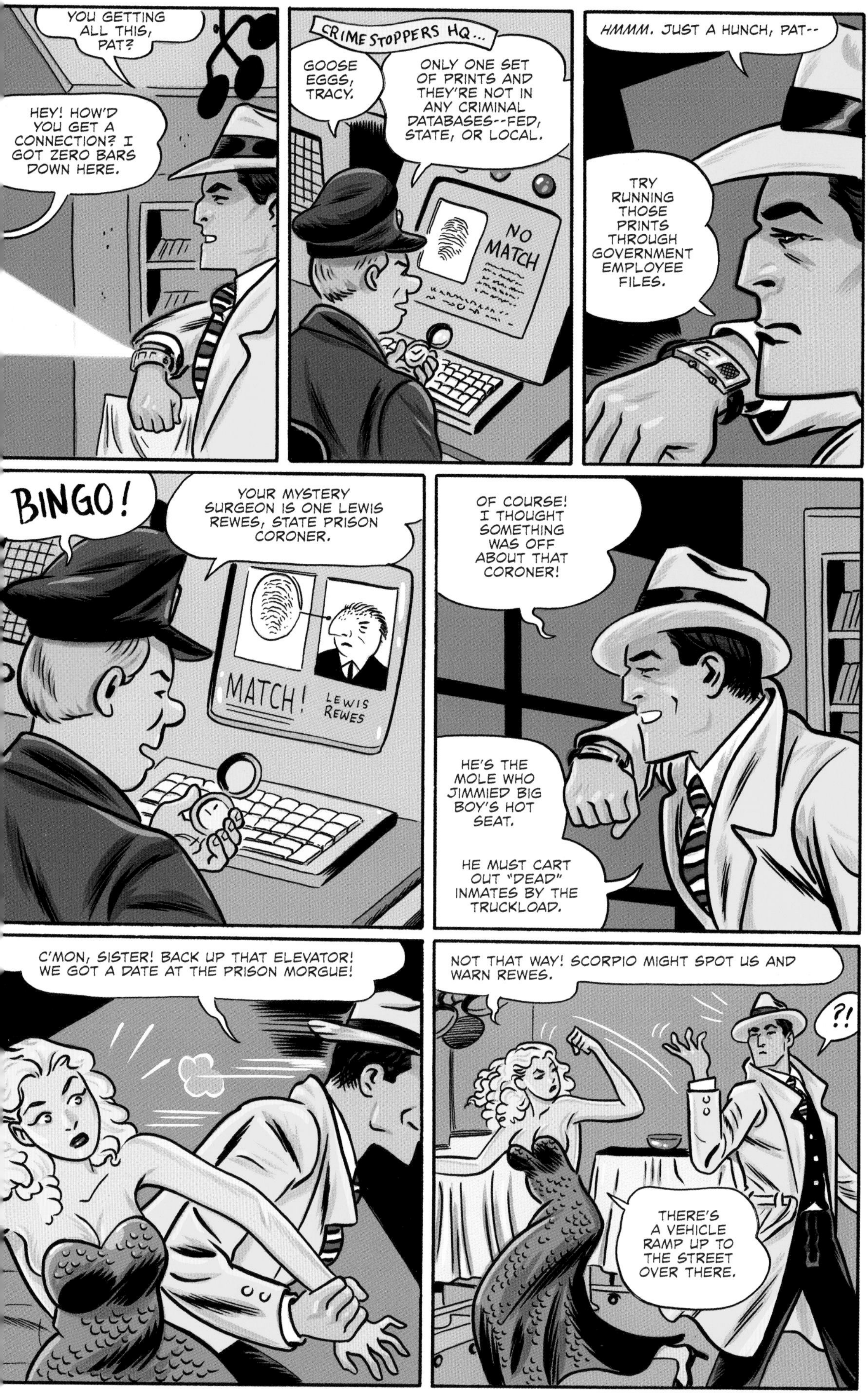
YOU GETTING ALL THIS, PAT?
HEY! HOW'D YOU GET A CONNECTION? I GOT ZERO BARS DOWN HERE.
CRIMESTOPPERS HQ...
GOOSE EGGS, TRACY.
ONLY ONE SET OF PRINTS AND THEY'RE NOT IN ANY CRIMINAL DATABASES--FED, STATE, OR LOCAL.
NO MATCH
HMMM. JUST A HUNCH, PAT--
TRY RUNNING THOSE PRINTS THROUGH GOVERNMENT EMPLOYEE FILES.
BINGO!
YOUR MYSTERY SURGEON IS ONE LEWIS REWES, STATE PRISON CORONER.
MATCH!
LEWIS REWES
OF COURSE! I THOUGHT SOMETHING WAS OFF ABOUT THAT CORONER!
HE'S THE MOLE WHO JIMMIED BIG BOY'S HOT SEAT.
HE MUST CART OUT "DEAD" INMATES BY THE TRUCKLOAD.
C'MON, SISTER! BACK UP THAT ELEVATOR! WE GOT A DATE AT THE PRISON MORGUE!
NOT THAT WAY! SCORPIO MIGHT SPOT US AND WARN REWES.
?!
THERE'S A VEHICLE RAMP UP TO THE STREET OVER THERE.

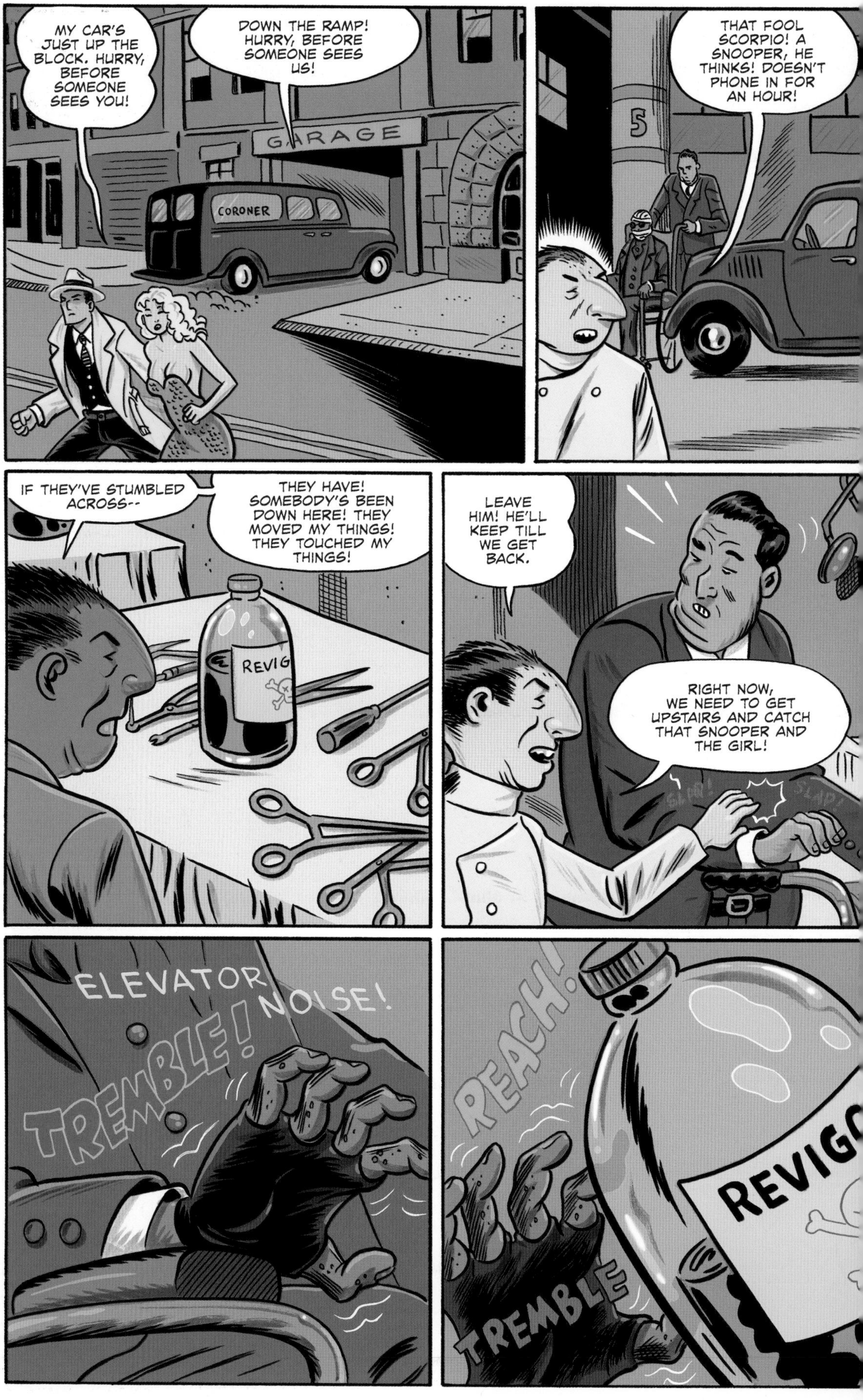
MY CAR'S JUST UP THE BLOCK. HURRY, BEFORE SOMEONE SEES YOU!
DOWN THE RAMP! HURRY, BEFORE SOMEONE SEES US!
GARAGE
CORONER
THAT FOOL SCORPIO! A SNOOPER, HE THINKS! DOESN'T PHONE IN FOR AN HOUR!
5
IF THEY'VE STUMBLED ACROSS--
THEY HAVE! SOMEBODY'S BEEN DOWN HERE! THEY MOVED MY THINGS! THEY TOUCHED MY THINGS!
REVIG
LEAVE HIM! HE'LL KEEP TILL WE GET BACK.
RIGHT NOW, WE NEED TO GET UPSTAIRS AND CATCH THAT SNOOPER AND THE GIRL!
ELEVATOR NOISE!
TREMBLE!
TREMBLE
REACH!
REVIGO
TREMBLE

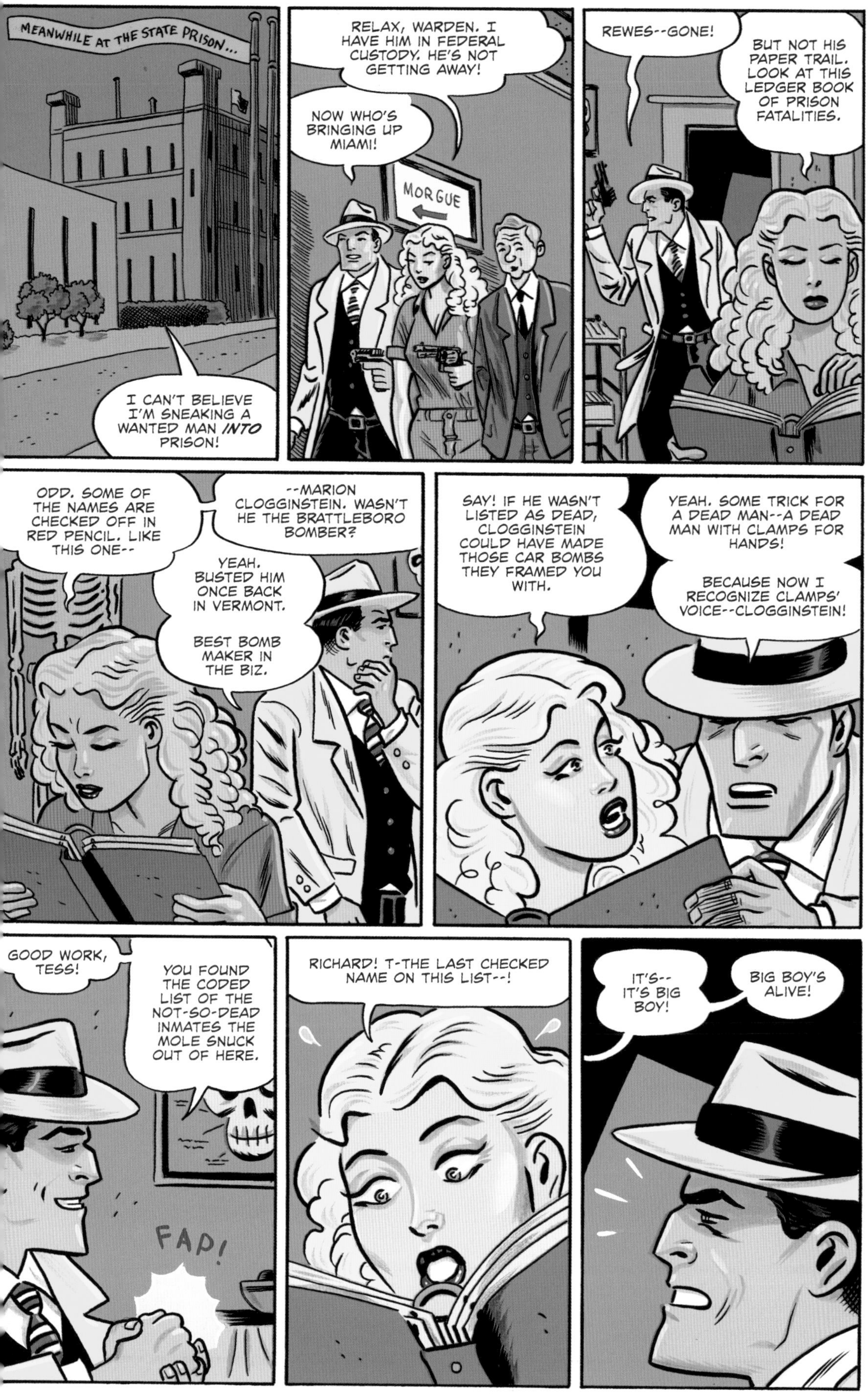
MEANWHILE AT THE STATE PRISON...
I CAN'T BELIEVE I'M SNEAKING A WANTED MAN *INTO* PRISON!
RELAX, WARDEN. I HAVE HIM IN FEDERAL CUSTODY. HE'S NOT GETTING AWAY!
NOW WHO'S BRINGING UP MIAMI!
MORGUE
REWES--GONE!
BUT NOT HIS PAPER TRAIL. LOOK AT THIS LEDGER BOOK OF PRISON FATALITIES.
ODD. SOME OF THE NAMES ARE CHECKED OFF IN RED PENCIL. LIKE THIS ONE--
--MARION CLOGGINSTEIN. WASN'T HE THE BRATTLEBORO BOMBER?
YEAH. BUSTED HIM ONCE BACK IN VERMONT.
BEST BOMB MAKER IN THE BIZ.
SAY! IF HE WASN'T LISTED AS DEAD, CLOGGINSTEIN COULD HAVE MADE THOSE CAR BOMBS THEY FRAMED YOU WITH.
YEAH. SOME TRICK FOR A DEAD MAN--A DEAD MAN WITH CLAMPS FOR HANDS!
BECAUSE NOW I RECOGNIZE CLAMPS' VOICE--CLOGGINSTEIN!
GOOD WORK, TESS!
YOU FOUND THE CODED LIST OF THE NOT-SO-DEAD INMATES THE MOLE SNUCK OUT OF HERE.
FAP!
RICHARD! T-THE LAST CHECKED NAME ON THIS LIST--!
IT'S--IT'S BIG BOY!
BIG BOY'S ALIVE!

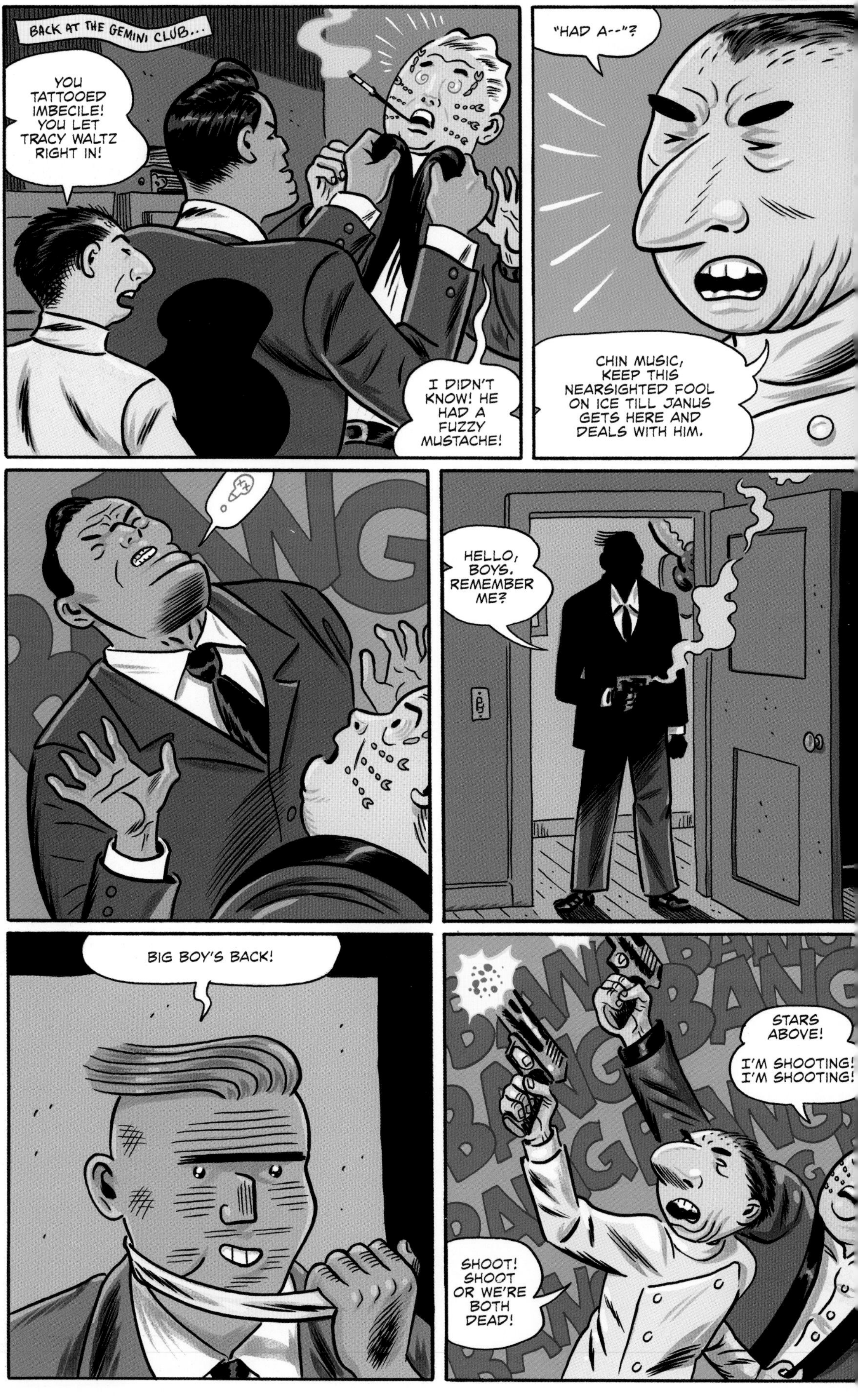
BACK AT THE GEMINI CLUB...
YOU TATTOOED IMBECILE! YOU LET TRACY WALTZ RIGHT IN!
I DIDN'T KNOW! HE HAD A FUZZY MUSTACHE!
"HAD A--"?
CHIN MUSIC, KEEP THIS NEARSIGHTED FOOL ON ICE TILL JANUS GETS HERE AND DEALS WITH HIM.
BANG
HELLO, BOYS. REMEMBER ME?
BIG BOY'S BACK!
STARS ABOVE!
I'M SHOOTING! I'M SHOOTING!
SHOOT! SHOOT OR WE'RE BOTH DEAD!
BANG BANG BANG BANG

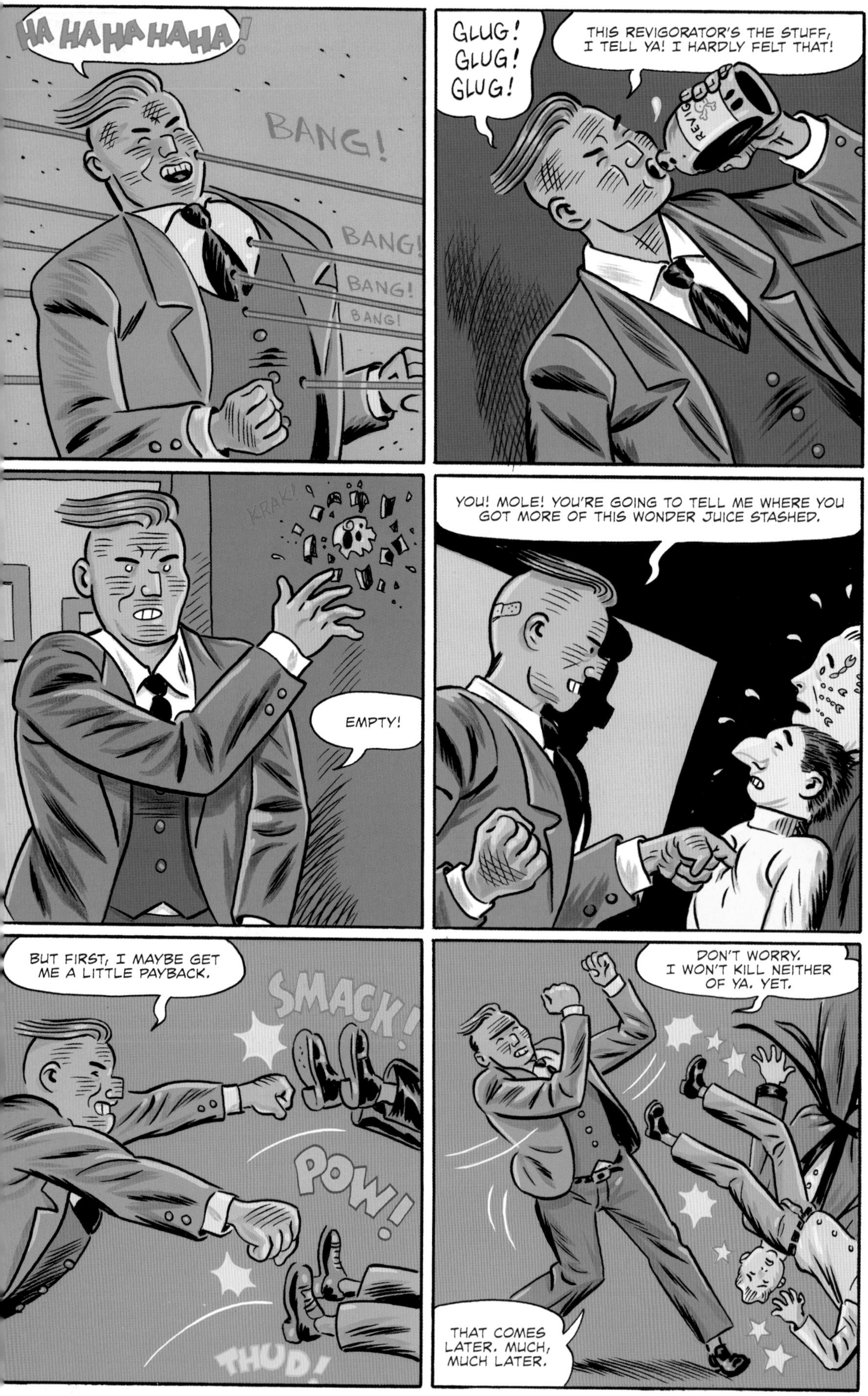
HA HA HA HA HA!
BANG!
BANG!
BANG!
BANG!
GLUG! GLUG! GLUG!
THIS REVIGORATOR'S THE STUFF, I TELL YA! I HARDLY FELT THAT!
KRAK!
EMPTY!
YOU! MOLE! YOU'RE GOING TO TELL ME WHERE YOU GOT MORE OF THIS WONDER JUICE STASHED.
BUT FIRST, I MAYBE GET ME A LITTLE PAYBACK.
SMACK!
POW!
THUD!
DON'T WORRY. I WON'T KILL NEITHER OF YA. YET.
THAT COMES LATER. MUCH, MUCH LATER.

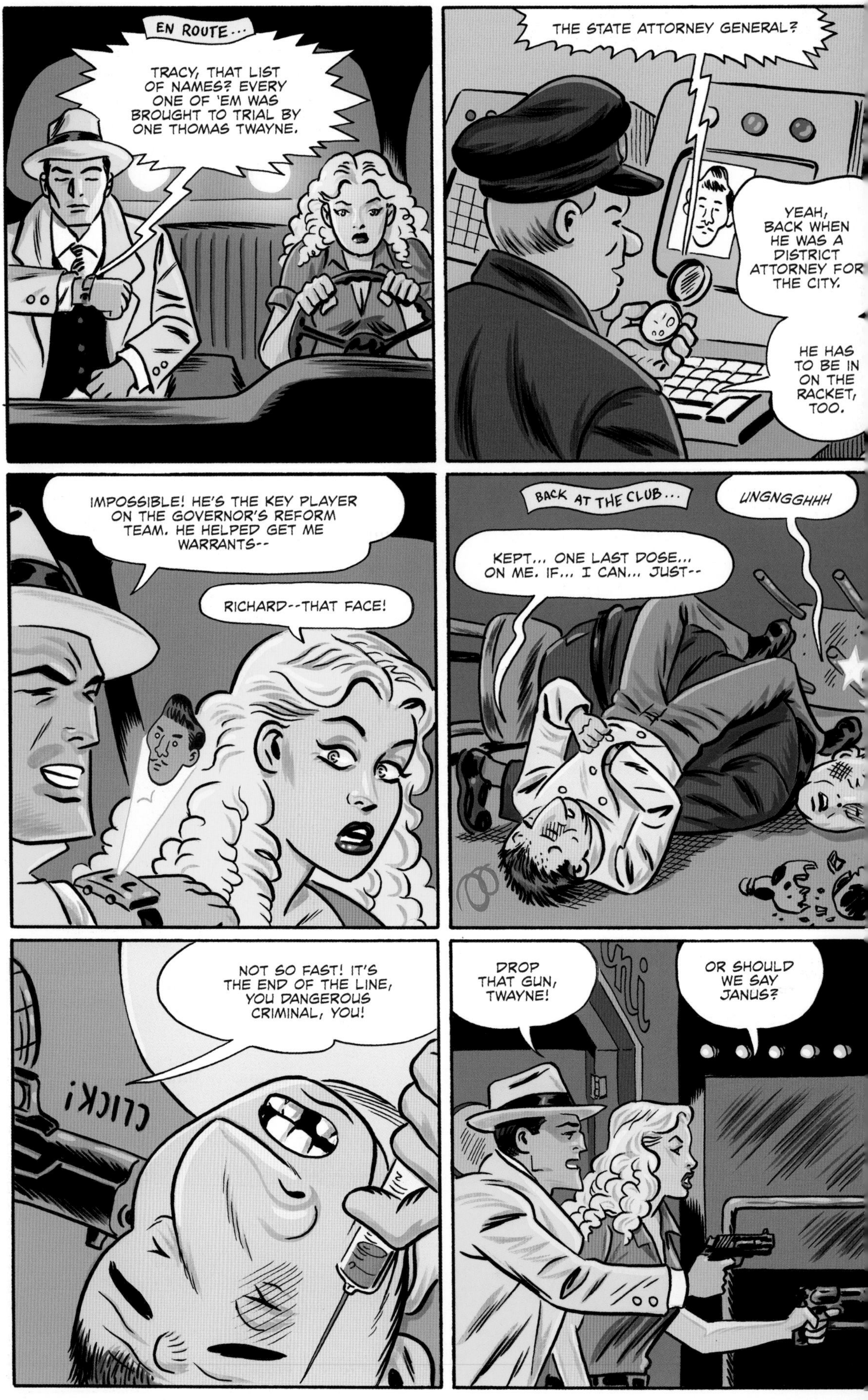
EN ROUTE...
TRACY, THAT LIST OF NAMES? EVERY ONE OF 'EM WAS BROUGHT TO TRIAL BY ONE THOMAS TWAYNE.
THE STATE ATTORNEY GENERAL?
YEAH, BACK WHEN HE WAS A DISTRICT ATTORNEY FOR THE CITY.
HE HAS TO BE IN ON THE RACKET, TOO.
IMPOSSIBLE! HE'S THE KEY PLAYER ON THE GOVERNOR'S REFORM TEAM. HE HELPED GET ME WARRANTS--
RICHARD--THAT FACE!
BACK AT THE CLUB...
UNGNGGHHH
KEPT... ONE LAST DOSE... ON ME. IF... I CAN... JUST--
NOT SO FAST! IT'S THE END OF THE LINE, YOU DANGEROUS CRIMINAL, YOU!
CLICK!
DROP THAT GUN, TWAYNE!
OR SHOULD WE SAY JANUS?

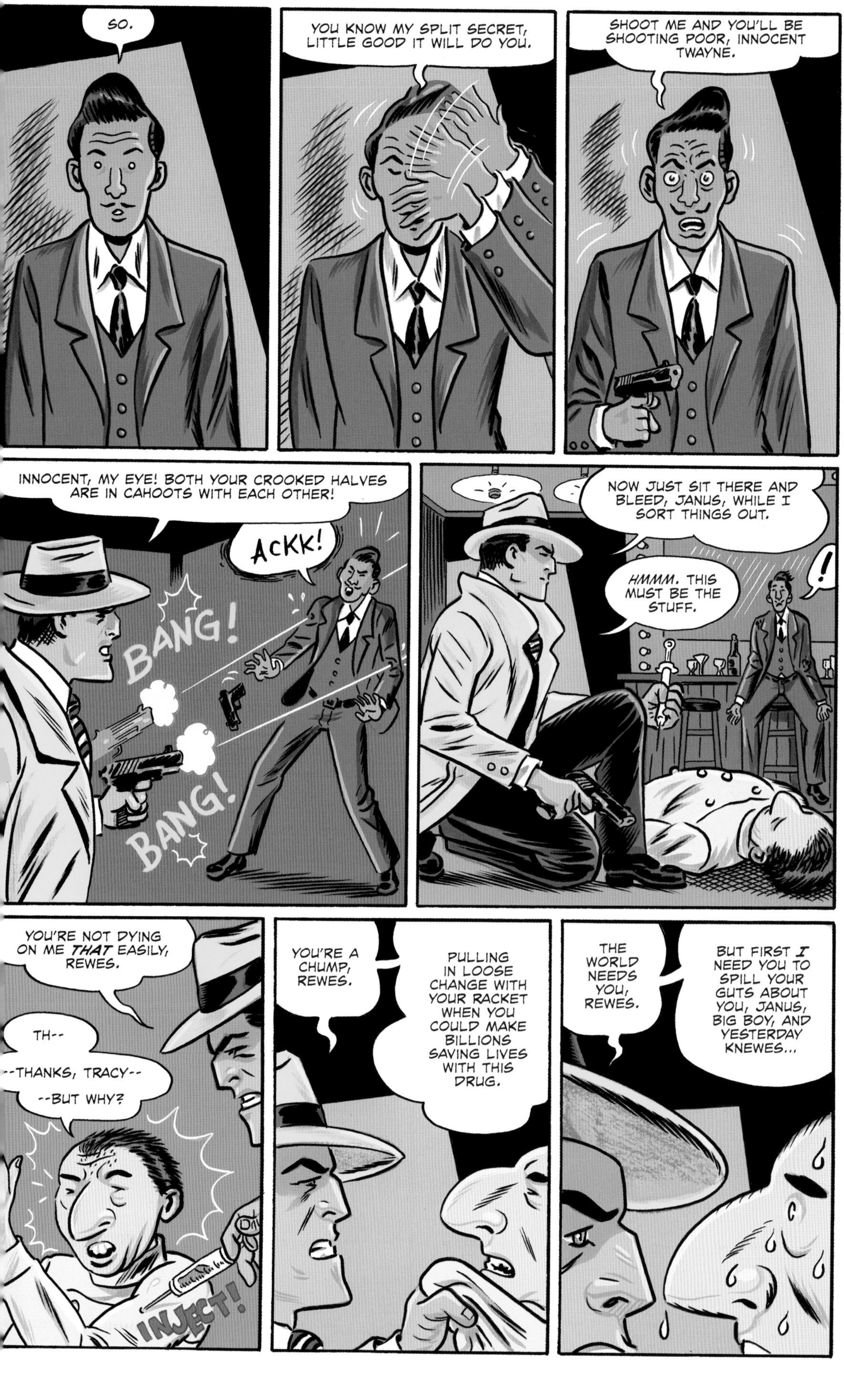
SO.
YOU KNOW MY SPLIT SECRET, LITTLE GOOD IT WILL DO YOU.
SHOOT ME AND YOU'LL BE SHOOTING POOR, INNOCENT TWAYNE.
INNOCENT, MY EYE! BOTH YOUR CROOKED HALVES ARE IN CAHOOTS WITH EACH OTHER!
ACKK!
BANG!
BANG!
NOW JUST SIT THERE AND BLEED, JANUS, WHILE I SORT THINGS OUT.
HMMM. THIS MUST BE THE STUFF.
!
YOU'RE NOT DYING ON ME THAT EASILY, REWES.
TH--
--THANKS, TRACY--
--BUT WHY?
INJECT!
YOU'RE A CHUMP, REWES.
PULLING IN LOOSE CHANGE WITH YOUR RACKET WHEN YOU COULD MAKE BILLIONS SAVING LIVES WITH THIS DRUG.
THE WORLD NEEDS YOU, REWES.
BUT FIRST I NEED YOU TO SPILL YOUR GUTS ABOUT YOU, JANUS, BIG BOY, AND YESTERDAY KNEWES...

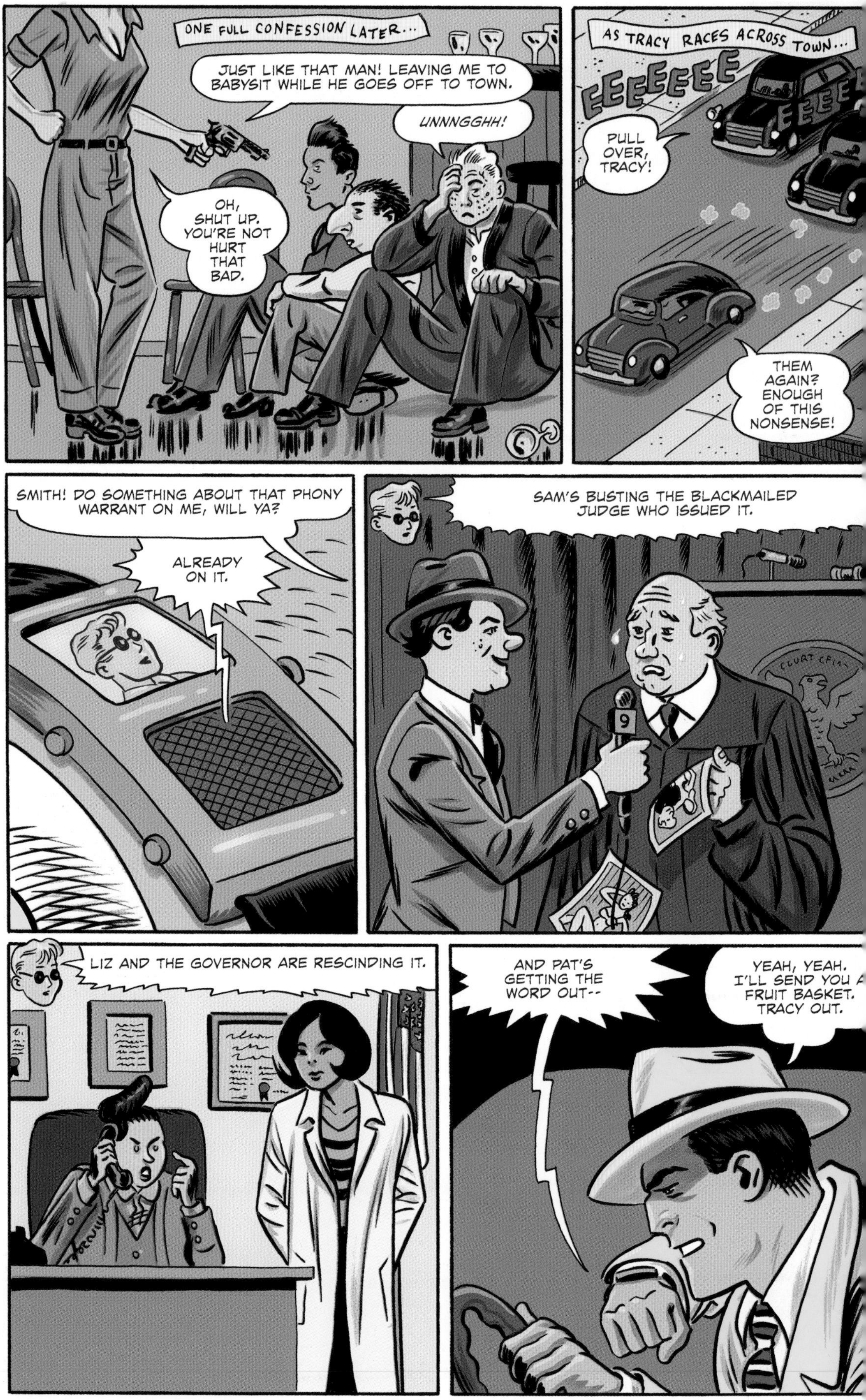
ONE FULL CONFESSION LATER...
JUST LIKE THAT MAN! LEAVING ME TO BABYSIT WHILE HE GOES OFF TO TOWN.
UNNNGGHH!
OH, SHUT UP. YOU'RE NOT HURT THAT BAD.
AS TRACY RACES ACROSS TOWN...
EEEEEEE
PULL OVER, TRACY!
THEM AGAIN? ENOUGH OF THIS NONSENSE!
SMITH! DO SOMETHING ABOUT THAT PHONY WARRANT ON ME, WILL YA?
ALREADY ON IT.
SAM'S BUSTING THE BLACKMAILED JUDGE WHO ISSUED IT.
LIZ AND THE GOVERNOR ARE RESCINDING IT.
AND PAT'S GETTING THE WORD OUT--
YEAH, YEAH. I'LL SEND YOU A FRUIT BASKET. TRACY OUT.

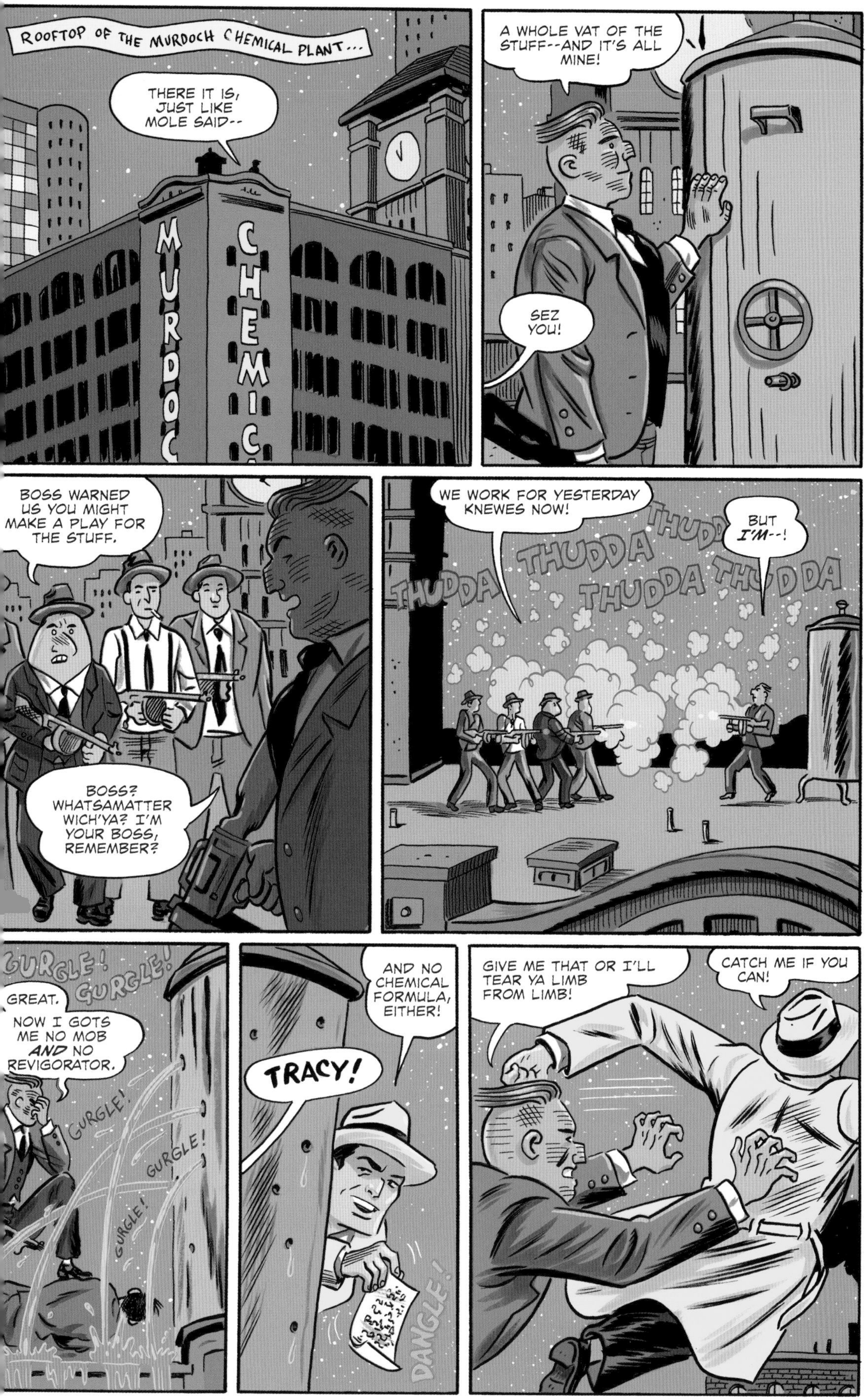
ROOFTOP OF THE MURDOCH CHEMICAL PLANT...
THERE IT IS, JUST LIKE MOLE SAID--
MURDOC
CHEMIC
A WHOLE VAT OF THE STUFF--AND IT'S ALL MINE!
SEZ YOU!
BOSS WARNED US YOU MIGHT MAKE A PLAY FOR THE STUFF.
BOSS? WHATSAMATTER WICH'YA? I'M YOUR BOSS, REMEMBER?
WE WORK FOR YESTERDAY KNEWES NOW!
THUDDA THUDDA THUDDA THUDDA THUDDA
BUT *I'M*--!
GURGLE! GURGLE!
GREAT. NOW I GOTS ME NO MOB ***AND*** NO REVIGORATOR.
GURGLE! GURGLE! GURGLE!
AND NO CHEMICAL FORMULA, EITHER!
TRACY!
DANGLE!
GIVE ME THAT OR I'LL TEAR YA LIMB FROM LIMB!
CATCH ME IF YOU CAN!

BACK AT GROUND LEVEL...

WE'RE IN TOO DEEP! IT'S EITHER TRACY OR US! GET UP THERE AND SHOOT TO KILL!

WE'LL CLAIM WE DIDN'T HEAR THE WARRANT GOT PULLED.

MURDOCH CHEMICAL

IT'S OVER, DUEFFERT!

THROW DOWN YOUR GUNS AND SURRENDER YOUR BADGES!

YEAH? YOU GONNA MAKE US, PATTON?

YOU AND WHAT ARMY?

SCREEEEEEE

ME AND THIS ARMY.

HONEST COPS OF TRACY'S SPECIAL SQUAD

STATE TROOPERS

ULP!

THAT'S ALL WELL AND GOOD, BUT BACK ATOP THE ROOF...

MIGHTY LEAP!

≶WHEW≶ BARELY MADE IT!

EASY HOP!

GIVE IT UP, TRACY! RUNNING ONLY MEANS YOU'LL DIE TIRED!

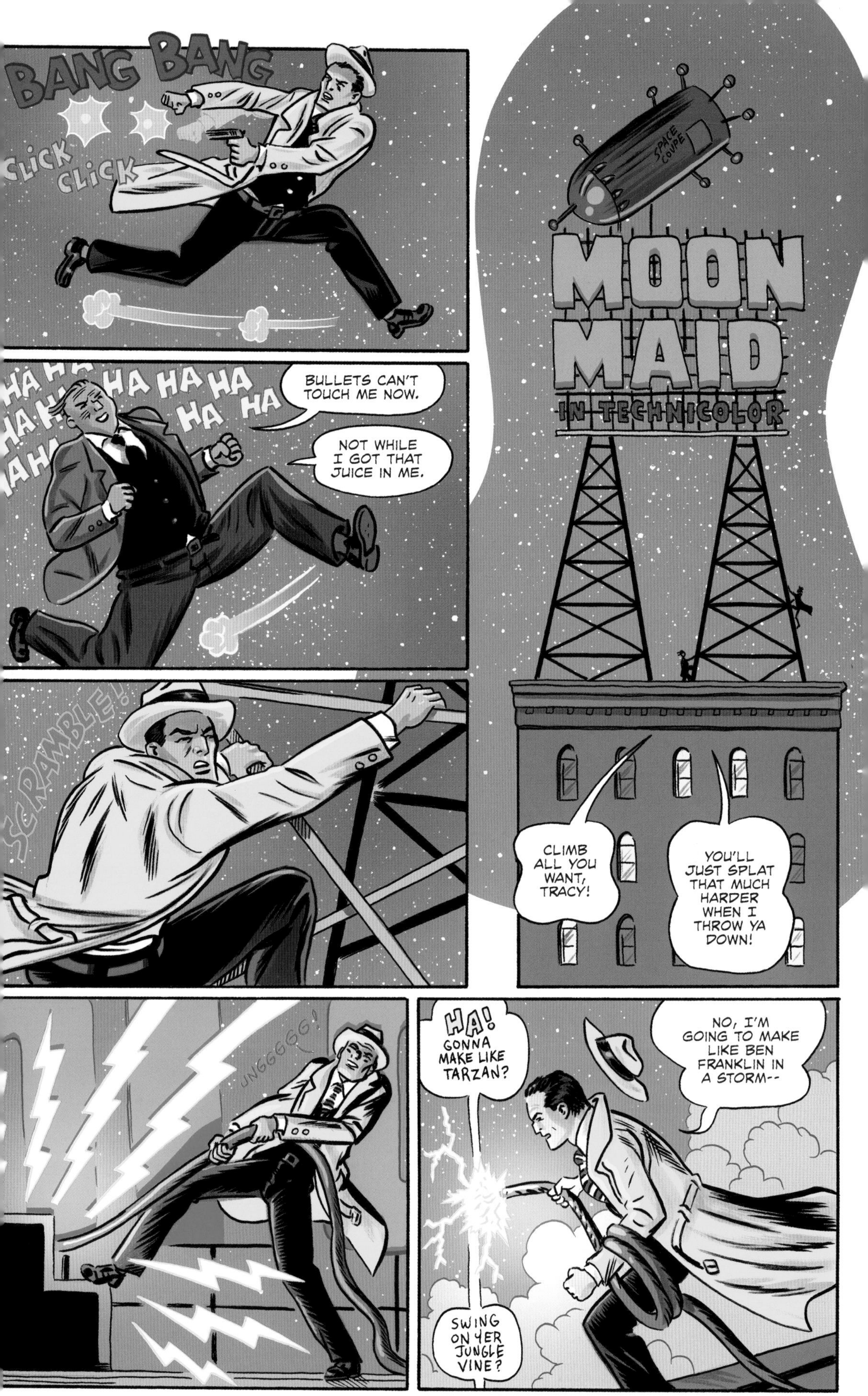
BANG BANG
CLICK CLICK
HA HA HA HA HA HA HA HA HA HA
BULLETS CAN'T TOUCH ME NOW.
NOT WHILE I GOT THAT JUICE IN ME.
SPACE COUPE
MOON MAID
IN TECHNICOLOR
SCRAMBLE!
CLIMB ALL YOU WANT, TRACY!
YOU'LL JUST SPLAT THAT MUCH HARDER WHEN I THROW YA DOWN!
UNGGGGG!
HA! GONNA MAKE LIKE TARZAN?
SWING ON YER JUNGLE VINE?
NO, I'M GOING TO MAKE LIKE BEN FRANKLIN IN A STORM--

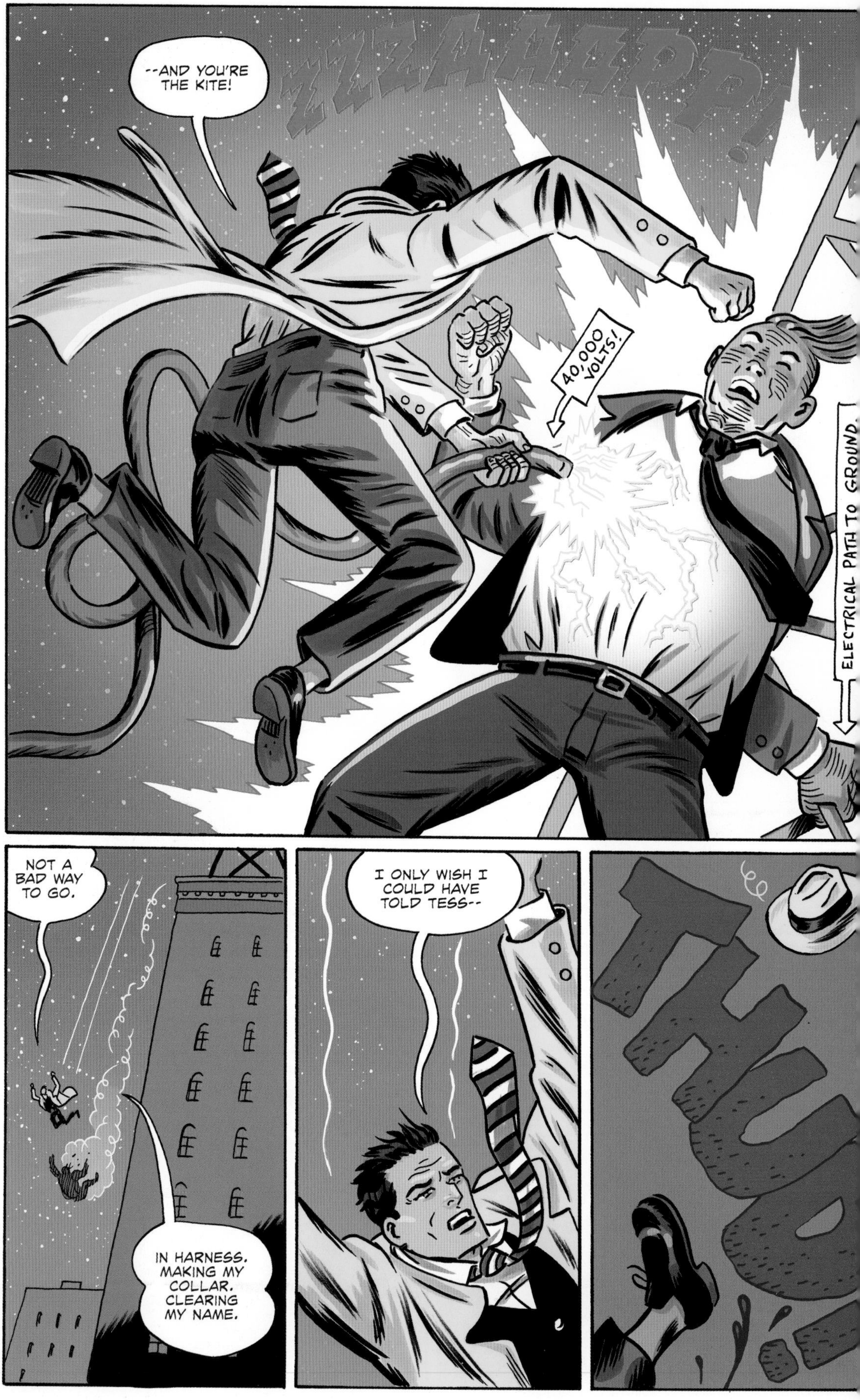

--AND YOU'RE THE KITE!
ZZZAAAPP!
40,000 VOLTS!
ELECTRICAL PATH TO GROUND.
NOT A BAD WAY TO GO.
IN HARNESS. MAKING MY COLLAR. CLEARING MY NAME.
I ONLY WISH I COULD HAVE TOLD TESS--
THUD!

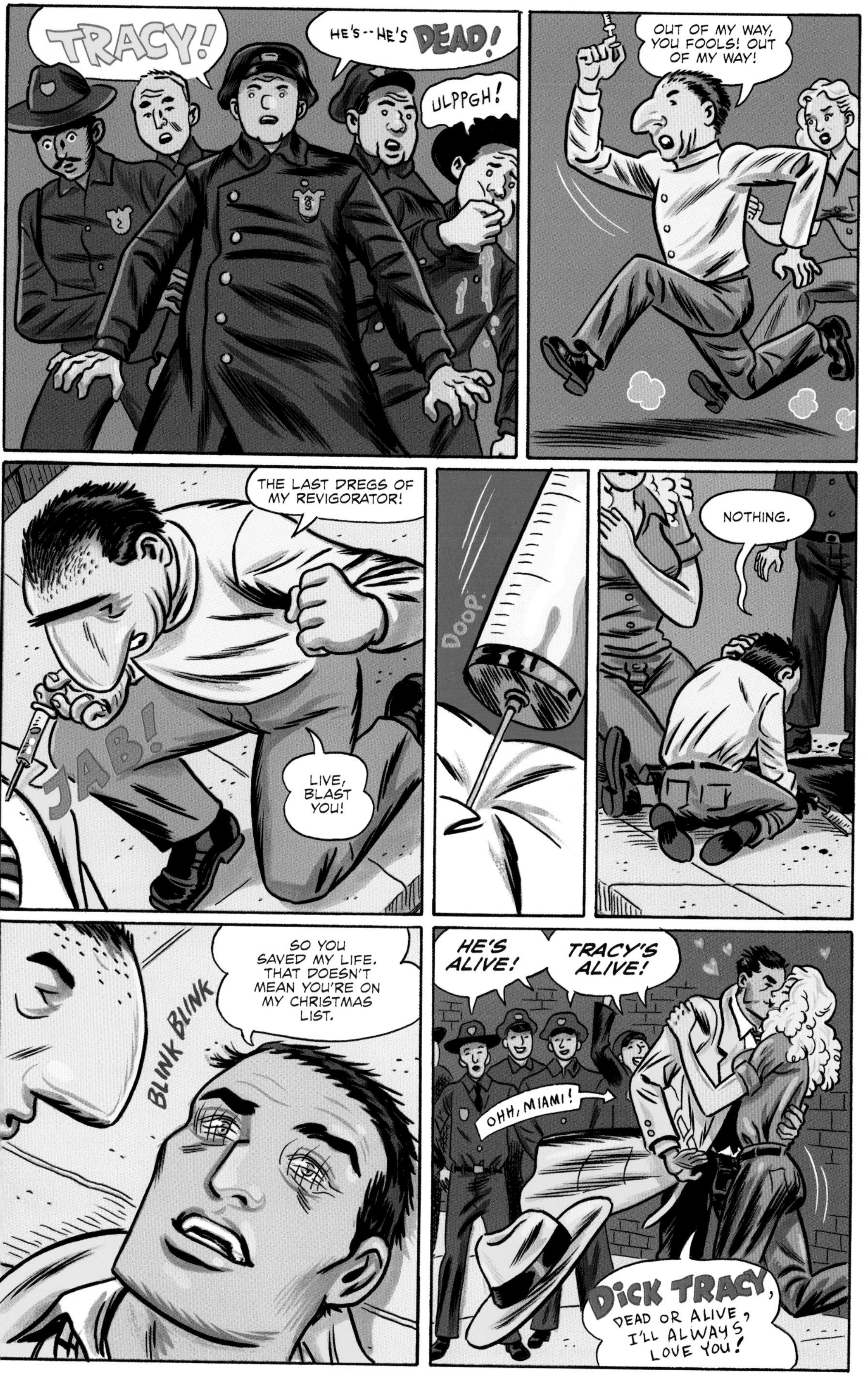
TRACY!
HE'S--HE'S DEAD!
ULPPGH!
OUT OF MY WAY, YOU FOOLS! OUT OF MY WAY!
THE LAST DREGS OF MY REVIGORATOR!
JAB!
LIVE, BLAST YOU!
DOOP!
NOTHING.
SO YOU SAVED MY LIFE. THAT DOESN'T MEAN YOU'RE ON MY CHRISTMAS LIST.
BLINK BLINK
HE'S ALIVE!
TRACY'S ALIVE!
OHH, MIAMI!
DICK TRACY, DEAD OR ALIVE, I'LL ALWAYS LOVE YOU!

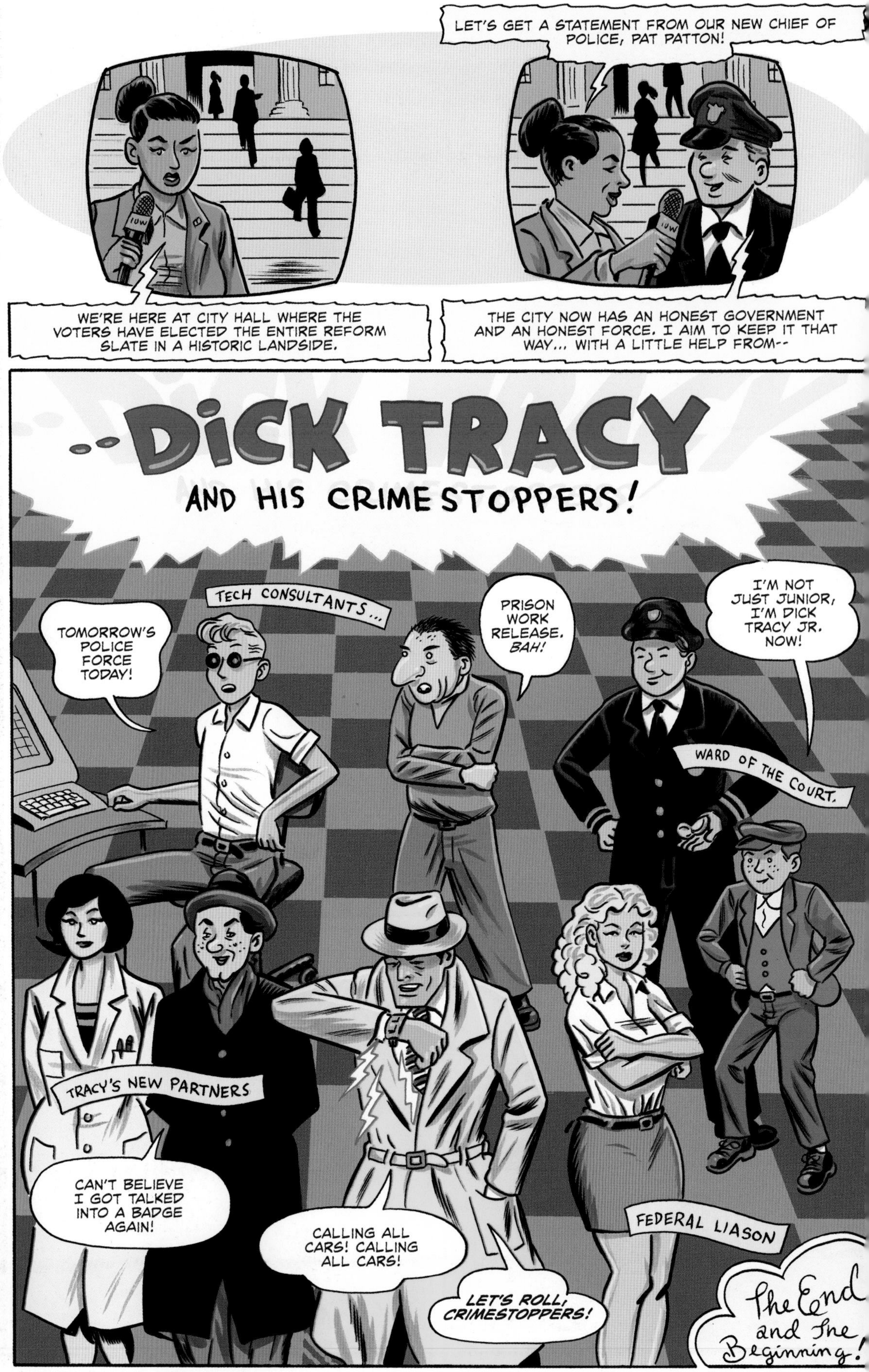
LET'S GET A STATEMENT FROM OUR NEW CHIEF OF POLICE, PAT PATTON!
WE'RE HERE AT CITY HALL WHERE THE VOTERS HAVE ELECTED THE ENTIRE REFORM SLATE IN A HISTORIC LANDSIDE.
THE CITY NOW HAS AN HONEST GOVERNMENT AND AN HONEST FORCE. I AIM TO KEEP IT THAT WAY... WITH A LITTLE HELP FROM--
--DICK TRACY
AND HIS CRIMESTOPPERS!
TECH CONSULTANTS...
TOMORROW'S POLICE FORCE TODAY!
PRISON WORK RELEASE. BAH!
I'M NOT JUST JUNIOR, I'M DICK TRACY JR. NOW!
WARD OF THE COURT.
TRACY'S NEW PARTNERS
CAN'T BELIEVE I GOT TALKED INTO A BADGE AGAIN!
CALLING ALL CARS! CALLING ALL CARS!
LET'S ROLL, CRIMESTOPPERS!
FEDERAL LIASON
The End and The Beginning!

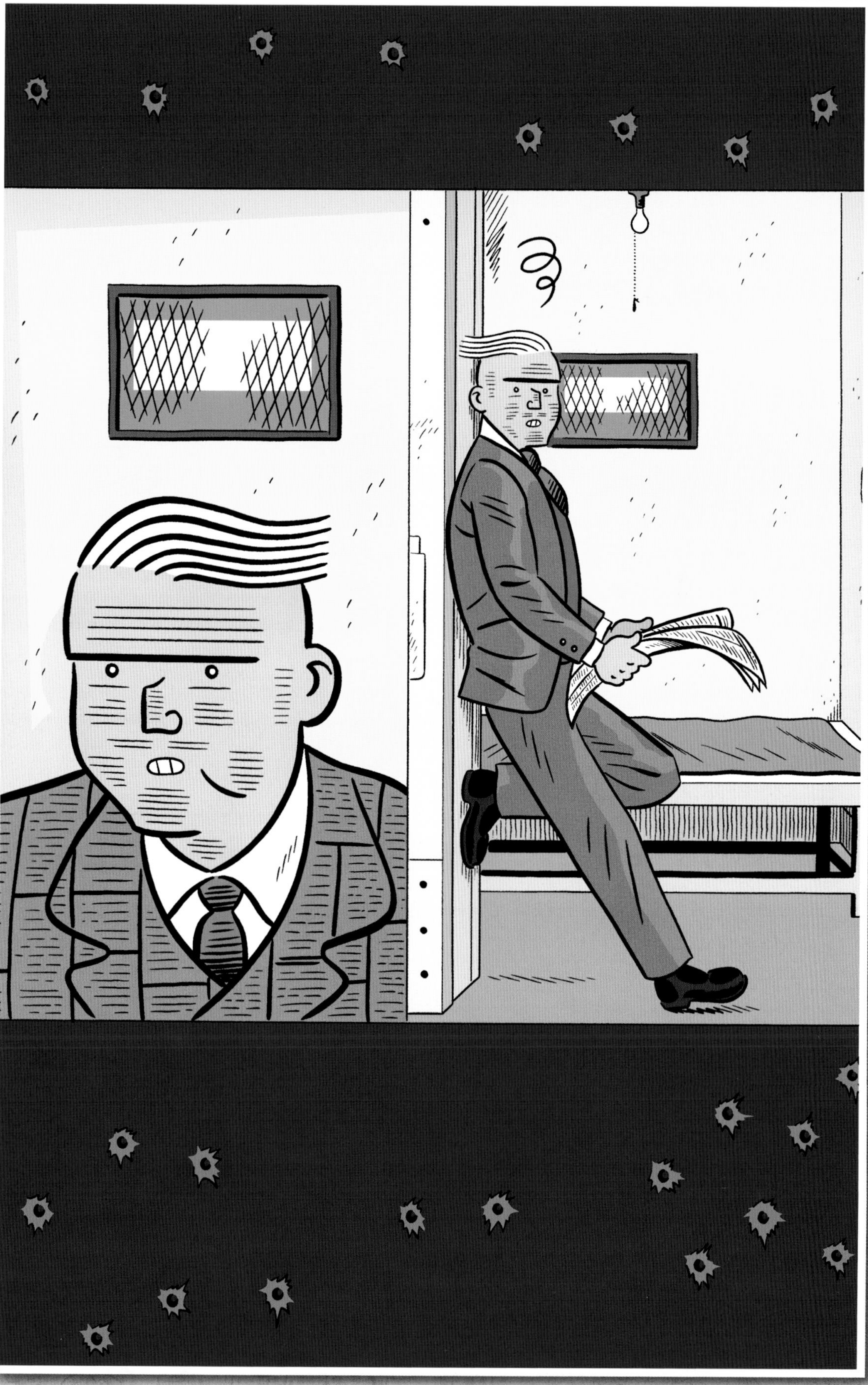

ART BY **RICH TOMMASO** | COLORS BY **AMY PLASMAN**

STRIP OVERVIEW

HISTORY

Since 1931, Chester Gould's *Dick Tracy* has thrilled millions with tales of good guys versus bad guys, while showcasing the latest criminology techniques and old-fashioned values. Tracy's knack for originality earned him a reputation as the quintessential detective who kept the streets safe. Through the years, Dick Tracy had numerous partners and sent thousands of rogues to the slammer (and many to their graves), but there was always more work to be done. The strip's innovative technology was popular, but it was the strange, weird and out-of-this-world villains (with their fun names and hideous faces) that gave the strip its huge fan base.

PREMISE

Gould invented Tracy to take down known mobsters such as Al Capone, John Dillinger, Bonnie & Clyde and Baby Face Nelson. "When I came up with the idea of Tracy, Chicago was in the throes of Prohibition gangsterism: what we needed was a cop who could stop it. I wanted a cop who could find a known hoodlum in the act of committing a crime and shoot him down without a moment's hesitation," said Gould. With that, he fashioned the most famous and successful detective of all time, Dick Tracy. Inspired by the image of the innovative Sherlock Holmes, Gould created new crime-fighting technology, including the two-way wrist TV, closed circuit TV police line-up and the engineless car.

SETTING

Although tough and no-nonsense, Dick Tracy is the most likeable and resourceful member of your local police force. A great detective, Tracy always gets his man. If he lacks the means to track down the thug, he'll invent something to get the job done. Tracy's beat includes terrorists, arsonists, mobsters and counterfeiters causing chaos in your city.

CREATIVE TEAM

Comics super-stars Michael Allred, Lee Allred, Rich Tommaso, and Laura Allred have teamed up to bring you an all-new take on one of the most iconic comic-strip heroes of all time. With Dick Tracy reimagined for the 21st century through a retro lens, *Dead or Alive* is a lock to be the pop-art event of the year!

On the following pages, we'll take you behind the curtain to see how the magic happens, from script to finished page.

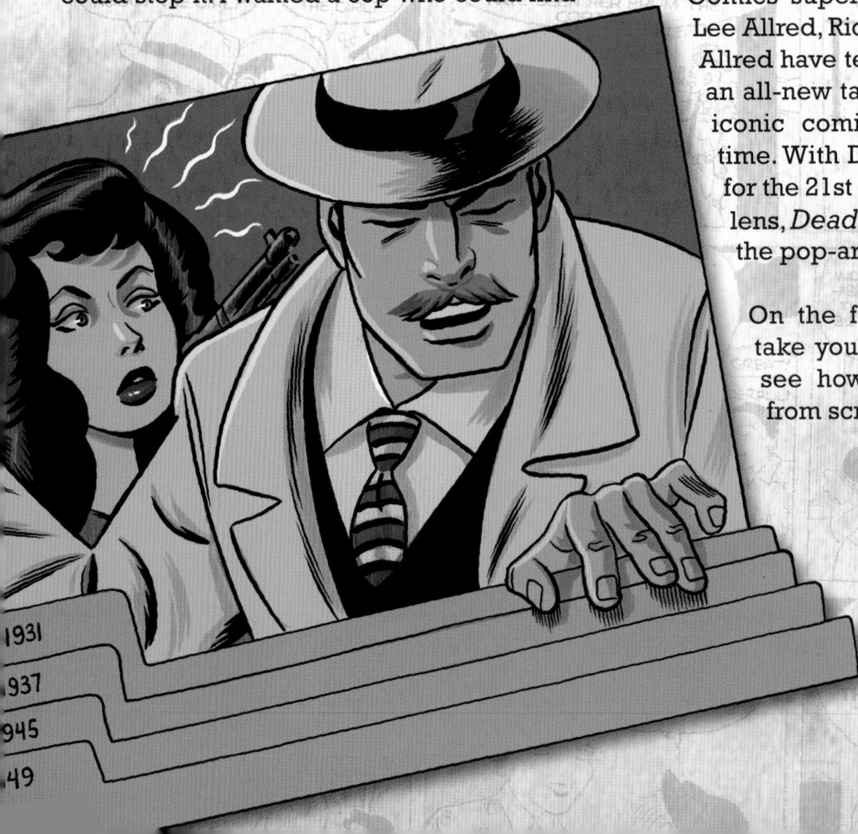

1931
937
945
49

TIMELINE

Through innovative crime-fighting techniques, a natural instinct for detective work, and devastating good looks, Dick Tracy keeps the streets safe from the most menacing villains in comic history.

1930s | *A tough detective joins your local police force.*

1931
After he submitted strips for a decade, the New York Daily News Syndicate accepts Chester Gould's strip about a detective.

• October 4, the first Dick Tracy strip appears in the *Detroit Mirror*; the first Sunday strip appears December 13.

• October 13, the opening sequence introduces readers to Tess Trueheart, a commercial photographer and daughter of a grocer. Tess is also Dick Tracy's fiancée. When Tracy arrives at the Trueheart family apartment to announce his engagement to their daughter, he walks in on thugs hired by Big Boy, a local gangster, robbing Tess' father. After Big Boy's gang kills Tess' father, Tracy joins the police force to search for Tess and bring the killers to justice.

• October 22, Tracy joins the plainclothes division of a big city police force.

• December 1, Pat Patton, an Irish uniformed cop, joins the cast as Dick's loyal friend.

• Notable villains include: Dubbs, Haf-and-Haf, Hy Habeas and Ribs Morocco.

1932
• In May, the Sunday pages merge with the daily continuity strip.

• In June, Gould introduces the idea of a telephone wiretap, and Tracy puts it to good use. This invention is still in use by law enforcement agencies today.

• June 9, Big Boy sets a death trap for Tracy—a car speeding toward an open bridge; this assassination attempt only steels Tracy's resolve.

• September 8, Tracy meets and takes a nine-year-old thief under his wing. Tracy adopts him and gives him the name Dick Tracy Junior. Chief Brandon sends Junior to the Big Boys detention home when he discovers Junior's fingerprints on a gun used in a murder. Tracy vindicates Junior proving that he was not the killer, and transforms him into a crack investigator.

• The Baby "Buddy" Waldorf case gives Dick Tracy increased publicity. Ripped from the headlines during the Lindberg kidnapping, Tracy hopes to rescue the baby of a rich socialite. Gould's version of the events gives the American people a happy ending to the true-life tragedy, when Buddy is returned to his family.

• Notable villains include: Alec Penn (a.k.a. Count Gordon, a.k.a. B. Bellas, a zoo keeper), Broadway Bates, Dan "The Squealer" Mucelli and Larceny Lu.

1935
• When Boris, a villain Tracy is detaining, escapes during Tracy's watch, Brandon demotes the dashing detective to a uniformed policeman. Tracy ultimately finds Boris, and the Chief reinstates him as a detective.

• In December, Tracy becomes a government agent (G-man) to help Jim Trailer catch Cut Famon.

• Notable villains include: Cutie Diamond and The Arsons.

1937
• October 21, The Blank, a villain notorious for having no face, makes his first appearance. For any other detective, catching a thief without a face might prove a difficult task, but not Dick Tracy. When The Blank attempts to kill Tracy in a decompression chamber, his partner Pat Patton saves him just in time, proving that crafty police work always prevails over evil.

• Notable villains include: Stud Bronzen.

1939
• Tess Trueheart and Dick Tracy experience problems in their relationship.

• July 11, Tess confirms that she intends to marry Edward Nuremoh. She claims that Tracy's true love is, and will always be, his job.

• July 30, Tess marries Nuremoh, a former baseball player. Unknown to Tess, the two-timing baseball player intends to divorce her to collect her inheritance. Then Nuremoh plans to marry his true love, Lola.

• Notable villains include: Scardol, John Lavir and Nat the Fur King.

1940s | WWII inspires Nazi villain character to challenge Tracy.

1941
• July 26, Littleface Finney joins the cast. He causes mayhem as a jewel thief, gang leader, and murderer. In one of the most gruesome arrests by Tracy, Littleface loses both ears trying to escape from the detective. Tracy puts him in jail on December 28.

• November 16, The Mole hits the scene as a vermin-visage known for his monstrous hand strength. He runs an underground hotel for runaway felons. Tracy captures him on December 21. He reappears in 1971.

• Notable villains include: Duke, Selbert, and Trigger Doom.

1942
• October 18, the first appearance of Pruneface, the Nazi gang leader notorious for his severely sun-damaged face. He is one of the meanest and most unforgettable characters in the strip.

• Notable villains include: Jacques, B-B Eyes, and Tiger Lilly.

1943
• April 15, 88 Keyes, the manic piano-playing killer, joins the cast. 88 arranges for the murder of millionaire A. B. Helmet so Helmet's wife can collect $200,000 in insurance money.
Tracy captures Pruneface and is lost in a blizzard with little Johnny Wreath.

• Mrs. Pruneface, also a vicious murderer, joins the saga. An Amazon woman with no nose, cavernous eyes, and a wicked smile, she captures Tracy to avenge her husband's death.

• December 21, Flattop Jones, a hired assassin, makes his first appearance. He later captures and attempts to send Tracy to his death beneath the pilings of a ship. Jones' family haunts Tracy for years as Angeltop and Flattop Jr. attempt to get even.

• Notable villains include: Laffy.

1944
• Tracy is appointed to Lieutenant Second Grade in the Naval Reserve where he tracks down Nazi spies.

• March 13, Vitamin Flintheart, an aging actor who is also a pill popping, Shakespeare-quoting ham, joins the cast in the case of The Brow as one of Tracy's good friends.

• May 22, The Brow, a wartime Nazi spy and informer, makes his first appearance.

• In September, Gravel Gertie joins the cast, bringing comic relief to the strip. Although Gould intended Gertie to be a minor character, she is so popular that Gould keeps her and eventually pairs her up with the smelly B.O. Plenty. The couple eventually get married.

• September 27, Shaky (a.k.a. Mr. Pappy), one of Gould's most famous villains, comes on the scene in a shakedown attempt on Rich Nat Banks. Named for his twitch and terribly shaky hands, Shaky quivered each time he got angry.

His condition was treated with a liquid nerve tonic to calm down his shakes. Shaky suffers a violent death frozen in a coffin of ice on Jan. 21, 1945.

• Notable villains include: Flattop and The Summer Sisters.

1945
• May 17, Breathless Mahoney makes her first appearance. The good-looking, money-hungry, blonde thief is fashioned after film star Veronica Lake. Breathless leads Tracy on one of the longest chases of his tenure on the force.

• In July, B.O. Plenty, a seedy, bewhiskered and smelly farmer joins the cast. This cussing, spitting and tobacco-chewing character with a big heart becomes a faithful friend of Dick Tracy.

• Notable villains include: Itchy, Measles and Splitface.

1946
• Jan. 2, Diet Smith, an industrialist and electronics innovator, joins the cast. Diet and his son Brilliant create futuristic gadgets to aid the crime-fighting team.

• February 10, Brilliant, son of Diet Smith, invents the atom light.

• February 13, Brilliant creates the two-way wrist radio, Dick Tracy's most famous gadget to date.

• June 14, Shoulders joins the rogues gallery. This villain is most famous for hiding 2,000 precious stones in his shoulder pads. He accidentally shoots himself as police surround him in an antique shop on February 22, 1948.

• August 18, B.O. Plenty and Gravel Gertie marry. Newspapers everywhere cover this fictional wedding as their cover story.

• November 24, Influence joins the cast as a reformed criminal. This blackmailing hypnotist experiences a religious conversion in prison. He aides police by hypnotizing witnesses to help them recall details of the crime.

• Notable villains include: Cueball, Gargles, Irma and Nilon, Rod Hoze, The Mar and Themesong.

1947
• The closed circuit TV police lineup makes its debut in the comics.

• June 1, Sparkle Plenty, daughter of B.O. Plenty and Gravel Gertie, is born. Like her parents, Sparkle Plenty is extremely popular with fans.

She inspires a line of dolls.

• Junior creates Crimestoppers, a club introduced by Gould to get kids excited about safety. The syndicate receives a flurry of mail from readers asking if they can create local branches of Crimestoppers.

• July 13, Brilliant concocts a miniature ring camera that Tracy wears on his finger.

• December 7, Mumbles, a singer and conman whose nearly incoherent speech becomes endearing, joins the cast. He is deadly!

• Notable villains include: Coffyhead, Gruesome and Hypo.

1948
• Battery-powered TV camera introduced to track criminals.

• September, Diet Smith devises an atomic-powered video camera with unlimited range.

• September 16, Brilliant creates Dick Tracy Telegard, an antennaless, portable television burglar alarm.

• October, Diet Smith reveals that Brilliant is his son.

• October 23, Pat Patton named Chief of Police. He appears in the strip until 1977.

• October 28, Brilliant is killed by Big Frost.

• December 26, Sam Catchem joins the cast as Tracy's sidekick until 1958.

• Notable villains include: Heals Beals, Big Frost, Sleet and Mrs. Volts.

1949
• April 14, Pear Shape, a Gould self-caricature, joins the rogues gallery. This villain is a racketeer and jewel thief whose weight-reduction scheme finances his dastardly deeds.

• September 11, Crimestoppers changes its name to Crimestoppers Textbook, offering tips for readers on how to keep their families safe.

• December 24, after an 18-year courtship Dick Tracy and his long-time fiancée Tess Trueheart finally marry. The event takes place nearly 20 years after the first strip where Dick Tracy comes to meet Tess' parents and her father is killed by Big Boy, leading Tracy to join the force.

• Notable villains include: Dyke Spike, Mousey, Sketch Paree, Sleet, Talcum Freely and Wormy.

ANNOTATIONS

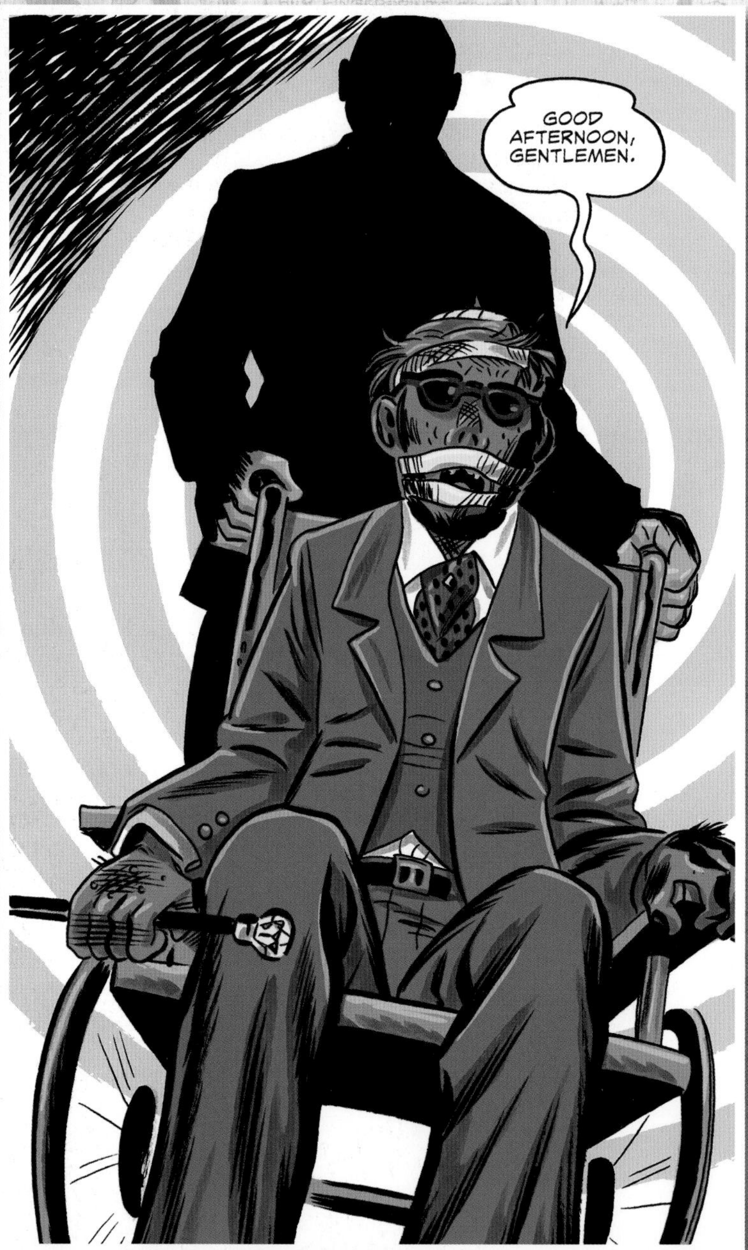
GOOD AFTERNOON, GENTLEMEN.

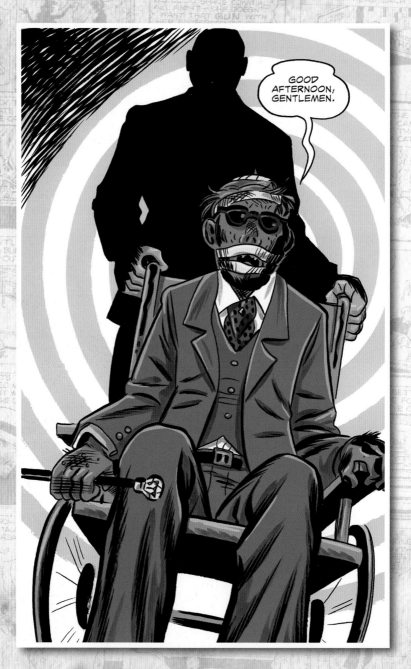

PAGE 6, PANEL 1:

Yesterday Knewes is modeled after the Crypt Keeper from **Tales from the Crypt**.

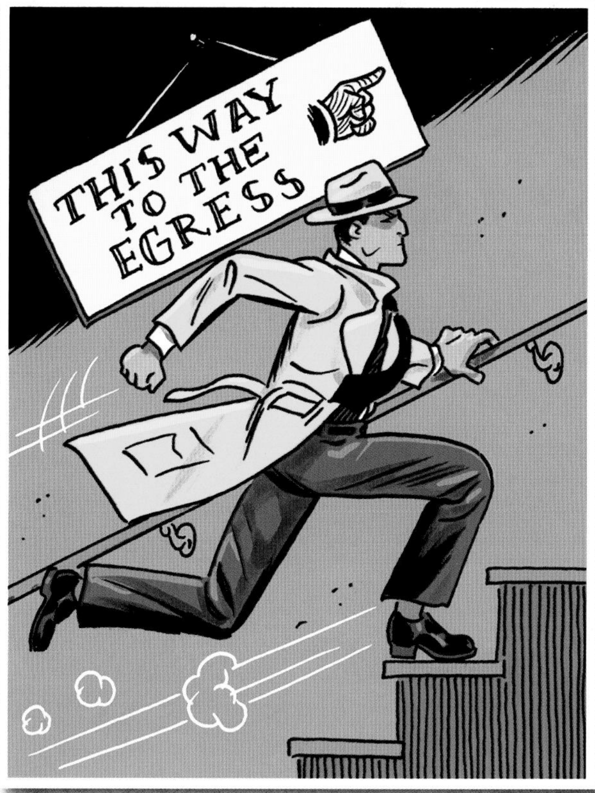
THIS WAY TO THE EGRESS

PAGE 11, PANEL 2:

"This Way to the Egress" sign—a reference to P.T. Barnum. The idea is that police HQ is nothing but a circus of clowns and freakshows.

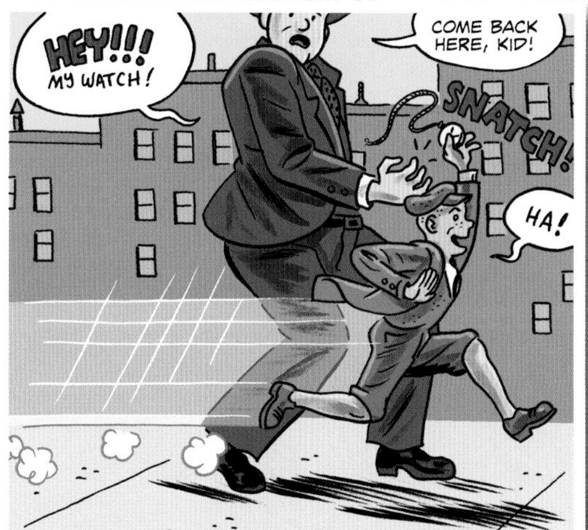
HEY!!! MY WATCH!
COME BACK HERE, KID!
SNATCH!
HA!

PAGE 15, PANEL 7:

Junior's introduction is an homage to the way he's introduced in the original Dick Tracy comic strips—in which he also steals a watch.

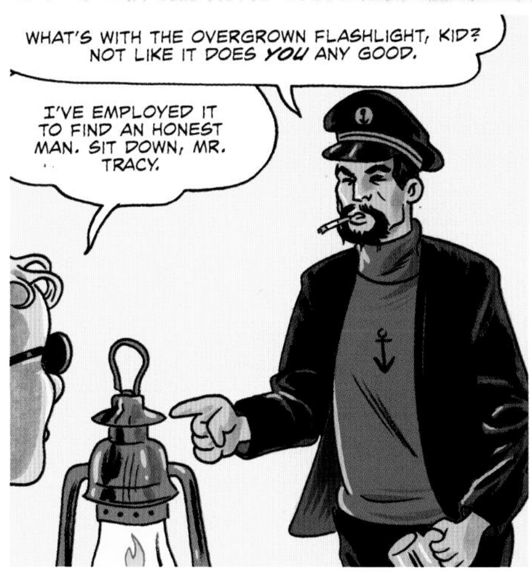
WHAT'S WITH THE OVERGROWN FLASHLIGHT, KID? NOT LIKE IT DOES *YOU* ANY GOOD.
I'VE EMPLOYED IT TO FIND AN HONEST MAN. SIT DOWN, MR. TRACY.

PAGE 17, PANEL 4:

Diogenes Lanthorn carries a lantern as an homage to the ancient Greek philosopher Diogenes, who carried around a lantern "looking for an honest man."

PAGE 2 *(6 PANELS)*

PANEL 1

We see the text to one of the fluttering newspapers. Newspaper front page like that one Rich did in SPY SEAL. Newspaper is named Telegraph Hill Telegraph. Top story above the fold: PEEPERS wanted as a serial killer, tough cop DICK TRACY driving force behind warrant.

Big main headline. Smaller sub-headlines. Black/white headshot photo of G. JEPSON PEEPERS. Another b/w photo of DICK TRACY elsewhere on the page.

MAIN HEADLINE: MANHUNT FOR SOFTWARE MOGUL PEEPERS

SUB-HEADLINES: CHIEF SUSPECT IN CLOUD CAM KILLER CASE DID PEEPERS' POCKETS NIX PREVIOUS CRIMES?

NEWS PAPER TEXT (use as little or as much as layout space dictates):

Bay Area residents were rocked today by the most powerful man in Silicon Valley, software mogul G. Jepson Peepers being named the "Cloud Cam Killer" serial murderer.

Peepers himself used company access to geo-track young female victims and turn off his own CloudPeepers security cameras, not some outside hacker as originally thought.

Sources reveal plainclothes detective Richard Tracy responsible for obtaining the warrant over objections of both city and state officials who've benefitted from CloudPeepers donations.

Peepers' arrest triggered panic in the Statehouse where Peepers acted as sugar daddy to politicians from the Governor on down to rookie state assemblymembers.

PANEL 2

Exterior A retro-looking jet airline sits on tarmac. The plane has CloudPeepers painted across its fuselage. It's PEEPERS' private/corporate airliner. One of those rolling staircases is wheeled up to the open passenger boarding door. PEEPERS dashes towards it.

In keeping with our modern-but-retro Animated Batman-ish look for Dick Tracy's world, I suggest using for the airliner the very retro-looking turbo prop/jet-combo Bristol Brabazon. (Those are inline jet engines on the wing roots between turbo props, btw.)

More art ref pics (Bing search): https://tinyurl.com/y92xbecj
YouTube newsreel showing this plane from various angles: https://youtu.be/7rgAW1pwsQo

1 PEEPERS (panting): *puff *puff*

2 PEEPERS: …I'll be safe…once I make it…to my plane…my private island…

PANEL 3

PEEPERS with satchel scurries up the boarding stairs. PEEPERS is nervous, sweating. Money $50 and $100 dollar bills -- continue to flutter out of the leather satchel he carries.

3 PEEPERS (panting): *pant* *pant* Made it!

PANEL 4

Top of the portable boarding stairs stands DICK TRACY. A vicious kick from TRACY sends PEEPERS sailing backwards in an arc Satchel bursts open, money flies everywhere. PEEPERS shouts TRACY's name. NOTE TO LETTERER: maybe use "Dick Tracy" logo for dramatic effect?

4 SFX (kick): THOK!

5 DICK TRACY: The warrant in my pocket says hello, Peepers.

6 PEEPERS (spikey): DICK TRACY!!

PANEL 5

Down on the tarmac. TRACY hauls up the stunned PEEPERS by the necktie. Money continues to fly everywhere.

7 TRACY: A word of advice, Peepers, in case you're thinking of putting up a fight --.

8 TRACY #2: I don't throw the first punch, but I throw the last. I don't shoot first, but I shoot to kill.

PANEL 6

Small panel (maybe insert panel in #5?) PEEPERS' eyes roll up in the back of his head and he faints dead away at TRACY's threat.

NOTE TO RICH: if you want to consolidate this into Panel 5, feel free. :)

9 SFX (SMALL): FAINT!

10 PEEPERS (weak and wavy): uhnnnnn…

Next, Rich "Two Times" Tommaso drew the page in pencils, following his layouts.

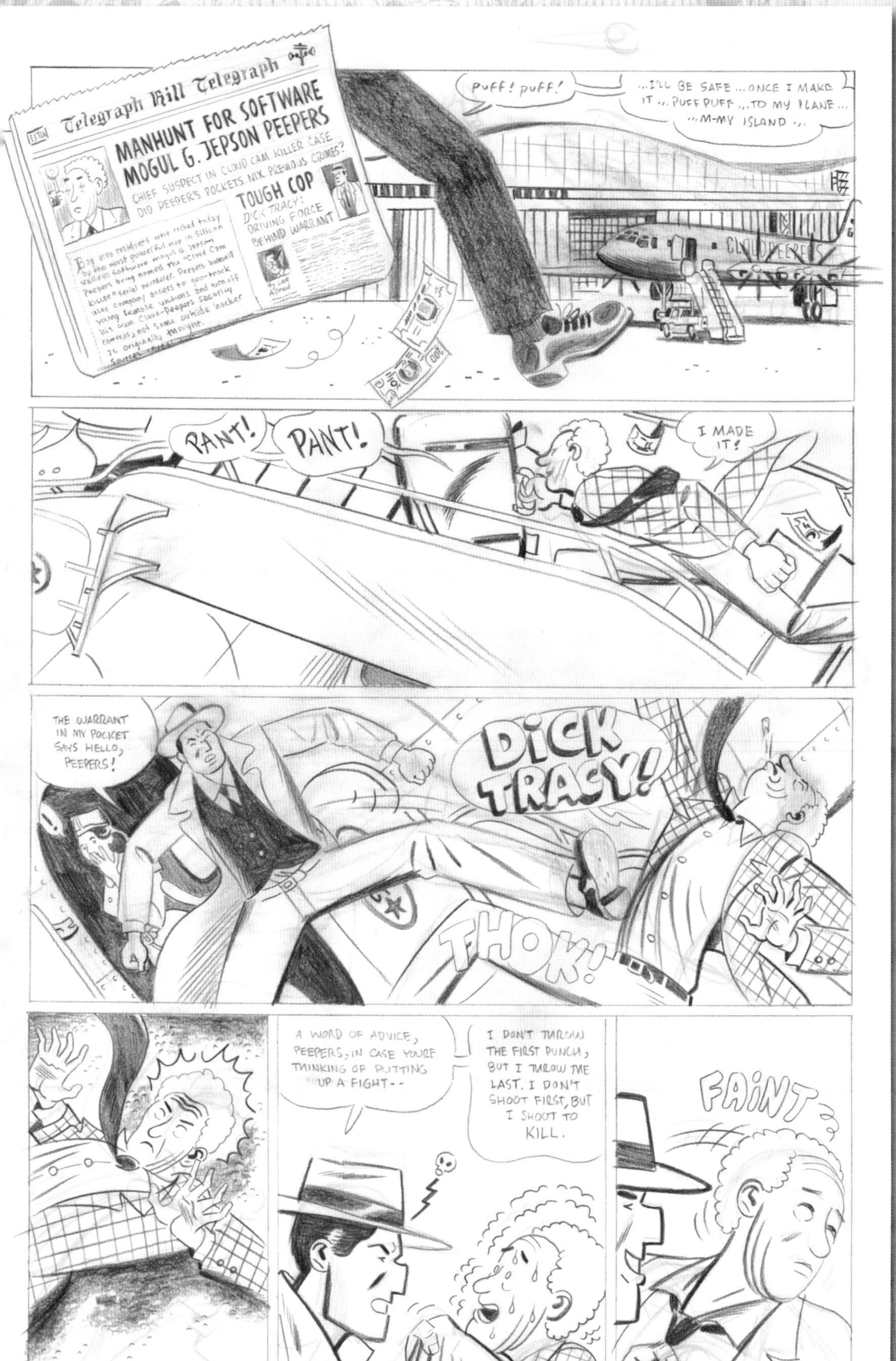

Telegraph Hill Telegraph
EXTRA
MANHUNT FOR SOFTWARE MOGUL G. JEPSON PEEPERS
CHIEF SUSPECT IN CLOUD CAM KILLER CASE
DID PEEPER'S POCKETS NIX PREVIOUS CRIMES?
TOUGH COP
DICK TRACY: DRIVING FORCE BEHIND WARRANT
PUFF! PUFF!
...I'LL BE SAFE... ONCE I MAKE IT... PUFF PUFF... TO MY PLANE... ...M-MY ISLAND...
CLOUDPEEPERS
PANT!
PANT!
I MADE IT!
THE WARRANT IN MY POCKET SAYS HELLO, PEEPERS!
DICK TRACY!
THOK!
A WORD OF ADVICE, PEEPERS, IN CASE YOU'RE THINKING OF PUTTING UP A FIGHT--
I DON'T THROW THE FIRST PUNCH, BUT I THROW THE LAST. I DON'T SHOOT FIRST, BUT I SHOOT TO KILL.
FAINT

Then, Michael "Mumbles" Allred laid down the India ink to finish off the line art.

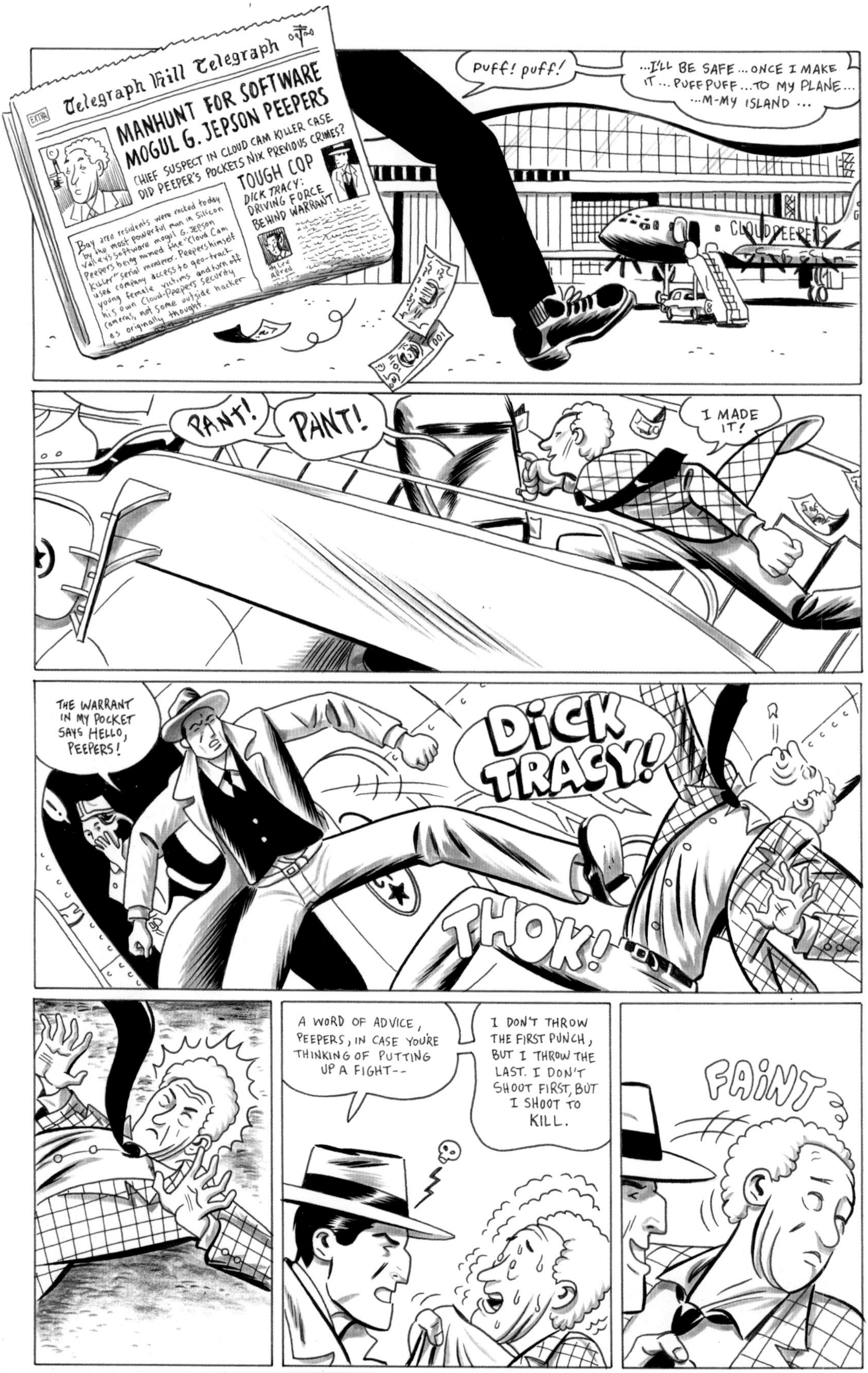

Telegraph Hill Telegraph
EXTRA
MANHUNT FOR SOFTWARE MOGUL G. JEPSON PEEPERS
CHIEF SUSPECT IN CLOUD CAM KILLER CASE
DID PEEPER'S POCKETS NIX PREVIOUS CRIMES?
TOUGH COP
DICK TRACY: DRIVING FORCE BEHIND WARRANT
Bay area residents were rocked today by the most powerful man in Silicon Valley's software mogul G. Jepson Peepers being named the "Cloud Cam Killer" serial murderer. Peepers himself used company access to geo-track young female victims and turn off his own Cloud-Peepers security cameras, not some outside hacker as originally thought.
PUFF! PUFF!
...I'LL BE SAFE... ONCE I MAKE IT... PUFF PUFF... TO MY PLANE... ...M-MY ISLAND...
PANT!
PANT!
I MADE IT!
THE WARRANT IN MY POCKET SAYS HELLO, PEEPERS!
DICK TRACY!
THOK!
A WORD OF ADVICE, PEEPERS, IN CASE YOU'RE THINKING OF PUTTING UP A FIGHT--
I DON'T THROW THE FIRST PUNCH, BUT I THROW THE LAST. I DON'T SHOOT FIRST, BUT I SHOOT TO KILL.
FAINT

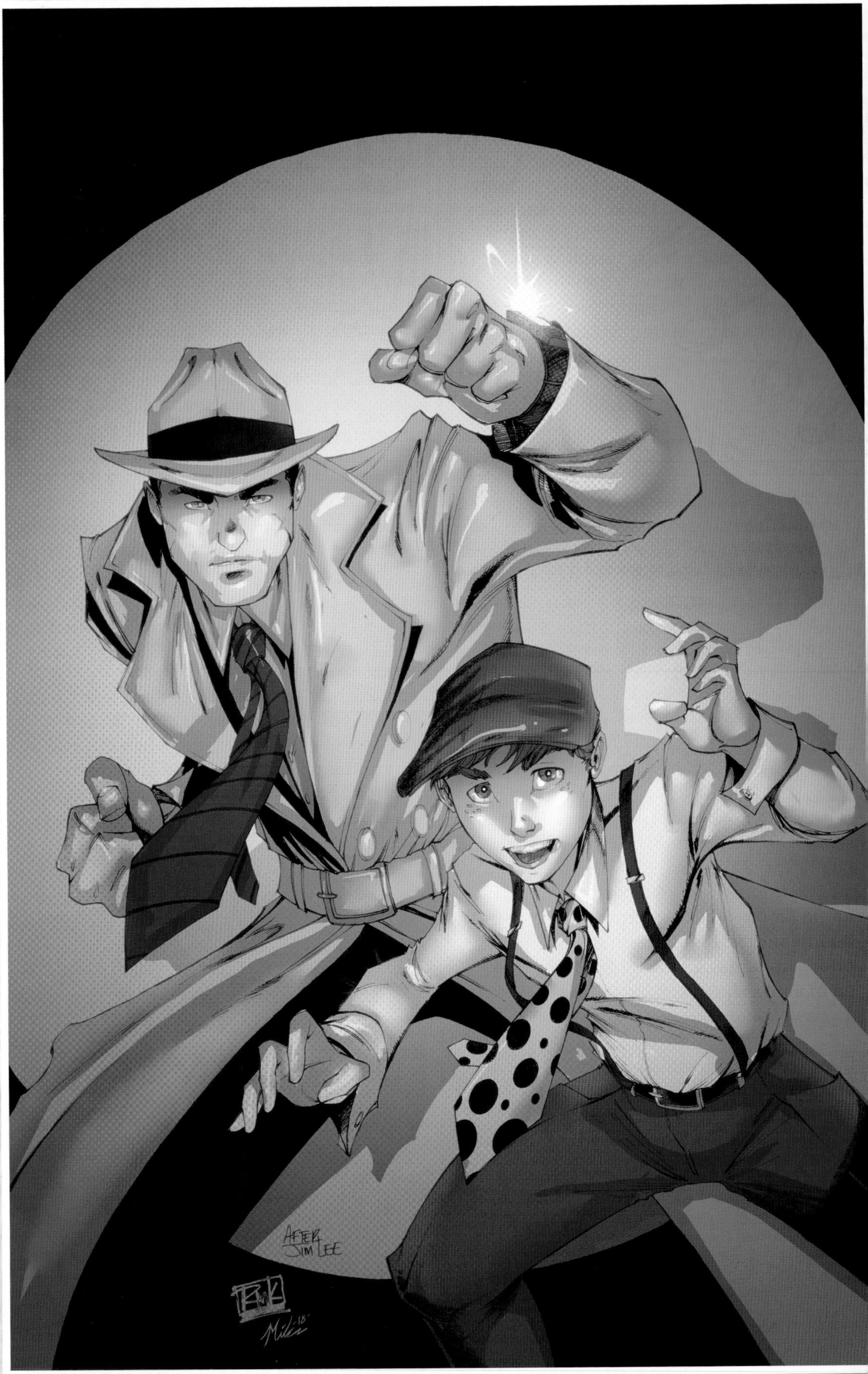
AFTER
JIM LEE

ART BY **RYAN KINCAID**

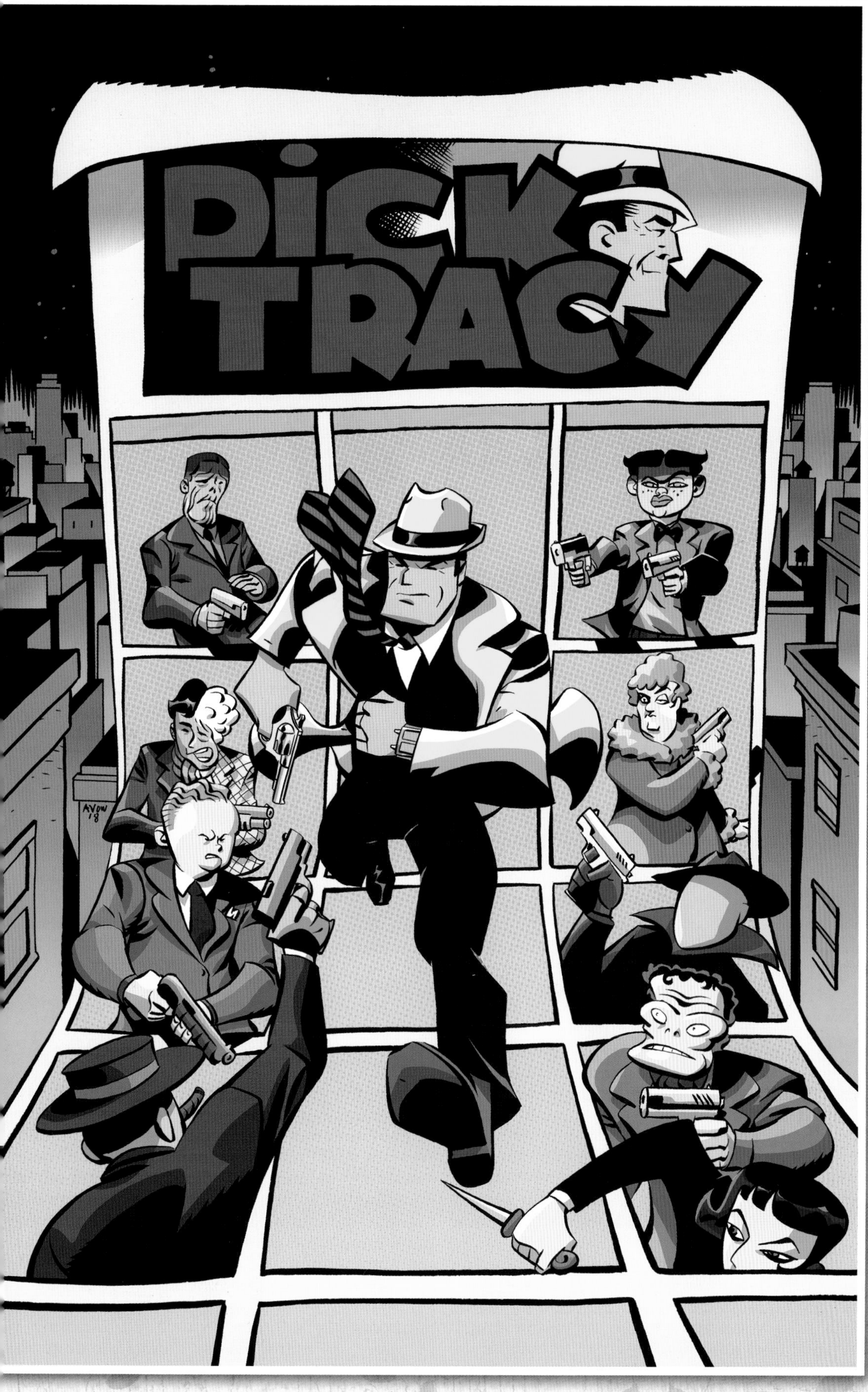
DICK TRACY

ART BY MIKE OEMING

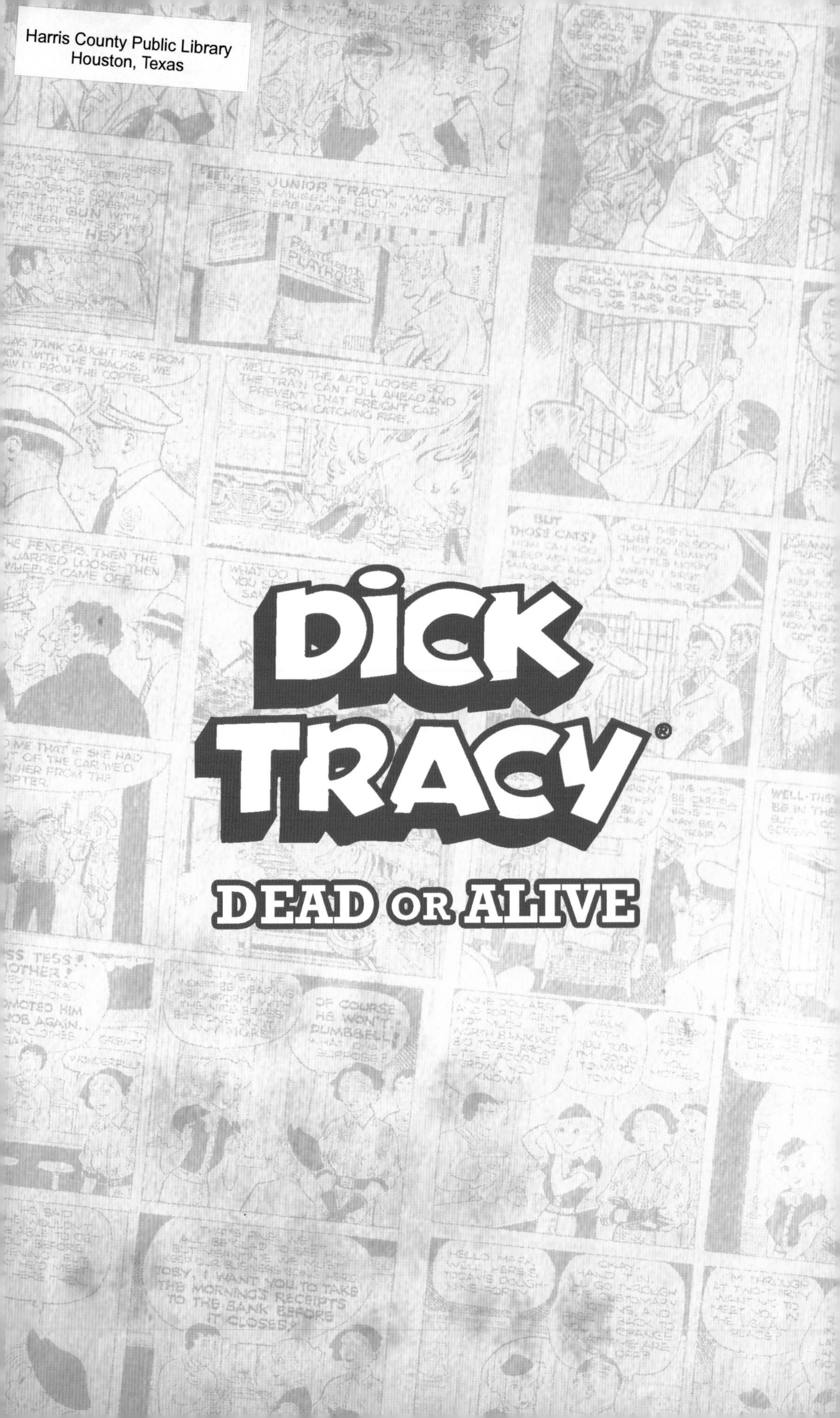
THAT'S JUNIOR TRACY—MAYBE HE'S BEEN SMUGGLING B.U. IN AND OUT OF HERE EACH NIGHT—
WELL PRY THE AUTO LOOSE SO THE TRAIN CAN PULL AHEAD AND PREVENT THAT FREIGHT CAR FROM CATCHING FIRE.
YOU SEE, WE CAN SLEEP IN PERFECT SAFETY IN THE CAVE BECAUSE THE ONLY ENTRANCE IS THROUGH THIS DOOR.
THEN WHEN I'M INSIDE, I REACH UP AND PULL THE ROWS OF BARS RIGHT BACK LIKE THIS, SEE?
TOBY, I WANT YOU TO TAKE THE MORNING'S RECEIPTS TO THE BANK BEFORE IT CLOSES.

DICK TRACY®

DEAD OR ALIVE